"Intruder battle cruiser. We grow impatient. The planet will be vacated, or all will pay the price."

His jaw tight, Kirk replied. "Kenisian vessel, we believe in settling our differences through discussion, not force, if at all possible." He didn't like the Kenisian's tone or threats, but now wasn't the time to mirror them.

After a long pause, Uhura sighed in frustration. "They've closed the channel, sir."

Spock was already studying his scanner when Kirk turned toward him.

"They're charging weapons."

"Shields." Kirk pounded the arm of his command chair. "All hands, battle stations."

"Battle stations," Uhura repeated over the intercom. "All hands to battle stations. This is not a drill. All hands, report to battle stations."

The captain tensed instinctively, as he had when he was a young, green ensign and first heard the call to battle. He told himself that this would change. It hadn't. He could still feel himself coiling up. He had gotten better at hiding it, but the feeling always remained.

To his side, Pippenge gripped the rail so hard it looked like he was trying to snap it in half. For him, a triumphant return home, planned for months in advance, had been tainted by the improbable.

"Evasive action, Mister Sulu." Kirk studied the tactical display, which he knew would be inadequate. "Mister Scott, we need those sensors."

"Aye, sir." Scott sped toward the turbolift. "I'll move the lads along."

STAR TREK®

THE ORIGINAL SERIES

CRISIS OF CONSCIOUSNESS

Dave Galanter

Based on *Star Trek*
created by Gene Roddenberry

POCKET BOOKS

New York   London   Toronto   Sydney   New Delhi

Pocket Books
An Imprint of Simon & Schuster, Inc.
1230 Avenue of the Americas
New York, NY 10020

This book is a work of fiction. Any references to historical events, real people, or real places are used fictitiously. Other names, characters, places, and events are products of the author's imagination, and any resemblance to actual events or places or persons, living or dead, is entirely coincidental.

First Pocket Books paperback edition May 2015

POCKET and colophon are registered trademarks of Simon & Schuster, Inc.

For information about special discounts for bulk purchases, please contact Simon & Schuster Special Sales at 1-866-506-1949 or business@simonandschuster.com.

The Simon & Schuster Speakers Bureau can bring authors to your live event. For more information or to book an event, contact the Simon & Schuster Speakers Bureau at 1-866-248-3049 or visit our website at www.simonspeakers.com.

Manufactured in the United States of America

10 9 8 7 6 5 4 3 2 1

ISBN 978-1-4767-8260-7
ISBN 978-1-4767-8261-4 (ebook)

For Simantha

"*He that studieth revenge keepeth his own wounds green, which otherwise would heal and do well.*"
—John Milton

ONE

Captain's log, Stardate 3458.2.

Enterprise *has arrived at* Deep Space 5. *We are ferrying home a delegation from the planet Maaba S'Ja. A xenophobic culture, the Maabas leaders have taken a political risk in signing this accord, which would open up trade with and offer protection to their world. Given the sensitive partisan atmosphere the Maabas president is dealing with, Starfleet Command felt that the "red carpet treatment" for the ambassador and his party was needed.* Enterprise *was the closest ship, and we have been tasked with the duty.*

When Captain James T. Kirk entered the transporter room, he found his first officer and chief medical officer already waiting. As usual, Dr. McCoy looked uncomfortable in his dress uniform, and Commander Spock only looked a bit more formal than when in his duty tunic.

"Fifteen minutes, Bones," Kirk told the doctor. "An hour at the most."

Tugging at his collar, McCoy frowned. "That's an hour too long."

"Of course," the captain said, "you'll have to put it back on for dinner."

"Why bother eating if this thing won't let me swallow?"

"I have the coordinates, sir," the transporter chief said as he worked the console.

Kirk nodded. "Thank you, Mister Kyle." Turning a bit toward McCoy, the captain allowed himself a slight smirk at the doctor's predicament. "I'd suggest a good tailor, but I think you like to complain."

"Well," McCoy said, "I'm not sure I have to stand here and be insulted."

"Actually, you do." Kirk motioned to Kyle. "Energize."

Humming to life, the transporter chamber brightened as six columns of sparkle manifested, swirled, and then solidified into humanoid forms.

"Ambassador Pippenge, welcome aboard. I'm Captain James T. Kirk." He stepped toward the platform, his arm outstretched for the Maabas greeting. He had spent the previous evening with the *Enterprise*'s archaeology and anthropology officer, Carolyn Palamas, taking a cram course in the Maabas's culture.

The ambassador descended toward Kirk, taking the captain's right elbow in his left palm. Then, unexpectedly, Pippenge held out his right hand. "Allow me to greet you in the Terran manner, Captain."

Kirk took the tall man's hand and shook it. It was an overly firm handshake; Kirk wondered which of the Federation politicians had taught it to him.

"My chief medical officer, Lieutenant Commander Leonard McCoy, and my first officer and science officer, Commander Spock." Kirk motioned to each in turn as the delegation descended from the transporter platform.

With great warmth, Pippenge reached for Dr. McCoy's hand and shook it happily. He then turned toward Spock. With some difficulty, the ambassador presented his best representation of a Vulcan salute. Having three fingers and two thumbs made it an interesting and somewhat awkward approximation. "Live long and prosper, Commander Spock." The words were in heavily accented Vulcan, without assistance of the universal translator. Clearly Pippenge was looking to impress his hosts.

Fingers splayed, Spock raised his hand in response. "Peace and long life, Ambassador."

Pippenge chittered, a sound which seemed like an expression of delight. "You recognized the greeting. I am overjoyed. I practiced all night."

"You honor us." Spock nodded in respect.

"My compatriots." The ambassador gestured with both hands to include the delegation behind him. "My assistant, Tainler. Attendants Nedash and Skent, and their adjutants Brintle and Ortov."

Kirk nodded pleasantly to all, but knew he was unlikely to remember most of the names. He trusted Spock could be called on to supply them, if the need arose.

Despite being easily ten centimeters taller than the Vulcan, Pippenge was anything but imposing. His thick black hair, streaked with bars of white in what seemed to be a stylistic choice, perhaps belied his age. Telling the years of an alien was often difficult for the captain, and he tended to ask, if culturally appropriate.

"We're pleased to welcome you aboard the *Enterprise*."

The rest of the Maabas party were not tall. Like most races, they came in all shapes and sizes, and several different color variations. Pippenge was a pale pinkish hue. His assistant, Tainler, was a more ruddy color. The others were different shades. One trait they shared were thin noses and deep-set eyes which made the bridges of their noses even more pronounced.

"We've arranged quarters for the journey," the captain said, motioning them toward the doorway. "But I hope you will all join me for dinner this evening, so we can become acquainted."

Bowing slightly, Pippenge pursed his lips. "We shall be delighted, Captain."

WHEN THE CABIN door chime rang, Lieutenant Carolyn Palamas was too busy to answer. She had no time for interruptions, but when the buzzer rang again she finally responded with an exasperated "Come in!"

Nyota Uhura, already in her dress uniform, entered as the door slid open for her. "Shouldn't you be expecting me?" she said. "*You* asked me to stop by."

"Oh, I'm sorry, Lieutenant. I just can't find my dress boots." She looked again in the closet she'd just closed a second before, then she pulled open every drawer of the dresser.

Leaning on the wall next to the dresser, Uhura smiled. "Firstly, we're off watch and Mister Spock isn't in earshot, so you don't need to call me by rank. Secondly, the difference between our dress and our duty boots would hardly be noticed by the captain, let alone the Maabas delegation."

Reaching back into the bottom drawer, as if the boots would actually fit there, Palamas scoffed. "*I* would know."

Uhura straightened and stepped fully into the room. "Well, they're not going to be in there. Would you like me to help you look?" She glanced around the cabin. "Not that there're that many places for a pair of boots to hide."

"I'm being silly, aren't I?" Standing, Palamas smoothed out her dress uniform, which also didn't look too different from her standard one.

"A little." Uhura smiled warmly. "I know you're not really concerned about boots."

Palamas smiled and shook her head. "I've been

researching the Maabas for a week, but that's not nearly long enough to give the captain everything he might need."

"He doesn't need everything," Uhura assured her.

"They're a fascinating people. Really they are. But I can't remember it all. With more time, I'd have everything at hand."

"When did the captain invite you?" Uhura asked.

"An hour ago," she admitted. Turning to her computer, Palamas reviewed the screen. "Did you know they all have internal communication implants? Direct cortex interfaces."

Coming to stand behind her, Uhura glanced over the material the A&A officer was studying: a mass of facts from technology to geography. "You're overthinking it. Why would the captain want to know the length of the growing season on their most southern continent?"

"I don't know. I told you, I didn't have time to prepare good notes."

Uhura smiled and took Palamas by the arms, turning her away from the screen. "Look, I've been to a lot of these. They're a piece of cake."

Palamas fretted, "I'd asked two days ago if I should attend . . . but he said it wasn't necessary. Now—"

"Carolyn, deep breath," Uhura said.

She straightened her uniform. "*Now*, he wants me there."

"He thought better of it." Uhura motioned

toward the door. "Just fill in the cultural details he might need. You did all the research. It'll come back to you as you need it."

"I didn't think he cared," Palamas said. "I wasn't even sure he'd read my report."

Nodding, Uhura guided the other woman toward the doorway. "I'm sure he did. Well, at least he skimmed it. He's the captain."

"What if I cause an international incident? What if . . ."

"Stop, or I'm going to point out your boots to him."

As the door to the corridor opened, Palamas turned back and begged, "Don't you *dare*."

WHEN KIRK ENTERED his private dining room, most of his senior officers and many of the Maabas dignitaries were already present. He recognized Tainler, Pippenge's assistant, though the ambassador himself had yet to arrive. She and two others of her party were engaged in some discussion with Spock. Palamas and Uhura talked with Scotty, who was in his dress uniform replete with kilt.

Just as the doors closed behind him, they opened again and the captain turned to see Dr. McCoy enter.

Kirk greeted him with an already bemused expression. "Bones, glad you could make it."

"I'm here," the doctor said. "If you want me cheerful, I'll need a drink."

The captain shook his head. "Not tonight."

"Oh? Why not?"

Hesitating a moment, Kirk knew there was a reason. He'd seen it in the report as a bullet point but couldn't quite place the why. Turning slightly to his left, he called for one of the two people who would know. "Lieutenant Palamas."

"Lieutenant," McCoy said pleasantly. "Our new archaeology and anthropology officer."

As she joined them, Palamas returned the doctor's smile. "I'm qualified in xenoarchaeology and xenopology as well, Doctor."

"Of course you are, my dear." He bowed toward her apologetically, the ever-suave gentleman when a pretty woman was present.

"The good doctor is wondering why no spirits for tonight's festivities." Kirk smirked slightly, letting Palamas know he was having a bit of fun at McCoy's expense.

"Oh, yes, sir." She turned fully toward the doctor, her face now grim. "The Maabas value one's mental capacity so much that—without law or statute—theirs is a dry planet, Doctor."

"They don't imbibe at all, any of them?"

"Not only that, but they'd be shocked that someone as learned and skilled as a physician would do so." Palamas looked at McCoy with such earnest sincerity that the captain wondered if she was always such a quick study.

"Cross *them* off the list for my next shore leave," McCoy muttered.

With a chuckle at the doctor and a nod to Palamas, Kirk sent her back toward the table just as the doors behind him opened again. Ambassador Pippenge and one of his attendants entered, and the ambassador greeted the captain and McCoy with a handshake. They were dressed ornately, with brightly colored robes that seemed to hang in a more formal arrangement than what they'd worn when they beamed aboard.

"I trust you found your quarters acceptable?" the captain asked.

Pippenge bowed pleasantly.

Kirk motioned them toward the table as he scanned the room and took a head-count, noticing the other Maabas were also dressed more formally. He liked that their formal attire was flamboyant. In many cultures the inclination was the opposite. "I believe we're missing one of your party?"

Scanning the gathering himself, the ambassador made his own count. "Skent seems to be delayed. I'm sure he'll be along."

"We'll be happy to wait," Kirk said.

"Oh, please, do not. His tardiness shouldn't put us all off schedule."

"Very well." The captain gestured toward the table, and they all took their seats. After brief toasts by both Kirk and Pippenge about the new relationship between the Maabas and the Federation, the first course was served.

The fare was a mixture of Terran, Vulcan, and Maabasian cuisine, and Kirk asked Lieutenant Palamas to explain the origin of each of the Federation dishes. To her credit, she was able to, and the ambassador was sufficiently impressed.

"The starbase provided the *Enterprise* with the . . . *karfis*, isn't it?" she asked Pippenge. "Fields of it grow quickly, and you can get two harvests a year from them, if I remember correctly."

"You do. You know a great deal about our planet," he said admiringly. "Do you know where it's grown?"

"Mostly in . . ." she hesitated searching her memory. "It's a northern province, near a popular seaport."

"Yes?"

"Heffron?"

The ambassador chittered. "Correct! I am very impressed."

With a bubble of quiet laughter, she demurred, but Kirk encouraged her with a nod. This was one of the reasons he'd decided to add Palamas to the dinner.

"The Maabas government has been generous with its hospitality," Palamas said. "Previous diplomatic missions learned your history, enjoyed its cuisine. Food is an important part of culture, don't you agree?"

Pippenge pursed his lips, and Palamas whispered to Kirk that this was the Maabas version of an affirming nod.

"There've been more than a few diplomatic missions, I understand," the captain said. "Your government has been fairly cautious about signing the treaty. Until recently."

"Yes," the ambassador agreed. "My people have been generally suspicious of other species—bordering on the xenophobic."

"Is that why you have no interstellar exploratory programs?" McCoy asked, taking a bite of his salad.

"Yes, Doctor." Pippenge shuddered, which Palamas quietly told Kirk was akin to a sigh. "After many years of searching for a new homeworld, and being chased from dozens of inhabited systems, we were too weary to seek the stars once we found a home."

"Understandable," Spock said, "for war refugees." The Vulcan never seemed to eat at these gatherings, and yet the captain knew his plate would be half empty when removed from the table.

"We try not to see ourselves that way. But there are our Days of Remembrance, and the Fast of Landing—when food stores waned before we were certain our new world's flora was not poisonous to us—and so on. I suppose in our hearts we will always be refugees."

"A shared experience," Kirk said, looking for a bright side to the sad history, "binds a society together."

His lips pursed again, Pippenge agreed. "Quite so. Quite so." Uncomfortable with the awkward silence that followed, the ambassador waved his hand around to indicate the starship. "Your ship and her crew are a marvel, Captain."

Kirk accepted the compliment modestly. "While your people's efforts did not focus on space exploration, your science does exceed ours in many areas."

"Nothing so elegant as this."

"If I may, Ambassador, I've studied the records of Maabas technological successes." Hands clasped on his lap, Spock looked both effortlessly comfortable and yet somehow formal. The first officer participated in ceremonial meals as precisely as he did everything else: with such measured care that it seemed effortless. His contribution was usually intense attention and the interesting observation. "Your terraforming effort, which has transformed one of your planet's lifeless moons into a thriving farming colony, is but one example of how you have surpassed Federation science."

Pippenge rolled his head around. Palamas whispered in the captain's ear that the motion was a cross between a bow and a shrug. "You're most kind, Mister Spock. The first Vulcan I've met in person, and not at all what I expected."

Spock's right brow arched slightly upward. "Sir?"

"Oh, no, I meant no offense." Pippenge was obviously flustered and embarrassed.

McCoy smirked and took a sip of water. "Offending Spock is a difficult task, Ambassador."

"Indeed." Spock nodded his agreement.

"I assure you . . . I only meant . . . we're not used to dealing with aliens." His eyes wide, Pippenge looked contrite. "Though, I must admit you do resemble the mythical phantoms that are said to haunt the ancient ruins of our planet."

"Does he?" Grinning, the doctor gazed at Spock, bemused.

"Phantoms?" Kirk asked, also entertained by the notion of Spock as a specter.

"Old stories," Pippenge explained. "Mostly, I think, told to keep people from exploring in unsafe areas. If one ventures too deep into the ancient ruins, a being of greenish pallor, an upswept brow, and pointed ears is said to destroy the individual with fire and lightning."

"Interesting," Spock said.

"Children's legends," the ambassador said. "Just folklore about demons who whisk you away when you do wrong. Again, I mean no offense, I assure you."

"I understand," Spock said agreeably.

"Meeting someone not born of your planet, even if you're aware they exist, can be a life-changing event. Here you are, among hundreds of aliens," Kirk pointed out. "You and your party are handling it with great grace."

Pippenge was quiet. He shifted his weight, leaning one way in his seat, then the other, but said nothing for quite a time.

What must he be contemplating? Kirk wondered. Since joining Starfleet, he'd always found meeting new life-forms exhilarating. Occasionally more than that, but always least that.

"Thank you, Captain Kirk." Pippenge hesitated and then said, "It has not been easy for my people. We know there are alien races on other planets, but they are not always friendly—most notably the one that pushed us from our homeworld. It was two millennia ago, but we remember. In the time since, we've isolated ourselves, and while we thought it was for our protection, it was also to our detriment. I think we are now ready to travel again among the stars."

"More aliens will come to Maabas now," McCoy said. "Are your people ready for that?"

That was one of Starfleet Command's worries as well. However, the Federation Council was untroubled. Their opinion was that a culture intelligent enough to make breakthroughs in science, to accept the Federation as an ally, could be eased into other frontiers, even ones alien to themselves.

"Most are, or we'd not have signed the treaty." The ambassador's quick reply made Kirk think this was one of Pippenge's political talking points. Likely many Maabas shared Dr. McCoy's concerns.

"Some aren't as eager," Kirk said.

Absentmindedly, the ambassador grabbed a dark strand of his hair and stroked it nervously. "No group is all of one mind, Captain." He chittered happily. "But we are ready to move forward." Standing, Pippenge thrust back the loose arm of his official robes and raised a fork as one might raise a glass. "Onward to the future."

"Here, here," McCoy said. The *Enterprise* officers in attendance applauded. The Maabas officials sang in a cheerful tone. Pippenge attempted both, and the captain couldn't help but smile.

There was much to celebrate. Most treaty negotiations didn't go as smoothly as they had with the Maabas. They'd asked for very little from the Federation: trade, protection, and cultural and scientific exchange. In return, the UFP wanted much the same. The previous surveys and exchanges, which had given Lieutenant Palamas the information in her report, had shown that the Maabas had great intellectual flexibility. In addition to their unique scientific research, their philosophy dovetailed nicely with that of the Federation. They were a united planet with a democratically elected government, there had been no wars since they colonized their planet, and they shared many of the same principles as the Federation.

Kirk raised his glass to make his own toast, but just as he was taking a breath, the door to the corridor slid open. Skent, the missing Maabas attendant, entered with an *Enterprise* security officer close behind.

The captain rose to greet them. "Mister Baumgartner?"

The guard frowned. "He was found on engineering deck, sir. In a restricted section."

Pippenge rose to confront his comrade. "Is this true?"

"An error," Skent said sheepishly. "I was merely exploring . . ."

The ambassador puckered his lips. "I see."

"A puckering of the lips is like a human shake of the head," Palamas whispered to Kirk. He hadn't noticed she'd joined him. The captain nodded his appreciation. This *was* just the sort of understanding of alien body language he needed from his A&A officer.

"Ambassador, you and your aide were also seen on the engineering deck." Kirk had seen the report earlier, but thought little of it. Guests could get turned around on a ship as big as the *Enterprise*. One occurrence could be easily dismissed. Two, however, made the hairs on the back of Kirk's neck stand up.

Was Pippenge displeased with Skent because he was where he shouldn't be, or because he was *found* where he shouldn't be?

"He had this on him." Baumgartner handed Kirk a small device that fit into his palm but had no obvious screen or method of input.

The captain rolled the object around in his

hand, then showed it to the ambassador. "Can you explain this, sir?"

"A scanning tool and recording device," Pippenge said.

Spock rose and joined the captain to his right. "A tricorder."

"Designed to interact with our computerized implants, yes." The ambassador was contrite and glared down at Skent. "Explain yourself, please."

"My brother is in the Science Directorate. He asked me to record anything of interest," the attendant said, unwilling to meet Pippenge's eyes.

"On the *Enterprise*?" Kirk asked.

"Anywhere."

The captain pressed his lips into a thin line and wondered if that would be taken as a sign of acceptance by the Maabas delegation. If so, perhaps that wasn't a bad thing. He didn't like it, but he didn't have evidence that there was any malicious intent.

"Mister Spock?" He handed the device to his science officer. "Please review the data collected and make sure nothing of a sensitive nature has been recorded."

Spock nodded. "Yes, sir."

"If you wish to satisfy your own justice, Captain, I understand," Pippenge said. "Though I assure you, there will be repercussions for Skent's rude actions."

This was just the kind of kink that Starfleet

didn't want in the relationship between the Maabas and the Federation. And, unless the device was a danger to his ship, there probably was no reason to be concerned. "We have a saying, Ambassador." Kirk motioned them all back toward the dinner table. "'No harm, no foul.'"

Pippenge bowed. "You are most gracious hosts."

Amiable smiles and mild discussion followed until the hour grew late and the ambassador and his party excused themselves.

As Kirk stood to leave as well, Palamas approached. "Thank you for inviting me, Captain. It was an interesting evening."

"I appreciated your attention to detail tonight, Lieutenant. Good night."

"Thank you, sir," she said pleasantly, and joined Uhura, who waited for her near the door.

"May I walk you back to your cabins, ladies?" Scotty approached them, and the three left together.

As the table was being cleared by yeomen, Spock approached Kirk. "I shall have a report on the abilities and contents of this device by the morning, sir."

The captain knew better than to dispute the timing of his first officer's sleep schedule or the prioritization of his work/personal-life balance. "Thank you, Mister Spock."

"Drink, Jim?" McCoy asked.

Kirk nodded. "I was thinking the same."

———

THE DOCTOR POURED himself another glass and held the bottle toward Kirk, who shook his head. "One's enough."

"Since when?" McCoy had loosened the neck on his dress uniform enough that the black undershirt showed through a V shape he'd opened over his chest.

"I'm on duty." The captain cradled the glass in his hand, sipped the drink just to keep nursing it, then placed it on the doctor's desk.

"Uh-oh, I know that look."

"What look?" His brows jutting upward, Kirk glanced at McCoy.

"The something's-bothering-me-but-I'm-not-sure-what look."

"Please," Kirk scoffed, but hesitated before continuing. "I'm sure it's nothing."

The doctor took another sip of his brandy. "I'm sorry. I mistook you for Jim Kirk."

At that the captain chuckled. "Am I that obvious?"

"Only on even-numbered stardates." McCoy topped up his snifter even though there was more yet to savor. "Tell your bartender all about it."

The doctor could be a good sounding board. Kirk lifted his glass and took another small sip, explaining, "Over the year the Federation and the Maabas have been negotiating, the main sticking point was the building of an orbital space station which could resupply and repair space vessels."

"Why was that a problem?"

Kirk shrugged. "I don't know. They didn't want to work on 'vessels of war,' despite assurances that Starfleet's mission was one of peace and exploration."

"Even Vulcan has spaceports where a starship can dock." The doctor sighed and shook his head. "If you can out-pacifist a Vulcan . . ."

"Suddenly, they change their mind and in a matter of a few weeks have signed a treaty. Why?"

"Reasoned debate caused a political shift?" Swiveling back and forth in his chair, McCoy frowned and offered a shrug as he speculated. "Some internal need for a specific resource they lack, which we have? An external threat of some kind?"

Pointing directly at the doctor, Kirk nodded. "That."

"Then why don't we know about it?"

The captain shook his head and looked down into the glass he lifted from the desk. "I don't know, Bones."

The bosun's whistle rang out, jarring him from further thought. "*Bridge to Captain Kirk.*"

He leaned toward the desk's comm panel and thumbed the button. "Kirk here."

"*Now entering the Maabas star system, sir.*"

"Ahead of schedule, Mister Sulu. Slow to impulse. Standard approach. Let me know when we make orbit."

"*Aye, sir.*"

"Kirk out."

When the doctor was sure Kirk had switched off the comm, he continued. "What's it got to do with the Maabas delegation snooping? Because that's what's really bothering you, isn't it?"

"I don't know." It was true that it bothered him, but he wasn't even sure it should. There were such things as innocent mistakes. The captain liked everything to add up, and with the Maabas, not everything did. "You remember the story Pippenge told?"

"Which?" McCoy capped the bottle, walked to the cabinet behind the desk, and stowed it away. "The man isn't lacking for stories."

Most ambassadors weren't, the captain thought. "The mythological demons that look like Spock."

The doctor laughed and after a couple drinks the sound was more throaty than usual. "You think Vulcans visited this planet years ago, threatening sightseers and correcting grammar?"

With a chuckle, Kirk shook his head. "Not exactly. But the Romulans . . . ?" He let the sentence trail off, and the notion hung between them.

"Not their general area of influence," McCoy said thoughtfully, nursing his drink.

"'Demons,'" the captain quoted Pippenge. "What'd he say? Upswept brow, pointed ears?"

"Yes." The doctor snickered. "They destroy you with fire and lightning."

"That could describe a weapon," Kirk said. "Or a transporter."

"You're reaching."

"Deep Space 5 is near the Romulan Neutral Zone." The captain tilted the glass toward himself and watched the liquid contents run against the bowl as he set it right again. "A Federation-Maabas alliance would be a concern for the Romulans." He raised the glass to his lips and took a sip, just as the bosun's whistle sounded again.

"*Bridge to Captain Kirk.*" Spock's voice this time.

Quickly he hit the comm button. Sulu'd had the bridge. For his first officer to be calling, something had changed. "Kirk here. What's wrong, Mister Spock?"

"*We're tracking an unknown vessel on an intercept course.*" The Vulcan's voice was calm as usual, but had a serious tinge.

"ETA?"

"*Four minutes, present speed.*"

"Go to yellow alert. I'm on my way."

Kirk put his glass down on McCoy's desk and twisted toward the exit. "We've got company."

The doctor followed him toward the door. "Romulans?" McCoy called as the captain sped up the corridor.

"Unknown vessel, Spock said, so let's hope not."

THE LIFT TO THE BRIDGE seemed too slow, but Kirk knew it was the same speed as always. When the doors slid open, the captain was shocked, but not surprised, to see Pippenge standing just outside the turbolift entrance. The security officer, his weapon already drawn, pulled the ambassador out of Kirk's way.

"I saw the yellow alert, and we were informed we were already within the bounds of our system," the ambassador was telling the officer.

At the captain's nod, the security man holstered his phaser and stepped back.

Kirk knew how important the treaty was, but his gut reaction was to have Pippenge forcibly removed from his bridge—perhaps confinine him to quarters. Thankfully, diplomacy overrode that urge. The captain said in his most level tone, "Mister Ambassador, I didn't call you to the bridge."

Nervously, Pippenge pursed his lips. "Yes, Captain, I'm very sorry. I was simply worried. Please forgive me." At least the man knew he shouldn't be there.

Kirk needed to focus on the situation—not the ambassador. He gently pulled Pippenge toward the command chair as the lift doors opened again. Scotty stepped out and hurriedly moved toward his station.

"I saw the alert, sir."

The captain nodded and descended to the command well as Spock moved to his science station.

"Report."

"Alert status confirmed, sir, all decks."

Lieutenant Sulu and Ensign Chekov were at the helm and navigation consoles respectively, quietly awaiting their orders.

"The vessel?" Kirk asked as he lowered himself into the center seat.

"Unfamiliar configuration," Spock said, already bent over his sensor cowl. "No answer to our hails. Intercept in three minutes."

"Spock, what do you make of her?"

The Vulcan flipped switches for a moment, then spun a dial on the side of the viewer. "Conventional warp drive assembly, highly energized plasma weapons, and I believe four forward and four aft torpedo tubes."

A small knot formed between the captain's shoulder blades. "Well armed."

"Also," Spock continued, "class-one shielding and significant armor plating."

"Life-forms?" Kirk asked.

Spock was ready with the answer. "Reading one-hundred seventeen individuals; however, parts of the ship are resistant to scan."

Not a Romulan vessel. Thoughtfully stroking his lip with a finger, Kirk wondered what new race this could be. Being heavily armed didn't necessarily mean they were a threat. The *Enterprise* was armed to defend herself, but such weapons could be seen as offensive by strangers.

Turning toward the sound of the lift opening again, Kirk noticed that Lieutenant Uhura had changed into her regulation uniform. With a nod to the relief officer, she slid smoothly into her chair.

"Visual, Mister Chekov."

"Aye, sir." The ensign tapped quickly at his console.

On the main viewscreen, the image changed from a relatively empty starscape to one where a small dot grew larger, noticeable only because an indicator on the screen pointed out that it was the vessel in question.

"Magnify," Kirk ordered.

A larger, more impressive view of the approaching ship centered itself on the viewscreen.

The data on Sulu's tactical display stated it was only slightly larger in length and width than *Enterprise*. Its mass was seven times greater. Where Kirk's ship had a certain grace, with lines that suggested a design of intended beauty, the unknown vessel was a chunk of a craft, not quite cylindrical. It had no curves—just coarse edges and multi-level ledges that shaped its form. If there were standard warp nacelles, they were hidden within the bulk of the hull. It was either painted dark or naturally so, and its gray form almost disappeared against the black starscape. *It looks*, Kirk thought, *like a crumbling brick. An imposing one.*

The captain nodded toward the alien ship. "Can we predict their weapons range?"

Spock, still suspended over his sensors, replied cautiously. "Not with any accuracy, but if forced to estimate, I would suggest approximately the same as our own."

"How good are your planetary defenses?" Kirk turned slightly toward Pippenge and met his gaze.

His hands tightly gripping the railing, the Maabas ambassador was clearly shaken by the question. His homeworld—or rather, his people's chosen world—was off the usual interstellar routes and therefore rarely got unannounced visitors. "Well," he said slowly, "we'd like to think quite good. But they've not been tested in actuality."

"Captain." Uhura turned toward Kirk, and he twisted to listen to her. "I'm receiving an answer to our hail." She had one hand still on her console and the other touching her earpiece. "Audio only, sir."

"Let's hear it."

The speakers crackled to life, and as the voice was interpreted, presumably accurately, Kirk felt his throat tighten.

"*Attention to all who stand in our way of Kenis Prime. Surrender our planet back to us, or be destroyed.*"

TWO

The aliens hadn't waited for a reply. They'd sped toward *Enterprise*, and the nearer they came, the more the viewscreen crackled with static.

Kirk spun toward Spock. "What's causing that?"

The Vulcan smoothly but quickly consulted his console. "They're attempting to overload our scanners."

"Aye," Scott said from the engineering station. "And it's working. We've got to shut down the sensor grid."

"The whole grid? How is that possible?" Kirk asked. Their systems were well shielded, had built-in redundancies. He looked at his chief engineer and saw a grave expression on the man's face.

Scott quickly nodded once. "Right now, sir."

"Do it," Kirk ordered, then twisted toward the helm. "Switch to passive sensors for maneuvering and targeting."

"Aye, sir," Sulu and Chekov said almost simultaneously, their hands punching at their controls.

From his console, Scott directed an ensign

at the auxiliary engineering station to key in the shutdown. The chief engineer then nodded toward Spock, who took the next steps.

The change that took place couldn't be heard or felt. On a personnel level, it meant hundreds of crew rushing to positions to double and triple check their stations. Kirk sensed a difference, not physically, but emotionally. His ship was hampered—his sight blurred.

The captain thumbed a button on the arm of his chair. "Red alert."

On the viewscreen, the image changed from a starscape view to a tactical display fed by extrapolated computer data. Instead of reaching out, *Enterprise* now waited for information to come to it, and the computer had to estimate what was beyond visual sight.

Kirk's eyes narrowed on the dot on the viewer that was labeled "HO1." Hostile 1.

"Who are they?" he asked Pippenge.

"I—I don't know, Captain. Truly I don't."

Looking for some hint to a possible deception by the ambassador, Kirk saw none. The man's expression edged toward shock, perhaps even embarrassment, but not mendacity. Still, there were lies people told others and those they told themselves. The latter were more difficult to divine.

Uhura pulled the captain's attention from Pippenge. "They're hailing, sir. Audio only."

Turning his gaze back to the ambassador, Kirk said, "On speaker."

"*Attention, battle cruiser. We have surveyed your ship and assessed your capabilities. We order you to remove yourself from this star system. At once.*" The voice, interpreted through the universal translator, sounded vaguely female but had an odd resonance familiar to Kirk which he couldn't quite place.

Glancing to Spock, the captain found the Vulcan raising a curious brow.

The captain motioned to Uhura. "Patch me in." She touched a button, nodded at Kirk, and he began, "This is Captain James T. Kirk of—"

Clearly dismissive, the alien woman cut him off. "*We are of Kenis Prime. You are not. All intruders will vacate our home.*"

"Intruders?" Kirk's brow knitted, and he swiveled to Pippenge for an explanation as he made a slashing motion across his throat to Uhura, ordering communications privacy.

"I don't understand." The ambassador puckered his lips slightly, which Kirk understood to be the same as a human shaking his head. "We are not born to this world, but I assure you the planet was long uninhabited when we found it."

"But there *are* ruins of a previous civilization," Spock offered.

"Of course," Pippenge agreed. "Ancient. Abandoned for millennia."

"Could *these* people have abandoned them?" Kirk asked. "You've studied the ruins."

The ambassador pursed his lips. "Yes. For years."

Hands behind his back, Spock stepped to the rail that separated the upper bridge from the command well. "What do you know of those who built them?"

"Myself?" Pippenge's eyes widened—a shrug. "Little. I am neither an archaeologist nor scientist."

"You call this planet Maaba S'Ja," Spock said calmly. "If memory serves, that means 'new world' in your language. Is it possible another race called it Kenis Prime?"

Thoughtfully, Pippenge paused to consider it. "I don't know. Perhaps. It does sound familiar," he said eventually. "But by an extinct society. Dead, long before we arrived."

"Not so dead." Kirk motioned to the viewscreen, indicating not only the representative dot of the hostile ship, but the actual vessel beyond the bulkhead.

"I—I cannot imagine," Pippenge said quietly, almost to himself.

"They want their planet back." It was as if Fate were laughing at him for thinking this would be a quick diplomatic run—*Enterprise* as taxi service. With the treaty signed, the Federation was now pledged to protect the Maabas, and a hostile vessel from a people posing as the original inhabitants of the protectorate planet qualified as a threat to be handled.

An audible, figurative poke in Kirk's eye, the Kenisian vessel signaled again. "*Intruder battle cruiser. We grow impatient. The planet will be vacated, or all will pay the price.*"

His jaw tight, Kirk replied. "Kenisian vessel, we believe in settling our differences through discussion, not force, if at all possible." He didn't like the Kenisian's tone or threats, but now wasn't the time to mirror them.

After a long pause, Uhura sighed in frustration. "They've closed the channel, sir."

Spock was already studying his scanner when Kirk turned toward him.

"They're charging weapons."

"Shields." Kirk pounded the arm of his command chair. "All hands, battle stations."

"Battle stations," Uhura repeated over the intercom. "All hands to battle stations. This is not a drill. All hands, report to battle stations."

The captain tensed instinctively, as he had when he was a young, green ensign and first heard the call to battle. He told himself that this would change. It hadn't. He could still feel himself coiling up. He had gotten better at hiding it, but the feeling always remained.

To his side, Pippenge gripped the rail so hard it looked like he was trying to snap it in half. For him, a triumphant return home, planned for months in advance, had been tainted by the improbable.

"Evasive action, Mister Sulu." Kirk studied the tactical display, which he knew would be inadequate. "Mister Scott, we need those sensors."

"Aye, sir." Scott sped toward the turbolift. "I'll move the lads along."

The bridge shook as the lift doors closed. Salvos struck against the shields. Without sensors they could not see them coming.

"Damage report."

Spock hesitated a moment before replying. He checked something off one console, then verified it before looking up at the captain. "No damage. But there is something."

Kirk rose toward the science station but gave a half turn to the helm before stepping to the upper bridge. "Maintain evasive, Mister Sulu."

Pointing to an external schematic of the *Enterprise*, Spock indicated three points. "Inert material spaced equidistantly between the secondary and primary hulls."

"What are they?" Kirk shook his head at his own thought. "Not explosives."

"Unknown." Spock flipped two switches on his console but little changed on the graphic above them. The mass reading suggested they were heavy, but that told them little. The power-output said null, but without active sensors, it was all a guess.

Leaning down, Kirk hit the nearest intercom button. "Kirk to engineering. Mister Scott, I want those sensors back now." He looked to Spock. "We may have to risk an overload to see what we're dealing with."

Silence, no reply from Scott. Kirk repeated himself. "Kirk to engineering. Respond."

Just as the captain glanced toward Uhura, she was already checking. "Sir, I'm not getting a response on *any* channel. Internal or external."

Spock immediately bent over his viewer while Kirk checked the auxiliary science station. Internal sensors were either as hampered as the external grid, or . . . "A dampening field," Kirk said. "From the . . . *barnacles* we just picked up?"

His first officer had a flicker of recognition at what he probably thought was a quaint—if not fully apt—term for the material placed on their hull. "I see no evidence the field emanates from them, but I believe they're amplifying one."

"We could remove them manually." The captain stared at the blips on the schematic. Foreign objects on *his* ship.

"Doing so in space suits would likely take two point three hours."

Time they didn't have. Was this a prelude to being boarded? To being destroyed?

"What about phasers?" Kirk spun toward navigation. "We'll carve them off." Maybe the act would take some hull plating with it, but force fields could be put in place in those locations once the dampening field was gone.

Chekov checked his controls at Kirk's request. "Phasers inactive, Captain." He shook his head and turned toward Kirk. "But torpedoes are available, sir."

"Thank you, Mister Chekov. We won't be torpedoing the *Enterprise* today." The ensign was probably only giving full information and not really suggesting they should fire torpedoes on their hull, but Kirk wasn't going to even entertain the idea. "Mister Spock, what about beaming them off?"

The Vulcan nodded carefully. "Possibly." He smoothly worked his console and began a computer simulation. After a few moments, he looked toward the captain. "Assuming Mister Scott gets our sensors online. It will take the majority of our battery reserves, channeled directly through the cargo transporters."

"Leaving us how much?" Kirk asked.

Without checking his computations, Spock answered. "Twenty-two point four percent of capacity."

"Risky." Kirk massaged his lower lip with his right thumb. If they wasted most of their battery power on this attempt, they'd be as good as helpless. But if it worked . . . well, that was the risk part, wasn't it?

He looked for the briefest moment at Ambassador Pippenge, who seemed as anxious as the crew probably felt. They were more accustomed to masking it. As the Maabas were alien to Kirk, what he saw may not have been anxiety. Still, there were some universals of body language and manner among humanoids, and the captain thought he knew nervous tension when he saw it.

"Captain, I have Mister Scott." Uhura pulled Kirk's attention back to the moment, and he moved toward her station to confer with his chief engineer, whom he quickly updated.

"*Well,*" Scott said, "*that explains it. Most systems are down, and I surely won't be able to get external sensors working while those devils're there.*"

"We'll need internal sensors. Then we need to reroute battery power to the cargo transporters," Kirk said. "Mister Spock will provide the details." He motioned to Spock, who moved to Uhura's station with a data card, while Kirk returned to the command chair.

"I am so sorry for all this, Captain," Pippenge said. His tone, even through the universal translator, was marbled with regret.

"Did you have any idea that *this* could happen, Ambassador?" Kirk looked at Pippenge sidelong, a hard stare which was meant to elicit the truth.

"My word, I did *not.*"

He was believable, the captain decided for

the third time. But having been fooled by others in the past, he kept searching Pippenge's manner and determining that the Maabas ambassador was forthright.

"Captain?" Spock called from Uhura's station. "Mister Scott will be ready to proceed momentarily."

"Aye, but one question, sir."

Kirk thumbed the intercom on the arm of his chair. "Go ahead, Mister Scott."

"Where do you want them beamed? Out into space with wide dispersion or into fatal orbit around the star?"

The captain had already pondered that question and knew exactly where he wanted the Kenisian amplifiers. "Neither," he said. "Hold them in the buffers."

Silence. Kirk imagined Scott's eyes had widened a bit. After a moment, the engineer confirmed the order. *"In the buffers, sir. That'll take some doing if we don't want 'em to degrade in the process."*

"They can degrade—after we study them." Kirk glanced toward Spock to confirm his science officer would be able to glean the information from the transporter circuits.

The Vulcan nodded once.

"Aye, sir. Stand by." In the background, Kirk could hear Scott ordering someone to bypass a troublesome circuit. There was a brief silence, then the soft clicking of controls and a slight dimming of

the power of bridge lights and consoles alike. *"We're ready, Captain."*

Kirk pulled in a long breath and let it out with one word. "Energize."

Over the intercom, Kirk could hear the hum of the cargo transporter. It was a slightly different sound than the personnel system. Designed for items of larger bulk and not confined to a small circular pad, the cargo transporter used more power. Some people who'd traveled by it said it was on the harsh side—not painful, exactly, but clearly not usually meant for living matter. Kirk had experienced it himself but hadn't noticed a difference. Perhaps it was just one of those old salts' tales.

As the hum diminished, Scott's voice rang out more clearly than before. *"Transport complete, sir. We have them in the buffer."*

Already there was an apparent change. The lights had come back to full strength, and the ship sounded herself again.

"All sensors are back on line," Spock reported as the main viewscreen returned to a starscape view.

"Mister Chekov, target the source of that dampening field."

"Torpedoes, locked."

"Fire," Kirk ordered without hesitation.

Enterprise spat forth two orange orbs of power that slammed into the bottom of the Kenisian ship and sizzled along its shields.

"Phasers. Fire."

Blue bars of energy connected *Enterprise*'s phaser banks to the underside of the other vessel. The explosions from the torpedoes had disrupted their shields enough that the phaser beams broke through, and a small explosion erupted from the Kenisian ship's belly.

Spock lifted his head from his scanner cowl. "I am no longer reading the dampening field emanating from their vessel."

"I hope they can't repair them," Chekov said.

Kirk nodded his agreement as he rose and pushed himself toward the upper bridge. "Correct me if I'm wrong, Mister Spock, but a dampening field of that strength would take a great deal of energy, would it not?"

"It would," the Vulcan agreed.

"Powerful ship." Kirk took a lingering glance at the Kenisian vessel on the main viewer as it turned slowly away, as if the *Enterprise* were going to bear down on it. "But why send only one?"

"We have no fleet," Pippenge offered, still standing above Kirk's chair, one hand clasped tightly on the rail. "Perhaps they have surveilled us."

Kirk wagged a finger at the viewscreen. "But did they expect to find *us* here?"

"They did not seem unprepared for the contingency," Spock said.

"Captain, they're hailing us," Uhura said.

The captain stepped back down to the center seat.

"We've bloodied their noses." Kirk tried to offer Pippenge some sort of comfort. "They may not be used to that." He motioned for Uhura to put them through.

"Only audio," Uhura said.

"Clearly we have underestimated you, Captain."

Kirk paused, choosing his next words carefully. They were lucky, this time, but it could have gone much worse. "We've both survived that initial mistake. Would you care to discuss the matter? Without the looming threat of violence?"

There was a bit of a wait for a reply, and Kirk assumed that the Kenisian captain was also choosing her words carefully. *"Yes, we would. We are humbled by your grace in this matter."*

"The United Federation of Planets prefers conversation to conflict. And the Maabas are now a protectorate of the Federation." It was one thing to put out one's hand in a gesture of peace, but Kirk thought it important to make a point that the Federation wasn't backing off the agreement with the Maabas. Not just for the Kenisian's sake, but for Pippenge's.

"We understand."

"We would host you, and a small delegation, here on the *Enterprise*, if you like."

Another pause, as she considered Kirk's proposal. If she refused, he wasn't sure what her next move would be.

"*We accept your gracious offer.*"

Pippenge released a puff of breath.

"Are you familiar with matter-energy teleportation technology?" Kirk asked.

"*Yes. We employ such a system for materials—not usually for living beings.*"

"We can transport you to our vessel." Sensing Pippenge's discomfort, Kirk met the ambassador's eyes and tried to give him as well as the Kenisian captain assurance. "No harm will come to you."

"ENERGIZE."

Chief Kyle slowly pulled down the sliders as the Kenisian captain materialized.

As the transporter effect's sparkle and hum faded, she made a long gasp, but she quickly recovered.

Kyle stifled a gulp as they all noticed her upswept eyebrows and gracefully pointed ears.

"Vulcanoid," the captain said quietly, and his science officer agreed with a tacit brow raise.

Her hair was auburn and arranged high on her head with well-maintained curls that sprang down on one side. Atop bright white slacks she wore a loose navy tunic which glittered at her neck and at the end of long sleeve cuffs. It could, Kirk realized, be either adornment or rank insignia. "That," the Kenisian said breathlessly, regaining her composure, "was an interesting experience, Captain."

Kirk instinctively stepped forward to help her as she nearly stumbled off the platform. "I've always enjoyed it." He took her elbow and guided her down the steps.

"I did not." She waved him off as she found her footing. "We don't use such a method for living beings. I was merely surprised by the sensation." Her eyes, large and dark, met his own for a long moment, then looked to where he still held her arm.

The captain pulled his hand back instantly. He looked from her to his first officer, and she followed his gaze.

When she saw Spock, her eyes widened but she quickly recovered from any shock and bowed her head slightly to all of them. "We are Zhatan, Kenisian Fleet Commander and Ambassador." She raised her left hand, showing an open palm facing up. Many cultures offered a greeting of good faith to show they had no weapon.

"I'm Captain James Kirk." He gestured toward the two men behind him. "My first officer, Commander Spock, my chief medical officer, Doctor McCoy."

Spock raised his hand in salute. "Peace and long life."

She scrutinized him with intensity when he

spoke, as if studying him in all ways possible. "You are of Vul-kuhn." The way she said it wasn't just odd to the ear, but had a bittersweet note to it.

"Vulcan," he corrected, lowering his hand.

Zhatan bowed her head, accepting that, but explaining herself. "In our mythology, Vul-kuhn."

"Mythology?" Kirk asked, and he motioned between Zhatan and Spock with his hand. "I take it there's some linked history here."

"Prehistory, perhaps," Spock said. "I am unaware of any Vulcan expedition or colony in this area. Nor have I heard of the Kenisians."

"We have been a spacefaring people for several millennia, Captain. While our origins are lost to time, there are many who have heard of Vul-kuhn—excuse me, Vulcan, and believe we are of their line."

Kirk wondered if that was possible—a people who could create an interstellar craft might lose their own history, and he knew that time could bury facts that grow into myths.

"We look forward to learning more about your people and culture and offering you the chance to know ours." The captain motioned toward the doorway, and the security guards who stood on either side. "If you'll follow these gentlemen, Madame Ambassador, they'll escort you to our briefing room. I'll meet you there shortly."

"Captain." Zhatan smiled a bit—and it was rather alluring. Was she flirting with him? As she stepped toward the door, however, she stopped and turned to Spock, smiling at him as well. "Will Commander Spock be joining us?" She didn't look at Kirk when she asked.

The Vulcan waited for his captain to nod his approval, and only then did he reply. "I will."

She looked at Spock a moment more, smirking again ever so slightly, then left with the security detail trailing behind her.

The Vulcan offered no expression. Was he being cooler than usual? Did he feel the allure of Zhatan that Kirk had?

By the look on McCoy's face, he had clearly sensed it as well.

After a short but awkward silence, it was the doctor who finally spoke. "You know, I may have to say this is fascinating."

Spock pursed his lips a moment, then disagreed. "Not as such, Doctor. There are accounts of more than one group of Vulcan explorers and adventurers who set out for the stars." He shook his head after seeming to search his memory. "I've just no recollection of this one, but their journey may never have been recorded."

"Adventurers?" Kirk was curious.

"Vulcan had its era of exploration and colonization before the time of Surak."

McCoy sighed, as if having a discussion with the science officer was exhausting him. "We know that, Spock. But how many colonies were begun and then lost?"

"Colonies would not be an apt description of such ventures."

"The Preservers?" Kirk asked.

Spock considered that a moment. "Possibly. The time before Surak was one of great dissension and conflict, and a race such as the Preservers may have removed a tribe of early Vulcans in an attempt to ensure the species persisted."

"Or," the captain said, "the Kenisians may share a history with the Romulans. A lost colony of theirs?"

The Vulcan nodded. "Also a possibility, though not necessarily the case. At different times, many factions, political groups, even entire city-states sought refuge in the stars."

"I thought Vulcans were good historians," McCoy said as Kirk headed into the corridor and they followed.

"Now, but not in the pre-awakening," Spock stated. "Wars, large and small, ultimately obscure history. And generally, antiquity is writ by the victors."

"THE KENISIAN PEOPLE do not want war with the Ma'abas."

In the briefing room, Ambassador Pippenge was seated, plainly nervous, halfway down one side of the table and directly opposite Zhatan. As the Kenisian ambassador had come alone, the captain decided to have only Pippenge join them. Kirk sat at the end of the table, next to Spock who was in front of the computer console. McCoy was next to Zhatan, and Uhura had joined them and was seated next to Pippenge. Scott glowered from the very end of the table, still smarting over what the Kenisians had done to the *Enterprise*.

Highlighting the tension, two security guards waited patiently just inside the doors.

"We are called the Maabas," Pippenge corrected, his voice much softer than it had been that morning.

"Mabas," Zhatan said, not quite right. "However one pronounces it, our point is we, especially, dislike armed conflict."

"No more than we." Pippenge spoke so quietly Kirk could barely hear him.

Zhatan clearly had—and she smiled. "Good. As ambassador, we are prepared to accept the peaceful surrender of your people."

Strange phrasing, Kirk thought. Was she royalty? Referring to oneself as "we" suggested that possibility. *Could Zhatan be warlord, ambassador, and queen, all rolled into one?*

McCoy scowled at the arrogance. "Very magnanimous of you."

Missing the sarcasm, Zhatan merely nodded her acceptance of the "compliment."

"You want us to surrender the entire planet to you?" Pippenge was incredulous. "There are billions of people—"

Zhatan cut him off. "We counted approximately four billion, three hundred twenty-nine million, five hundred seventy-seven thousand, four hundred thirty-two."

"A-a-approximately," Pippenge stuttered.

"We're not factoring in birth and death rates, though it is safe to say the number has at least increased since we scanned the planet."

"Must come with the ears," McCoy muttered, and Kirk cast him a harsh glare.

Zhatan turned toward the doctor. "We beg your pardon?"

"You say 'we.'" Kirk drew her attention from McCoy, and Zhatan swiveled toward the captain. "May I ask why?"

"Us?" she said, seeming to think Kirk didn't understand the word.

Kirk and Spock shared a quick glance.

"Could you define 'us,'" Kirk pressed.

"Us," she said matter-of-factly. "Meaning 'we.'"

"We," he repeated. "More than you, an individual."

Suddenly Zhatan nodded, a smile curling her lips. "Yes, we see your confusion now." She motioned to Spock. "Those of Vulcan may be able to explain better than we."

The captain felt his face tighten. He was becoming annoyed. "Spock?"

"I'm afraid I'm at a loss, Captain." He looked to Zhatan. "Please specify."

"There is a word you may know: *Shautish-keem.*"

In Spock's eyes, Kirk saw a flicker of understanding. "A very old myth."

Zhatan smiled more deeply—almost a grin—which on someone who was of Vulcan descent always looked a bit off. "We are no myth."

"You only?" Spock asked. "Or perhaps your caste?"

"All Kenisians."

Whatever it was Spock now understood, he was clearly intrigued. Kirk saw the Vulcan straighten a bit, more focused than usual, even for him. "Care to explain, Mister Spock?"

"*Shautish-keem* is a method . . ." He paused and corrected himself. "The myth of a method—"

Zhatan frowned at that amendment, but Spock continued.

"—from Vulcan prehistory—of preserving the consciousness of one's ancestors within the mind of their progeny."

Silence weighed down on them for what seemed like a long while, until McCoy finally spoke. "Well, Spock may understand, but I'm not sure I do."

Kirk was glad he didn't have to ask.

"As an example," the science officer offered, "the

wisdom of a matriarch, before her passing, may be passed on to a selected relative so that her memories would not be lost."

"Her consciousness," Zhatan corrected, sounding a bit annoyed. "Not just her memories."

"Some kind of permanent mind-meld?" Kirk asked.

"In theory, a far more complicated process. Not practiced, if it ever truly was, since antiquity."

"We," Zhatan said proudly, "have always been this way." She looked to McCoy, whose mouth was a bit agape. "Do you grasp our nature now, Doctor?"

McCoy took a moment to contemplate his reply. "I think so. Family dinner with your crazy aunt, every moment of every day."

"Bones," Kirk chided, then turned back to Zhatan. "We're not just talking to you, but to one of your ancestors?"

"More than one," she said.

Spock's brows shot up. "Not merely a duality, but a true multividual?"

Uhura gasped, as clearly she understood the implications.

"The Vulcan word is *sha'esues*," Spock said. "A collective of distinct consciousnesses held within one mind." He looked squarely, even disbelievingly, at Zhatan. "A very unlikely condition."

"Our sense is that you deem it unlikely so as not to call it 'impossible' and be proven wrong."

Nodding, Spock accepted that appraisal.

"We assure you," Zhatan continued, "this has been the way of my people for our entire history."

Silence settled on that thought. Kirk wondered just how many personalities were within Zhatan. How did they communicate to her? Was she a primary personality, with control over the others, relegating them to mere voices, or did they "possess" her, for lack of a better term? In either case, how large was his audience?

In reality, it might not matter. Kirk often had to negotiate with more than one person—a council, a prefect on a short leash, a ship's commander who answered to higher ranking officials. Perhaps this would be no different.

Ambassador Pippenge seemed to come to the same conclusion. "If I may, Ambassador Zhatan, you are both intelligent and, most certainly, learned in many areas." Palms down on the table, he spread his fingers wide and pressed down slightly, releasing his tension physically rather than through his voice. "Why did you attack us?"

Even though the attack was on the *Enterprise*, Pippenge said "us," Kirk noticed.

So did Zhatan. "Us?"

"Once in our star system, the *Enterprise* is our guest," Pippenge explained.

True, though with the treaty already signed, *Enterprise* was an aligned vessel.

"At the time, we thought it a Maabas warship." Zhatan dismissed the attack with a wave of her hand, as if her perception that the *Enterprise* was the enemy justified the attack.

Pippenge pursed his lips. "We have no warships."

At that statement, the Kenisian ambassador and war commander grinned. She seemed to smile a lot, Kirk thought, and he wondered if it was a smile from Zhatan, or if it was a variety of consciousnesses that turned her lips upward. Could he ever know who was behind the ominous grin? How, he wondered, did her . . . *condition* work?

"No warships. Isn't that interesting," she said, staring at Pippenge, and though it was phrased as a question, it clearly was not.

"We're prepared," Kirk said, pulling their attention back to him, "to negotiate a peace between your two peoples."

"What is your interest in this planet?" Zhatan asked the question, but Kirk sensed a different tone than before. Again, he wondered just who within her was doing the asking.

"Cultural and scientific," Kirk replied. "The Federation's treaty with the Maabas fosters that exchange."

"One doesn't need a treaty to exchange ideas. One only needs a method of communication." Zhatan nodded slightly, as if she'd won some point in a debate. "What else does your treaty cover?"

Kirk was no fool, and now *he* smiled to let her know that. "You're asking if Federation protection is part of the agreement."

Still smiling, she nodded.

"It is," Kirk said, a bit more coolly, and gave Pippenge the briefest of supportive glances.

"Protection from?"

"Threats." Kirk's one-word answer hung there, and as Zhatan considered it, her smile faded.

She leaned back a bit in the chair and steepled her fingers in a manner that Spock often had. "Will you fight a war for them?"

"I don't think that will be necessary." Kirk felt his face tighten again, and he knew his smile had long faded as well. "Will it?"

THREE

"We do not wish war with you."

The captain could see Zhatan was hesitant. The phrasing bordered on equivocation. She might not want war, but that didn't mean she wasn't willing to fight one.

"She" was perhaps an inappropriate pronoun. Were there different sexes within this woman?

"No one *wants* war," Kirk said. "But wars are still fought." He looked squarely at Zhatan. Her high cheekbones were devoid of makeup, but he noticed a natural, healthy green tinge. "The question isn't if you *want* war, it's will you *make* war?"

Zhatan let that question sit for quite a long time, and it was an uncomfortable moment. She blinked at Kirk a few times, then said, "As you might imagine, we are of more than one mind on that question."

It sounded like a pun, and Kirk thought he heard Scott snort, but there was no humor in Zhatan's expression.

"Some," she continued, "are strongly in favor of talking with the Maabas—and the Federation."

Zhatan leaned back, frowning. "And some are very adamantly against that course."

"How do you balance all those different personalities?" Uhura asked in a gentle, forgiving tone, as if she knew it was a difficult task and was sympathetic to it.

"There *is* some effort involved in keeping us all working with each other rather than against," Zhatan admitted.

"Since the time of Surak, Vulcans have established certain mental disciplines to control their emotions. The Kenisians may have developed something similar," Spock said.

Zhatan—or one of the personalities within her, at least—disagreed, but leveled her comment to Uhura, who'd asked the original question. "Kenisian mental controls do not struggle with the emotions of one mind, but a far higher number. Spock compares the gripping of twigs by a small primate to the intricate construction of a musical instrument by a master craftsman. Hardly apt."

Eyebrows arched, Spock looked at Zhatan with some intent. Had he been insulted? If so, he'd not rise to the bait.

It was difficult to look at the Kenisian and not think "Vulcan," but that would be a mistake. Whatever genetics they might share, Zhatan's demeanor was not like that of any Vulcan Kirk had ever met. Culture and philosophy weren't inherited but learned, and a Vulcan who was without an adherence to reason was a disconcerting thing.

And Zhatan did unsettle Kirk. Her initial demeanor had been far more thoughtful, he noticed—even somewhat demure at times. Now her voice was anything but.

"So, you're not hampered by this? It's not difficult?" McCoy asked.

"Not in the least."

"The whole is greater than the sum of the parts," the captain murmured.

Zhatan seemed pleased with that phrasing, and she nodded her approval.

"Just how many 'people' are in ya?" Scott spoke for the first time during the meeting, and the Kenisian commander paused to examine the engineer before she answered. Was she giving the several different personalities within her enough time to evaluate him and decide their answer?

"Four hundred thirteen," she replied simply, and seemed to enjoy Scott's quiet gasp.

"That's . . . almost the crew complement of this vessel." Kirk tried to wrap his mind around the concept. It was difficult enough commanding that number of people—what if their thoughts were merged with his own? How would he cope?

Did hundreds of personalities decide what Zhatan said? Who she loved? What she wore? Did one like stripes while another liked polka dots? Was one a rash commander while another was more cautious? Who was "she" and what part did "they" play?

"Are they all deceased?" McCoy asked.

She paused, and her expression turned sad for a moment before recovering. "Most are long decayed. Some are merely infirm, however, and unable to abide their physical forms any longer." Zhatan motioned down her trunk, indicating her body. "Kenisian culture breeds selectively for this purpose."

Did Zhatan see her body as her own, or was it given to whatever personality needed to live on through it? What happened if she were struck by disease and there were two possible treatments, and the incorporated minds disagreed as to which course to take? Was there a vote?

Zhatan seemed amused at his obvious confusion. "For you it is an alien concept, we can see. But this method allows past generations to live on."

"Logical," Spock said.

"Is it?" Dr. McCoy leveled a sideways glare. There was something in Zhatan's description that had ruffled McCoy's feathers.

The Vulcan's brow furrowed for a short instant as he explained his reasoning. "The Kenisians reduce their drain on resources while keeping alive the knowledge and culture of a far larger population."

"Death, Mister Spock, is a natural part of life. Cheating that could make a person—or a people—

arrogant." McCoy turned to Zhatan and added a softer note. "I mean no offense, Ambassador."

There was something to what McCoy was saying, Kirk thought. If an entire people were immortal, they might look down upon beings with one natural life span.

"We are not offended," she said, and smiled at the doctor with the same electric connection Kirk had felt leveled at himself and Spock. "There *is* difficulty, at times, reconciling the values of the older generations with my own."

So was there effort to control her situation, or wasn't there? She had now offered each a separate explanation.

"Which of the generations within you," Kirk asked pointedly, "want Maaba S'Ja back?"

"All of them," she replied without hesitation. "We understand that the Maabas have considered this their home for thousands of years, but it was ours far longer."

"Then why did you abandon it?" Pippenge's voice was low and thick with emotion. Since he was hunched over the table, the ambassador's height wasn't evident, and he looked like an already defeated man.

Kirk noticed he didn't say "leave," but chose the word "abandon."

In contrast to Pippenge's tone, Zhatan's was smooth and strong. "We were invaded and driven from our world. But having survived, despite our oppressor's attempts to end our lives, we are ready to return home."

Pippenge looked as if he'd tasted something sour. If the Kenisian vessel was but one of a fleet—or even if it was alone—the Maabas were at an extreme disadvantage. "We are a peaceful people—"

"As were we," Zhatan said, but in her eyes Kirk saw no sadness, despite what her voice tried to impart. "The ravages of war transformed us. It's not a change we care to visit on you, but we want what is rightfully ours." This last sentence sounded more threat than anything else.

"Perhaps we . . ." Pippenge began so quietly that Kirk instinctively leaned a bit closer. "We could . . . share this system."

Zhatan seemed to consider it, and then, in a flurry, asked Pippenge several questions. "Divided how? What if you're living on a piece of land that was once ours? Perhaps one of your people now owns a farming valley that belongs to another and that individual wants to see it tilled by his progeny? What if we don't care for certain technological developments you've introduced into our ecosystem? What have you done with our buildings and artifacts? In what museum or under what microscope have you spirited away our culture?"

Pippenge opened his mouth a moment, then

closed it and remained silent. He had no answers to those questions.

For her part, Zhatan seemed almost as uncertain as Pippenge. Her eyes darted from Kirk, to the Maabas ambassador, to Spock, and back again. What kind of battle was going on within her, and which of several factions would win out?

The captain held out his hand, both figuratively and literally. "This is what treaties are for. We may not be able to work out the details in one meeting, but over time an agreement can be forged—without violence. Without bloodshed." He looked into Zhatan's eyes and tried to connect with all the minds she harbored. "Let the Federation mediate. Let us help."

Kirk's attempt at persuasion was seemingly lost on her. "We're not sure that is agreeable to our comrades both within and without," she admitted. "Tell me, Captain." Turning fully to Kirk, Zhatan met his eyes. Perhaps she was trying to discern his true intentions—as if he wasn't being forthright. "Will you stand in our way if we take back what is ours? We have no quarrel with the *Enterprise* or your Federation."

This question was exactly what Kirk hadn't wanted to hear. How could he answer? He didn't know the extent of the Kenisian fleet, their alliances, their resources.

At the same time, the Federation would not sign a treaty with the Maabas, then abandon them. While the agreement didn't make them a member of the Federation, it promised them protection. The Maabas were not some pre-warp civilization that couldn't be interfered with. They were, in fact, on the path to Federation membership.

"We don't want a quarrel with you, either." Kirk decided to walk an ambiguous line with Zhatan, rather than directly answer her question. "Take our proposal for mediation back to your people. All of them." He opened both arms as if the offer sat between them. "Discuss it—thoughtfully—knowing that both your cultures and peoples would benefit from a lasting peace."

Hesitating for an uncomfortably long time, Zhatan finally nodded to herself—or perhaps to one of the multitude of minds within her—and reached out her hand to Kirk. "Your words will be considered."

He took her hand, ready to forge an agreement based on a meeting of the minds. The captain felt good about it and his concerns melted away. He was sure an accord could be reached. The Maabas would make an agreement with the Kenisians, and if they didn't, it would be their loss.

But the Federation shouldn't take sides, Kirk decided. Not only were the Maabas intruders to this system, but the Federation was as well.

In fact, it would likely be best if *Enterprise* left. Yes, he should leave and never return.

I should tell Chekov to set a course back to DS5,

Kirk thought. *That would be the best option. The Maabas aren't worth our blood. Nothing is.*

He let go of Zhatan's hand and moved to the intercom on the table.

The captain hesitated, his thumb hovering over the control. *Set course,* Kirk thought. *Leave this system.*

It's the right thing to do. Wasn't it? Let the Maabas handle their own affairs. Who are we to force ourselves into this dispute?

The treaty had a protection clause, but the decision to take action could be left up to Starfleet Command.

I can recommend to Command that we don't get involved; that the treaty with the Maabas was a mistake. A new treaty with the Kenisians would be just as fruitful. More.

"We shouldn't be here," Kirk said softly. "We must leave."

Spock leapt from his seat and stepped between the captain and Zhatan. "Release him."

Kirk blinked several times. "Spock, what're you doing?"

Motioning the guards forward, Spock had them take Zhatan in hand. Each security officer took an elbow and drew her back.

"Release him," Spock repeated, and the words seemed foggy to Kirk—distant. "Now."

The captain looked at Zhatan and she returned his gaze. She smiled brilliantly, friendly and peaceful.

And yet, it seemed out of place. Wrong, even. As if no one should be smiling just now, but for a reason Kirk couldn't quite remember.

The Vulcan stepped toward Zhatan and the guards. Pulling his hand back, he slapped her across the face—twice.

"Sp-spock?" Kirk blinked again. *What's happening?*

"Spock, what the devil are you doing?" McCoy rushed to make sure Zhatan was okay, but the Vulcan blocked his attempt.

"Stand back, Doctor."

Spock struck her again, Zhatan grunted in pain, and Kirk felt his knees collapse.

The deck came up to greet him and then diffused into nothingness. He tried to push himself up, but wasn't sure the thought could connect to an actual movement. There was no sensation outside his last, fleeting thought, *I am alone.*

SICKBAY.

Jim Kirk could smell it—that air-scrubbed aroma that was less a scent than a lack of one. He could feel the light on his eyelids as he tried to pull them open. The overwhelming brightness wouldn't allow it, but he was able to partially open one eye. Above him stood a blurry McCoy.

"Neck . . . hurts," Kirk managed to croak out,

and he seemed to announce it at the same time he realized the sharp pain.

"I'll get you something for that." McCoy's tone was warm, laced with concern.

"No," Kirk said, his voice a slow syrup. He would use the pain—let it be the sensation that pulled him back to reality.

At the same time, his muscles were weak. The captain struggled to move, as if a force field were pushing down on him. Kirk inched himself up against it, and McCoy helped by grabbing an extra pillow and placing it underneath his head and neck.

Once propped up, Kirk relaxed into it and the light became a bearable glare. The neck pain, while still throbbing, spread itself in all directions, becoming a head-and-upper-back ache.

To McCoy's right stood Spock, hands behind his back. Past him was Nurse Chapel, who was biting her lower lip, a hypo grasped in her hand.

"What happened?" Kirk's voice scraped like gravel.

"You were assaulted," Spock said matter-of-factly. "A type of Kenisian mind-meld. It began when she touched your hand and continued after physical contact was broken."

Kirk felt his jaw slacken, and his mouth opened in shock. He noticed it was dry. *"After?"*

"Ambassador Zhatan is an extremely strong telepath." Spock said "ambassador" as if the title was dubious. "She's being held in the brig."

The captain swallowed hard. "Water."

Chapel moved to get him a cup and was back with it quickly. He took a sip, held its coolness on his tongue for a long moment, then let it drift down his parched throat.

When Kirk spoke again, his voice was near normal. "How long was I out?"

"About twenty minutes." McCoy glanced at the medical scanner readout above the biobed.

"What exactly did she do?"

Looking to Spock, McCoy deferred to the Vulcan's expertise.

"When she touched your hand, Zhatan initiated a mental link. I sensed it in your hesitation from that moment on. Subconsciously you were fighting the meld."

"You sensed it?"

Spock nodded slowly, once. "I am familiar with the body language, for lack of a better term, of such an encounter."

Pulling in a deeper breath, Kirk took one more sip of water and sighed. He was feeling more himself again. "You struck her."

"To break her concentration," Spock said. "After Zhatan refused my demand that she release you."

Swinging his feet over the edge of the bed, Kirk sat up. While his head swam a bit and a wave of nausea washed over him, he used the pain to steady himself.

"Jim, I'm not sure—"

Kirk waved off McCoy's concern. "I'm fine. I'm fine." He placed his feet on the deck and stifled the urge to buckle at the knees. Standing shakily he looked at Spock. "We need to confirm she's out of my head."

With tacit acknowledgment, Spock kept one hand behind his back and placed the other on the captain's face.

The Vulcan's fingers pressed lightly against the left side of Kirk's head: near his ear, at his temple, his cheek, his nose, and his jaw. In a sudden jolt Kirk had felt before, the pressure to these areas increased—as did the pain in his head and shoulders as he held his head in place against Spock's touch.

As if from afar, Kirk felt Spock's presence in his mind. It was only for an instant, then the Vulcan pulled away and the sensation was gone.

"Zhatan is not present," Spock said, his right hand returning to his left behind his back.

Kirk nodded his thanks. "Then let's go talk to her."

On the way to the brig, the captain's anger broiled in his belly. By the time Spock and he arrived, Kirk had to keep his voice from being a snarl. After years of diplomatic missions, he was well practiced at that.

The captain stood in front of the brig's force field and motioned to the guard to turn it off.

With a sizzle, the field was gone, and Zhatan stepped into the corridor to greet Kirk and Spock.

"Unprovoked violence," the captain began, his tone tighter than he'd wanted, "is unworthy of an ambassador in the middle of negotiations."

"We are sorry, Captain." She bowed slightly, and Kirk couldn't tell what was in her eyes. There were hundreds of people behind that gaze. How was he to know which were sincere and which were subversive?

"Are you?" he asked.

"We're afraid there are times when the disparate personalities within force an action which some do not desire."

Kirk nodded. Overtly, he had to accept that excuse—mainly because doing anything else would not be useful. What he really wanted was to tell Zhatan to get the hell off his ship.

Instead, he reiterated Ambassador Pippenge's offer. "The Maabas are interested in pursuing peace. The Federation is happy to mediate in order to find a way for both your peoples to coexist—if not in harmony, then at least civilly. We've done this for many opposing factions, and I have no doubt that with time, a proper accord can be reached. One that is agreeable to all." Kirk couldn't smile, as he normally might. Instead, his speech was pro forma. "We urge you to take this proposition to your people—*all* your people, as I said—and consider it as the best path for all involved."

"Yes," she said simply—even sadly. "We shall do so."

Kirk motioned toward the guards. "These men will escort you to the transporter room. We'll inform your ship to expect you." He then looked to the security team. "Mister Baumgartner, make sure neither you nor Lieutenant Sentell touch the ambassador." On that note, Kirk gave Zhatan a final polite bow.

When she and the security men were gone, Kirk just stood there, looking after her.

"Captain?"

Kirk shook his head. "I'm fine, Spock." He began moving down the corridor, and his first officer followed. "What did you find in Skent's device?"

"Nothing sinister," Spock said. "Notes on his journey, holographic images of the delegation at various locations, including the *Enterprise*. None were a risk to security."

"Good. Where's Pippenge?" Kirk turned and headed for the turbolift. "I want him on the bridge."

The Vulcan nodded, and before they entered the lift, he contacted security to have them escort the ambassador.

When they arrived, Sulu was in the center seat. With a nod, he relinquished it to Kirk and replaced the substitute helmsman at his own station.

"Standard orbit, Mister Sulu." Moments after Kirk lowered himself into the command chair, Pippenge and his escort stepped from the lift. The guard took up post at the lift doors while the ambassador stepped down into the command well, an excited chitter emanating from his throat. "Oh, you're uninjured! I am very glad, Captain. Very glad." He grasped Kirk's right hand in both of his, and the four-thumbed grip was noticeably tight.

Still a bit weary from his ordeal, the captain could only manage the slightest of polite smiles. He was concerned, and Pippenge could likely tell. Certainly the ambassador's own anxiety was etched into his pale pink features.

"The Kenisian vessel has retreated from the Maaba S'Ja system," Spock reported from the science station. "They're holding position at the edge of our sensor range."

Kirk nodded and motioned Spock toward him.

The Vulcan stepped down, flanking the captain on his right as Pippenge did on his left.

"Maybe they've estimated our scanner range incorrectly." Kirk stroked the edge of his chin with a forefinger and looked toward the viewscreen. On it, the Maabas homeworld spun slowly. Correction, adopted homeworld.

"Or," Spock offered, "they understand the scope of our sensors and are sending us a message."

"What message?" Pippenge asked.

" 'We're not done here,' " Kirk said.

"Perhaps they are showing respect, leaving the system while they contact their leaders to discuss our terms." Pippenge looked hopeful at the prospect

of such a conclusion, but one could tell he was trying to convince himself as much as anyone else.

"Maybe." *Or maybe not.* Kirk wasn't ready to
believe the Kenisians were so amiable. The forced
mind-meld told him that. "Why *this* planet?" he
asked, nodding toward the globe on the viewscreen.

"Perhaps a cultural or emotional reason which
escapes logic," Spock offered. "Being Vulcanoid
doesn't assure one a rational philosophy."

"Neither does being Vulcan." Kirk smiled playfully. He was feeling more himself with every moment.

Ignoring the jibe, Spock merely agreed. "Indeed.
Reason at all levels is a volitional act, not one of
instinct."

"You're a war-weary people," Kirk mused, trying to understand the Kenisian mind-set. Or was it
minds-set? "You've been living on another planet for
thousands of years. You learn another people now
inhabit the world you were pushed from—which
wasn't your own world to being with . . ." Kirk looked
at Pippenge and continued. "No offense, Ambassador, but what's so special about your planet?"

Head rolling around in a Maabas-style shrug,
Pippenge began his answer slowly. "Maaba S'Ja
is temperate and fertile in many areas, especially
the largest northern continent. Water and natural
resources are not overly plentiful but it is surely
not a lifeless husk. We did, as you noted, have to

terraform one of the natural satellites, due to our increasing numbers."

Sulu had obviously been paying attention, and he turned toward them from his helm. "There are at least three other planets in this sector equally as habitable."

Kirk nodded and considered that. He appreciated input from his senior officers, and Sulu knew that such commentary was valued. Having been an astrophysicist, the helmsman could often be called upon for the kind of assessment he'd just offered.

"Mister Spock?" Kirk swiveled toward his first officer. "Let's assume there's something more to this story that we're missing."

Spock nodded.

"Of what do you speak, Captain?" Pippenge asked.

Kirk turned back and smiled, and then looked to Spock again, still holding his playful expression. "I don't know. But if there *is* something, I'd bet Mister Spock can find it."

Both of the Vulcan's eyebrows rose, and he pressed his lips into a thin line. "If," he began slowly, "I may have access to the Maabasian databanks, I shall endeavor to investigate."

"Of course, of course." Pippenge bowed. "I shall see to it immediately." He clenched his jaw tightly, then released. "Chifger? This is Pippenge. Commander Spock from the Federation *Starship Enter-*

prise will communicate with you regarding Maabas Central archives. Please see to his every request."

Kirk knew they used implanted communicators, and while he understood the privacy it afforded them, he'd never liked the idea. Starfleet had experimented with them for a time, but rejected their use when they were found to be no more secure than communicators and far more painful when an enemy sought to remove or destroy them.

After a pause, the ambassador puckered his lips. "No, he is to be given *full* access. Yes, yes, on my authority." Pursing his lips, Pippenge thanked Chifger and clenched his jaw again. "If you will contact my associate on subspace channel five-five-two, he will grant you access and answer any questions you may have."

Spock bowed his head in acknowledgment and retreated to the upper bridge. Once at his station, he picked up an earpiece and initiated the transmission.

Placing his left hand on the captain's forearm, Pippenge delicately pinched Kirk with his two thumbs, drawing his attention. "Captain, may I speak with you privately?"

This was Kirk's bridge, and those within earshot were in his strictest confidence and held his inalienable trust. Of course, Pippenge didn't know this, and that he trusted the captain of an alien starship was impressive for someone from a previously xenophobic culture. Still, the captain didn't want to abandon the center seat. The Kenisians were sitting out there, just at the edge of sensor range, and it made the hairs on the back of his neck stand on end. Stepping up to a more private section of the bridge was the most he was willing to do.

"Certainly." Kirk led Pippenge toward the viewscreen.

Pippenge whispered, "I must know, Captain, will you help us if the Kenisians refuse to come to an accord?"

That's the question of the day, isn't it? Kirk thought.

When he didn't answer immediately, the ambassador pushed on. "While we have a defensive force, it's not interstellar. However large or small the Kenisian fleet is, we can't rebuff a full-scale attack."

Feeling the urge to bite his lower lip, Kirk studied the ambassador. He hoped he wasn't outwardly expressing the real concern he felt. Logistically, the *Enterprise* may have been able to defend the planet from a ship such as Zhatan's. But they certainly couldn't hold out against several more of them.

The nearest Federation starship was the *U.S.S. Farragut,* but it was at least ten days away at maximum warp. If the Kenisians brought a fleet—or even a small squadron of ships—they would outgun the *Enterprise*, and there would be massive loss of life before reinforcements could arrive.

Is a planet worth it? Would the Kenisians agree to an orderly migration if the Federation offered to help find the Maabas another planet?

Glancing at the viewscreen to his right, Kirk watched the M-class planet spin lazily beneath them. *A rock*, he thought, *like many others*. Add water and air, it became an ecosystem; in some ways fragile and rare, in others robust and comforting. It had supported life for how many millions of years before the Kenisians happened upon it? And despite a war that left its cities in ruin, that rock was able to sustain another race for thousands more years.

Neither people were native to the planet. But what did "native" mean? Pippenge was born on a planet he called home. Was he native? Did one have to spawn from a planet's oceans as humans did on Earth to call a planet their own?

Spock was half human, but born and raised on Vulcan. To which planet could he be considered native? What of a human born on Mars? Or Alpha Centauri? Were they aliens in their own homes?

This wasn't an issue of the Maabas forcing the Kenisians from their homes and the aggrieved party now wanting back what was stolen. Someone else did the forcing, and the Maabas were refugees when they found the Kenisians' *adopted* planet. Both peoples had been lost. Both had found the rock below and clung to it in their need.

Why was one to be considered to have more right than the other? Especially when the current residents had offered to share their world?

"Will the Federation help?" Kirk echoed the ambassador's query. Finally responding, the captain said, "Mister Ambassador, that's why we're here."

FOUR

"You made the right call, Jim." Admiral Withrow's office filled the main viewscreen. His large desk bisected the image on the screen and the Starfleet insignia behind him framed his bushy red hair. *"The Federation Council wants Starfleet to give our full support to the Maabas."*

"Agreed, Admiral, but if the Kenisians are serious in their threats, *Enterprise* will need support." Kirk leaned forward slightly in the command chair. Something told him Zhatan was very serious, and he hoped he'd imparted that to Withrow.

"I'm recalling the Exeter, *but she's three weeks from your position."*

"The *Farragut*?"

Withrow's eyes flicked to someone out of view, then quickly back. *"Yes, they're closer, but otherwise engaged and can't be diverted.* Exeter *is the next closest. Even if* Farragut *finished on time, she couldn't get to you before* Exeter."

"I see." Three weeks was a long wait. What was happening with the *Farragut* that Withrow saw the *Enterprise*'s situation as a lower priority? Kirk could only imagine. But as weighty a responsibility as a captain's command was, the braid of an admiral was far heavier. It wasn't a position Kirk envied. "Very well, sir. We'll hope for the best and prepare for the worst."

"*I'm sorry, Captain. I wish I had better news.*"

Kirk sighed slightly. "So do I."

"*I know last time you were in my office, I'd promised you an exploratory mission, Jim. Next one, I promise.*"

A smile tugged at Kirk's lips. "I'll hold you to it, Bob."

A yeoman with a clipboard leaned in to the picture. The admiral signed with only a glance at what it contained. "*Can I assume the Maabas government has officially asked for this support?*"

The captain nodded. "The ambassador and his delegation are beaming down to confirm it as we speak."

"*Keep us informed.*" Withrow's brows knitted in concern. "*Good luck, Jim. Starfleet out.*"

The viewscreen reverted to the image of the planet below. Conferring with Command had not gone as Kirk expected.

He turned to Uhura. "Lieutenant, let the Maabas delegation know we've apprised Starfleet of the situation and . . ." How should he phrase the fact that *Enterprise* would be the only hope the Maabas had for three weeks? "They will have Starfleet's full available support in the most timely manner possible." *Closer to a month than not*, Kirk thought. "Let them know how long, but assure the Maabas *we* will be here."

And hopefully we'll be able to stop the Kenisians.

PIPPENGE AND HIS PARTY materialized directly where Captain Kirk said they would: just inside the anteroom to the Maabas High Court. It was a comfort to see home, even if it was the more sedate foyer to the beautiful courtroom. The anteroom was filled with colorful glass sculptures and lighted tables that told stories to those waiting. And the temperature here was more agreeable than aboard the *Enterprise*.

Their own teleportation technology allowed only for station-to-station transport. Pippenge had hoped the scientific exchange with the Federation would allow such accurate and untethered travel to revolutionize Maabas mobility. Now, all he hoped for was a way to keep his world.

Norla, one of President Moberte's adjutants, gasped when she saw the materialization process had completed. "Amazing," she said. "Quite amazing."

The ambassador pursed his lips in acknowledgment, and when he didn't smile, Norla's own happy expression quickly faded.

"What is wrong?" she asked.

"Much." Pippenge handed her the diplomatic packet he'd been carrying and walked past her toward the Court chambers. "I must consult with the council immediately."

She stopped him before he reached for door. "They are voting. There can be no disruptions."

Huffing out an annoyed breath, Pippenge turned back to his delegation.

"Barge in, Ambassador," Skent said. Turning to Norla, he explained, "This is a matter of great importance."

"What has happened?" she asked.

Ortov, one of the young attendants who had spent much of the voyage to and from the Federation space station in silent contemplation, finally spoke. "A race calling themselves the former inhabitants of this planet has named it as Kenis Prime and claimed it as their own."

Pinching her nose, Norla lowered her head and began to shudder.

"It is unjustified," Tainler said.

Pursing his lips, Skent agreed. "But they have the means to wage war, and we do not."

"This is why I must speak to the council now," Pippenge snapped.

Motioning the ambassador quickly away from her, Norla relented. "Go, go."

Pippenge reached quickly for the Court door.

"Please wait for me here," he told the others as he entered the council chamber.

The Court was where the elected heads of all the Maabas provinces conferred about any action or incident of planetwide interest. There were seventeen representatives seated around an oval table. There had always only been that number. No matter how populated a district became, it was worth one-seventeenth to the Court. In the past, that had caused many an argument. Why should a district with a million people get the same representation as one with three million? Tradition. When the Maabas arrived on their new world, the bulk of the people were spread across seventeen huge vessels. Those ships held the majority of the refugees from their old world, and while looking for a new home, each vessel had counted as a single vote in the exiled court. When they disembarked, many stayed together with their former shipmates. Some had not and people were free to move where they desired. Over time, some provinces thrived better than others, and so population disparity arose.

Pippenge, from the largest district, had never cared for that construction. But since it had worked—as much as any government can—for so long, it was highly unlikely to change.

The tall ceiling and curved walls of the room allowed all voices to be well heard without artificial amplification. However, the sessions were recorded both for posterity and broadcast.

When Pippenge entered without announcement, he had to wait until the vote being taken was complete. Whatever they were discussing passed by three votes, and the small gallery chittered its approval.

Making his way directly to the Court's president, Pippenge leaned down and whispered, "We must consult under closed session, with haste."

President Moberte had known Pippenge many years and had appointed him to his ambassadorship. She flickered the lights of the hall with a button on the table before her, pulling the attention of all in attendance to her decree. "Closed session is called and granted without dissent." Moberte did not wait for verbal opposition, and the attendants ushered the gallery audience to the exits.

By the time Pippenge made his way to the small podium directly opposite the president, all eyes were on him.

"The *Enterprise* has been attacked," Pippenge began, and he told the Court of the last few hours' ordeal in as much detail as he could, including Zhatan's assault of Captain Kirk.

As soon as the ambassador bowed his head, showing he had completed his statement, he was peppered with questions.

"Is Captain Kirk well?"

"Why did *Enterprise* not hold this person on charges?"

"Should we say 'these persons' if she is truly this multividual as was described?"

"If she is Vulcan too, perhaps Kirk's Vulcan first officer supported the attack and when it was unsuccessful he liberated her."

"What does the Federation say about all this? Will they honor the treaty?"

"If this happened while in our space, have we jurisdiction to prosecute the Kenisian woman? Women? Whatever she is."

Holding up his hands, Pippenge clacked together the nails on his four thumbs and asked for quiet. "Please, please, listen to me."

The room quieted down only when President Moberte flickered the lights again.

Snorting two breaths from his nostrils, Pippenge was frustrated. Most of the Court's questions had been answered already, if they'd only listened more closely. But as he had been speaking, aides were handing written comments and queries to the Court members, and they were more than likely fixating on how they should react rather than on what Pippenge told them.

Pulling in a deep breath, the ambassador answered all their questions as he remembered them. "Captain Kirk is well and unharmed by the attack. The *Enterprise* was not in orbit when the Kenisian commander assaulted him, and I believe her government would claim the space in which the attack took place was disputed. She is not a Vulcan, but they probably share some distant lineage." He took another breath, and focused only on the president's expression as he continued. "Commander Spock was the one who discerned the attack and stopped it from injuring the captain. As for the Federation, they have been apprised of the situation. They are sending help, but it will take some time. Captain Kirk, as their representative and at their behest, has—as I indicated—pledged the *Enterprise*'s support."

Many quiet whispers and side discussions broke out until Moberte flickered the lights yet again. Silence reasserted itself.

Nehrin, from the smallest district, who represented a mostly agricultural province, was the first to raise his hands and clack his thumbnails in an attempt to be heard. "Pippenge, you've met this woman, or whatever she or they may be. Do you believe they're willing to share this planet? And if so, how much land would they demand?"

Strigle, from the mostly industrial area, clacked to be heard next. "The question is why would they agree to share when they must know we haven't the force to repel them?"

"Is this truth?" Moberte asked. "Pippenge has seen but one ship. Where is this force you fear?"

"They attacked the Federation ship, stouter than anything we have. If they do not fear a vessel that could lay waste to this planet, why should we not fear them?" D'ricci shouted. While one of the more logical Court members, he also had a more negative, fatalistic outlook on life.

"The *Enterprise* rebuffed their attack, and with their skill forced the Kenisian into parley," Moberte reminded the Court.

Pippenge counted several affirmative expressions. Even D'ricci pursed his lips in agreement.

One of the newer Court members, recently elected from a coastal province whose chief enterprise was tourism, clacked her thumbs to speak.

She was an older woman, her hair now red with age, but she made no attempt to hide her years. Pippenge had never spoken directly to Lodi, but had always found her quiet and thoughtful in Court proceedings.

"You trust this Captain Kirk." Her voice was strong, though lower than one might expect. Pippenge assumed it was because she spent much of her time outdoors, perhaps at the resorts so prevalent in her community.

"I trust him," Pippenge said. "For those who wish it, I can offer the chance to meet him. You're surely as good at judging character as I, if not better." He smoothed their feathers a bit with that last comment, but that is what ambassadors did. "He is forthright, and having visited with his Federation leaders for these last few weeks, I assure you they *are* how they represent themselves." He puckered his lips. "We would not have signed the treaty otherwise."

"Then, if you believe this is the right path," Lodi said, linking her hands together, "we are committed. The Federation is more experienced with interstellar relations, and we should heed Captain Kirk's recommendation—and yours—as to how to resolve this crisis."

Pippenge hadn't thought of it as a crisis, but it was. People liked to say how this issue or that could mean the fate of the planet hinged on one thing or another, but here was a situation where that assessment was not hyperbole.

His gut told him to trust Kirk. His experience told him the same. But what if he was wrong?

Looking from face to face, not just the Court members but their aides and lastly President Moberte, Pippenge wondered if he should reconsider his advice. Perhaps they should offer the Kenisians an out by agreeing to find another planet. A migration would take years and be a hardship, but it wasn't impossible.

The president clacked her left hand's thumbnails together and called for a vote. "If dissent is to be held, let it be heard."

There was silence as all bowed their heads. This, Pippenge thought, was the true strength of the Maabas. They had been through so much turmoil together, so much loss that required them not just to depend on one another but to *respect* one another, that the end result was a true harmony. Perhaps that was why they'd resisted exploring the stars for so many years. They knew other people cultivated acrimony and disdain for their brethren, and the thought of becoming that frightened the Maabas.

"Thank you," the ambassador mouthed silently to the president.

Moberte pursed her lips. "You may inform Captain Kirk of the Court's agreement and our trust in him."

THE LAST THING Kirk saw in Pippenge's eyes before he beamed down was a look of overriding trust. The captain hoped that it wasn't misplaced.

When he returned from the transporter room, he walked directly to the bridge science station. He'd left Spock the conn, but the Vulcan had not abandoned his computers for the command chair. For Spock, being in command did not require a center-seat presence. He and Palamas had been poring over the records provided by the Maabas, and the first officer clearly felt his best efforts were to focus on that task.

"What've you got?" Kirk asked them.

Flipping a series of switches, the first officer

activated one of the viewers over his station. A spectral analysis wavered and faded, replaced by the data Spock required.

"While our own sensors were down, Maabas monitoring stations—which are quite sensitive—recorded a series of rigorous sensor scans aimed at the planet, all emanating from the Kenisian vessel."

Kirk studied the graphs. As soon as the *Enterprise*'s sensors had been hampered by the dampening field, the Kenisian ship had begun intensively scanning the planet. Why?

The captain rubbed the back of his tight neck. "They were distracting us."

"From what?" Palamas asked.

"They're looking for something." The captain leaned over and punched up pictures of where the Kenisians had scanned. "Defenses? Centers of industry? Resources?"

The Vulcan disabused the captain of that notion. "I had assumed so. They gave such locations cursory investigation." He pointed at several spots on one particular Maabas continent on the screen. "But these sites, here, here, and here. These were of paramount interest."

Having familiarized himself with the basics of the planet's physical and political geography, the captain was at a loss to understand why the Kenisians would be intent on those locations. "But there's nothing there."

"Nothing of which we're aware," Spock corrected.

"We did find this, sir." Palamas toggled a switch and another graphic overlaid the first. Several new dots, pinpointing different locations, filled the map. Three hit exactly where the Kenisians had been scanning. "Ruins. All sites with archaeological evidence of the civilization which predates the Maabas."

"Kenisian ruins." Kirk flipped another switch and returned to the previous graphic, limiting the sites to the three the Kenisian ship had been most keen to scan. "The Maabas have investigated all of these sites?"

"Yes, sir," Spock said. "Their records reveal that a great deal of Maabas technological advancement has come from either direct discovery of ancient technology at these sites or has been inspired by what was unearthed."

Of course, Kirk thought. Finding a planet with a past civilization as advanced as—or more advanced than—one's own would spur a technological revolution. World after world had such growth once they discovered warp drive and met other races. In fact, such an exchange was one of the reasons the Federation sought a treaty with the Maabas. To learn and grow through cultural and scientific exchange was a primary reason for the *Enterprise*'s mission to seek out heretofore unknown civilizations.

"The Kenisians were pushed from this planet,"

the captain said. "And they left something behind. Something important."

Spock agreed. "Presumably."

"We've got to find it," Kirk said, a new tension knotting his shoulders. "Before they start a war to get it back." And if they did, the captain wasn't sure the Kenisians would lose.

Likely considering the same concerns, Spock pursed his lips grimly. "Zhatan, as a battle commander, would likely have a confounding strategy."

Kirk pulled in a long breath and let it slowly out. "It's hard enough to predict one opponent. How would we do against a chorus of them?"

"WHY DO WE WAIT, Zhatan?" As always, the most restless among them was Tibis.

She looked down at her screen and watched the Kenis system from afar.

"So long we have waited. Why do we wait?" another asked.

"Why do we wait?"

"Why do we wait, Zhatan?"

"Why?"

Tibis was the instigator, the mind that unsettled the others and agitated them to discussion.

Why was Zhatan here, looking doubtful in front of her crew? She need not even be on the bridge. She could be alone.

Except alone for her was not as other individuals might regard the concept.

"We must not wait."

"Why do we wait?"

"Why?"

"Because something in Kirk's mind tells us to avoid conflict with him, if we can bear more delay," she told them.

"We cannot bear it."

"No, we cannot."

"We cannot."

"We cannot."

"We cannot."

The Federation ship sat in orbit of Kenis Prime. It mocked them from afar. And it angered many.

"We cannot abide, Zhatan."

"We cannot."

"We saw all, and Kirk's mind is a weak cognizance," Tibis charged.

But Zhatan remembered all too clearly his will and how difficult it was to attempt to corrupt it. *"We are not all in agreement."*

"Who are you to disagree with us, child? Have we not always guided you to safety? Listen to us." When Tibis couldn't get her way through argument, she patronized. And others followed suit.

"Listen to us."

"Listen, child."

"Listen."

"Listen to us."

Zhatan closed her eyes, shutting out the image of the *Enterprise* around *their* planet. A planet they never walked on with her feet, but she had seen it again and again in her memories.

"Kirk is formidable," the commander insisted.

"Enterprise can be overcome."

"With cunning and experience," Tibis reminded them.

"We have experience. We are history. Listen to us."

"Listen to us."

"Listen."

"Listen to us."

"He will defend the Maabas," Zhatan warned. *"He is virtuous and will honor his commitments."*

"The Maabas are insignificant."

"Kirk is insignificant."

"He will fail."

"He will fail."

"We will succeed."

"Have trust."

"Have faith."

"Have courage and trust."

"We will succeed."

"Our time is now. We will succeed."

"Maabas are insignificant."

"Humans are insignificant."

Zhatan rubbed her neck, massaging out an ache. *"Kirk's first is of Vul-kuhn. We have not seen his mind, but know its strength."* She touched her jaw, where Spock had struck her. Her neck still hurt from the blow.

"Spock is weak," Tibis assured them.

"His mind is weak."

"His cognizance is insignificant."

"He does not shautish-keem.*"*

"His is not sha'esues.*"*

"Spock is weak."

"Insignificant."

"Our time is now."

"Have trust, child. Have trust."

"Trust," Zhatan said. "Yes." *Doubts were for feeble minds, were they not?*

"Do not let doubt weaken you," Tibis chided. *"We are strong."*

"Together."

"Together we are strong."

"Together we are decisive."

"Listen to us."

"Listen."

"Listen."

"Listen."

FIVE

The Maaba S'Ja star shone brightly on the steppe the records had referred to as the Gloskik Plain. The air had a chill here and less oxygen than Kirk was used to. It was uncomfortable. Which was why McCoy was along, though he lagged behind Spock and Pippenge, as well as the ambassador's aide, Tainler.

"Come along, Doctor." Kirk tried to keep a gasp from his voice. "You're falling behind."

There was one security officer behind McCoy and one who took point just in front of Spock. Next to Kirk was Lieutenant Palamas, who continued to provide useful information based on her study of the Maabas.

"Damned transporter," McCoy huffed. "Could have put us down closer to the site."

"I'm afraid that's my fault, Doctor," Pippenge said with requisite remorse. "We transposed a coordinate number."

"Mister Ambassador, I was sure those were the right coordinates, but I see now I must have made a mistake." Like all Maabas, Tainler had a computerized implant, the display of which was written right to her visual cortex. It was clear she was looking through some data as she scampered alongside him.

Pippenge waved off Tainler's apology with a dismissive hand. "Please think nothing more of it. A brisk walk is just what we need to clear our thoughts."

"I could never live with an implant," Palamas whispered to Kirk. Like many humans, especially those serving in Starfleet, Palamas was horrified by the idea of unnatural biological alterations. The hubris of augmenting humans led to one of the most horrific conflicts in Earth's history, the Eugenics War, and was outlawed in the Federation.

Kirk glanced back at Crewman Kaalburg, then forward toward Ensign Ottenbrite. Neither of his security team were having problems breathing. Or, like their captain, they were trying to hide it.

"Have you been here before?" Kirk asked Pippenge.

"No, I'm afraid. I'm more an administrative animal than a scientific one."

"I didn't mean the archaeological site." Kirk gestured to the land around them. "I meant this countryside."

"Oh, here? No." Pippenge surveyed the flat land with its peppering of grasses and brush.

The plain could have been Mongolia or a terraformed part of Mars, by the looks of it. Natural beauty took many forms, and an even expanse of prairie or a lush jungle each held their own innate allure, especially for someone who worked in outer space.

"As a youth, my caretakers would suggest outings to nature areas with plant growth and waters and the like." A mild disdain leaked into Pippenge's tone. "I was not . . . I'm not sure how to say it."

"An outdoorsman?" Kirk offered.

"Yes! That is a delightful word. I was not an outdoorsman. I was raised in the city, and preferred my studies and activities with comforts, not insects and harsh conditions."

Listening to the dry grass crunch under his boots, Kirk wondered if he had not been raised on a farm, close to nature, might he have shared Pippenge's attitude? The captain couldn't imagine not enjoying the sun—any sun—shining on his face, warming it, feeling the breath it gave to all things on any world that lived.

"Here," Spock announced, studying his tricorder.

All stopped and looked around at the empty plain. Huffing lightly, McCoy trudged up alongside Kirk and stuck a hypo into his arm.

The captain spun toward the hissing sound.

"Tri-ox." McCoy turned the hypo on himself and pressed. "I wouldn't give you anything I wouldn't prescribe for myself." He then injected Palamas, who'd pleasantly offered her arm to him.

"Comforting." Kirk nodded toward Kaalburg and Ottenbrite.

"Yes, them too." McCoy injected both security officers, then turned back to the captain.

"None for me, thank you, Doctor." The Vulcan continued to scan with his tricorder.

"I wasn't going to offer, Mister Spock." McCoy placed the hypo back into his small medkit. "I know that green blood is accustomed to a thinner atmosphere."

"And," Spock said, moving off toward the left, "it wishes to remain unaccustomed to your potions."

Grunting his disapproval, McCoy said nothing.

"An entrance." Spock pointed toward the ground three meters to his left. "A slab of refined material which I believe is a hatchway."

"Yes," Tainler said. "This should be it."

"It will be locked," Pippenge said, turning to his assistant. "Do you have the code?"

Tainler's eyes darted around at her internal display. "I am finding it now."

When she suddenly smiled, the hatchway groaned open, sliding away to reveal a great chasm into which dirt and sand fell.

Kirk went to the edge and looked in. Steps led downward at a steep decline. Below he could see a landing that led to another staircase with a more reasonable pitch.

"When's the last time anyone was here?" Pala-mas looked down through the hatch.

"Fourteen years ago," Tainler said after a brief pause to recall the data. She then seemed to be reading from a document she'd called up on her internal computer. "'Mitash Gles dig site will lose funding this season, along with seven other ar-chaeological locations, as the Science Directive has suggested no more information can be gathered.' Dated thirty-seventh of Ashko season."

With a nod from the captain, Ottenbrite knew she should stay and guard the opening. Kirk took the first step down, followed by Kaalburg, Spock, and Palamas. Then Pippenge, McCoy, and Tainler followed.

The atmosphere was dry, cool, and rather stale, but the stiff breeze that forced in from the hatchway also freshened the flat air with surprising speed.

"There should be lights," Pippenge said, and looked to Tainler for confirmation.

She pursed her lips, then puckered them, then pursed them again. "Found them."

The lights slowly came up—glowing panels in the ceiling. When the room was fully brightened, an elevator to the right became visible, offering an-other mode of descent from the stairs.

"I assume all this," Kirk said, making a circling motion with his index finger, "is Maabas architec-ture."

"Yes," Pippenge said, repeating the circling motion himself. "The elevator leads to a central processing room where archaeologists, scientists, and engineers worked. From there, a connection to an underground complex built by the previous civilization—"

"The Kenisians," Palamas interjected.

"Yes, I suppose so. Anyway, from there one has access to several corridors in what we believed was a research facility."

"Buried underground?" McCoy asked.

"It's not uncommon," Palamas replied.

Tainler flattened her lips. "Scientific research may deal in compounds and materials which pose a danger to the population, and so several layers of rock and dirt act as a natural vault. It's one of the reasons there are intact ruins."

Kirk wasn't sure if the woman was accessing that explanation from a database or had studied the field.

"Don't most spacefaring races shift dangerous experiments offworld?" McCoy asked.

Pippenge moved toward the elevator doors and they creakily opened, a little gasp of stale air escaping as they did. Lights came on inside and Pippenge stepped in, Tainler at his side.

McCoy turned to Kirk, crooking a thumb over his shoulder at the elevator. "This is safe?"

The captain shrugged and stepped into the elevator. "It's fourteen years old."

Spock, McCoy, Palamas, and Kaalburg followed suit and the doors closed.

"Oh, it's far older than that," Pippenge said as the elevator descended slowly. "I believe this installation had been operational for nearly one hundred and fifty years."

"Wonderful," McCoy groused, then whispered to Spock. "How long is that in Earth years?"

"The universal translator is programmed with both Earth and Maabas solar information, Doctor. As you heard it, one hundred and fifty years is one hundred and fifty years."

"Oh, right." McCoy gnashed his teeth.

Slightly bemused, Kirk shook his head at the exchange.

"I assure you, Doctor, Maabas construction is very reliable." Pippenge tried to sound encouraging, but the groaning sound coming from the elevator didn't assure the passengers.

They arrived at what Kirk assumed was the bottom of the shaft with a dull clunk. After a moment of awkward inaction, a pneumatic hiss accompanied the slow opening of the doors.

The lights were already on and as they stepped out, Kirk noticed the air was fresher than the level above.

"Fresh air?" Palamas asked.

"As soon as we activated the elevator," Tainler said, "the air handler system was initiated."

Efficient, Kirk thought.

Before them was a central hub of computers—
empty chairs with powered-down consoles which
looked like stations on a Federation starbase. The
captain reminded himself that while Earth explored
space, the Maabas concerned themselves with discovering the world they'd adopted.

The walls were a mixture of manufactured composite materials and stone, using the natural structure of the planet's crust whenever possible.

Several hatchways led out of the room. Kirk
counted eight, all labeled in the Maabas language
which looked to his eye like a mixture of Korean
and cuneiform. "To the Kenisian areas, I assume."

"To the ruins," Pippenge said. "Yes."

An interesting change of phrasing, Kirk realized, but the ambassador wasn't wrong. They had to
keep in mind that just because Zhatan said this had
been her planet, that didn't mean it was true.

"I believe," Spock said, taking a reading off his
tricorder, "that I can utilize these systems to scan
the entirety of the ruins."

"That is their purpose," Tainler said.

Spock moved toward the central console. "Will
you help me?" he asked Tainler.

Bowing, the Maabas woman joined him.

Kirk nodded to Kaalburg. "Secure the elevator."

The crewman returned to the open lift, keeping
one leg inside it and one out.

"Oh, I'd not do that," the ambassador said. "Good

way to lose a leg. At any secure installation, the elevator will return to the top automatically. Extremeties notwithstanding."

Kaalburg quickly stood erect, just inside the lift, looking for the stop control. "Thanks."

"Ride up and stand guard with Ottenburg," the captain ordered.

"Aye, sir."

Kirk, Pippenge, and McCoy walked the perimeter of the room, looking through the hatchway windows as they passed. Lights were not on, so the corridors were black, and the light coming through the glass did little to displace the gloom.

"Lieutenant?" The captain motioned for Palamas to join him.

Leaving Spock and Tainler at the central console, she walked to where Kirk, Pippenge, and McCoy stood. "Sir?"

"You identified this as the site the Kenisians were most interested in."

"Yes, Captain. Their sensors focused mostly on this ruin."

"How did it differ from the other two sites they scanned?" Kirk peered out the hatch window closest to him, imagining that years ago the installation was a hub of activity with dozens of Maabas combing through its secrets.

"This was by far the largest site," Palamas said. "I can find out by how much, if you like."

The captain shook his head.

As usual, McCoy asked the most pointed question. "So the Kenisians think there's something here, but if the Maabas have studied these ruins for over a century, why didn't they find it already?"

Palamas shrugged. "I believe that sometimes to find something, you have to know what to look for."

"True," Kirk said.

"We've been examining ruins left in haste and damaged by war for years," Pippenge explained.

"Zhatan obviously knew what she was looking for," the captain said, "if not specifically where to look."

"They knew once they scanned the planet, sir," Palamas added.

Kirk nodded, then looked at the ambassador. "What if you *did* find it? But didn't know what you had?"

Pippenge considered Kirk's hypothetical a moment, then—perhaps consulting his own internal computer database—said, "I don't believe so, but I'm not an expert on these matters. It would seem this site revealed many small and interesting discoveries, but nothing paradigm shifting."

"What kind of discoveries, Mister Ambassador?" Palamas asked.

Again, Pippenge paused before answering. "Honestly, I don't know what to make of them, myself. I believe most of them related to interpreting other sites."

"Like the Rosetta Stone," Kirk said.

Pippenge pursed his lips. "I do not understand this reference."

"A carving found on Earth," Palamas explained. "The same text was written in three languages, providing a key to deciphering ancient hieroglyphs."

"Oh, perhaps, perhaps."

The ambassador was rather noncommittal to the notion, but it was less disinterest, Kirk thought, and more because he was out of his depth within the fields of archaeology and anthropology. Being an expert in those areas was why Palamas was on the landing party.

As the three approached Tainler and Spock, the captain asked, "What've you found?"

"The coordinates the Kenisian vessel was explicitly scanning." Spock pointed to a display which was without graphics and showed only a jumble of Maabas text.

"You can read that?" McCoy asked.

"After a fashion." The Vulcan looked to Tainler. "Correct me if I'm wrong, but the referenced chamber is at the lowest level found and the most protected in the original construction."

Tainler flattened her lips. "It is. But as I said, little was found here." She pointed to the same display.

"Just several vaults holding storage containers of a solid compound we could discover no purpose for. We believed it to be a construction material, since the vaults were constructed of a similar compound."

"An inert solid to us, perhaps," Spock proposed. "But many compounds are inert until a catalyst is introduced."

"Scientists did experiment on the compound, with all known catalysts." Tainler's lips puckered in the negative. "They found nothing."

"Indeed." Spock emphasized his point with a raised brow. "All *known* catalysts."

"One can't experiment with the unknown." Tainler's tone was defensive, and Kirk assumed she was feeling put-upon by all the recent revelations. Having an assumed-long-dead civilization return and claim your home had to shake the Maabas to their core.

"I meant no offense," Spock said. "I merely suggest that there may be a science here to which we are unaccustomed."

Rolling her head in acceptance of that, Tainler was demure.

"Are there Kenisian computer banks here?" Spock asked.

"Yes," Pippenge said. "They are still at the end of that hallway." The ambassador pointed toward a hatchway.

"They were accessed and copied, but never translated," Tainler provided.

"In fact," the ambassador said, "it was one of the first items the scientific exchange between our people and the Federation was going to undertake. We know you have a larger xenolinguistic database."

The database, Kirk realized, might not be necessary. If the Kenisians were truly Vulcan offshoots, then Spock might be able to decipher the ancient archives.

The Vulcan clearly had the same idea. "I will need access to those records."

Pippenge did not hesitate. "Of course. Tainler?"

"The system should have them." She moved to activate a series of switches on the console in front of them.

Kirk's communicator beeped, and he excused himself. Taking a step to the side, he flipped it open.

"Kirk here."

"Scott here, sir. The Kenisian vessel is gone."

The Kenisian ship had been at the extreme range of the *Enterprise*'s sensors. Maybe it was gone, or maybe it was just out of sensor range. "Mister Scott, I want you to survey the system. See if you can find them."

"Leave orbit, sir?"

"I need to know if they've gone or are just hiding."

"Aye, sir." Scott sounded skeptical. Or, more likely, his mother-hen concern was poking through.

"Drop back into orbit every two hours to make contact if it makes you feel better."

"Aye, it would."

"Kirk out."

"Is there a problem?" the ambassador asked.

"Overprotective chief engineer," Kirk told Pippenge with a smile.

The captain turned toward Spock and Tainler and peered past them to the console display. The screen was filled with both Maabas characters and glyphs that looked vaguely Vulcan. Not that the captain was an expert on either language.

Kirk knew Spock would report as soon as he'd learned anything. But with the Kenisian vessel unaccounted for, the captain needed answers now.

"What have you found?"

"The language in the Kenisian databank *is* similar to some ancient Vulcan dialects, though I believe it may have more in common with certain Romulan patois. Interestingly, I even see some roots in common with ancient—"

"Spock."

His first officer understood, but wasn't able to help. "I'm sorry, sir. Nothing as yet."

Kirk sighed, and he turned away, allowing Spock and Tainler to return to their work.

The captain decided they should take advantage of the extra computer stations. He clapped his hands together eagerly. "Lieutenant Palamas, bring your tricorder. We're going to see if we can't learn something ourselves."

Kirk wasn't sure whether scanning the Maabas

databanks would be useful or not, but he had to keep active. There was always the possibility that they might discover something Spock and Tainler wouldn't.

After a while, he found nothing of import. His anthropology and archaeology officer, however, was having a field day.

"This is remarkable," Palamas said yet again. "The Maabas found a computer with near sentience that they were able to reverse-engineer in under ten years. That's an amazing feat given the limitations of their scanning equipment at the time. In fact, that helped them improve their sensors so much that future discoveries accelerated threefold."

"Interesting, Lieutenant," the captain said, "but not especially helpful."

"Sir," she said, "this could be quite useful in mapping a more complete technological record. We should be able to trace back exactly which technologies were influenced by the ruins and which were more inspired by original Maabas innovation."

"But what are the Kenisians looking for?"

She nodded. "Oh, of course. I'm sorry, sir."

"It's easy to get distracted." The last thing Kirk wanted to discourage in his people was the thirst for knowledge.

As they continued their investigation, every so often Palamas would chime in with another factoid about the ruins that wasn't especially pertinent.

After two hours, Scott checked in, but had no news. There was no sign of the Kenisian ship.

Soon after Scotty's report, Spock called the captain over.

The *Enterprise* officers stepped over to the console where Spock and Tainler were working. Pippenge and McCoy gathered close behind. Kirk asked, "You've found something?"

"Yes," Spock said, and he gestured to a graphic of a molecular bond as it rotated on the screen in front of them. "This is the inert compound the Maabas scientists found, but thought useless."

Staring at it, Kirk searched his memory for something similar. Chemistry wasn't his strongest subject at the Academy. "I don't recognize it," he said.

"Neither do I," McCoy said.

Pippenge made a face that seemed to say "Don't ask me."

The captain raised his hands, palms up. "Spock."

"It is unknown to Federation science, but according to this data, it is a synthetic composite with qualities similar to paralithium, dilithium, and trilithium."

"Synthetic dilithium?" Kirk was aghast, and he shared a concerned glance with McCoy and Palamas.

"I do not understand," Pippenge said, his brow furrowed in worry.

"Dilithium is used in controlling warp propulsion and is inert," Spock said matter-of-factly. "But this synthetic dilithium is not, despite sharing certain qualities with the inert dilithium. These notes suggest that it is highly unstable with the correct catalyst."

"Our scientists ran simulations," Tainler said. "It's not an explosive. Not with any catalyst we attempted."

"But it is housed," Kirk pointed with his thumb to the hatchways behind them, "kilometers underground."

"With good reason," Spock said. "While we may not know the catalyst that would unleash its destructive power, this is not a compound one would create and keep in high quantity without reason."

"The Kenisians know what the catalyst is," Kirk said.

"Doubtless," Spock agreed.

"But," said Kirk, pacing and thinking aloud, "they don't have this synthetic dilithium. And they need it."

"What's it called?" McCoy's voice was thick and his blue eyes were a bit glazed over. The captain knew him well enough to know that the doctor was considering all the dangerous, explosive possibilities.

Spock checked the display. "It has been labeled *Iikum na'hubis*."

"*Iikum* is an old Vulcan word for compound," Palamas said.

"Correct." Impressed, Spock nodded toward the A&A officer.

"I've studied the ancient civilizations of all the Federation's founding members, sir," she said proudly.

"It must be difficult to synthesize," Kirk said, shrugging toward the hatchways. "Or they wouldn't need to raid this ancient warehouse."

"There is one more thing," Spock told them.

McCoy bristled. "Isn't there always?"

Spock explained, "I don't believe the containers in which this compound is stored are merely holding vessels. They may be prototype weapons."

"Torpedoes?" Kirk asked.

"More like mines." Spock flipped two switches, and the display changed to a picture of one of the ancient Kenisian weapons. "There is no delivery system, no primer, no catalyst, but I believe there are chambers within the containers intended to hold the catalyst when called for."

Kirk frowned. "This was a weapons factory."

"A testing facility, but it amounts to the same."

"They want to destroy us." Pippenge's voice wavered, and he nervously stroked his hair between the two thumbs of his left hand. He looked to Tainler, who appeared equally worried.

"No, they don't," Kirk assured them.

Spock motioned to the display. "If the *na'hubis* is as powerful as the data suggest, using it would destroy not only this planet, but the entire solar system."

"Damn," McCoy whispered.

"Mister Ambassador, the Kenisians want the *na'hubis*. There is no logic in destroying what you hope to claim."

"With respect, Mister Spock," Pippenge said shakily, "for good or ill, people are often motivated by motives other than logic."

"How much of this *na'hubis* is here?" Kirk asked.

"Fourteen containers, if these records are correct. Enough to destroy an entire space sector, if detonated properly."

"Properly?" McCoy snapped. "How is a detonation that destroys a space sector proper?"

"Please calm yourself, Doctor. 'Proper' meaning a correct process for a specific end. I was not making a moral judgment."

McCoy opened his mouth to respond but Kirk shook his head slightly, warning him off.

"And the danger to my people?" Pippenge asked again.

"None," Spock said. "Again, without the proper catalyst, it is, as your scientists found, quite harmless."

"Why go to war to acquire it?" Kirk tried to rub a knot of tension from his neck, but it wasn't going away.

"Perhaps to protect it," Spock suggested. "I'm not familiar enough with the compound to be certain. However, it could be used to produce a chain reaction, and that might cascade out of control, destroying more than one's intended target."

"A doomsday device?" Palamas asked.

Kirk shook his head. "Let's hope not."

"The Kenisians' intent is unknown," Spock said grimly. "But the possibility of wide-scale destruction cannot be ruled out."

"They may not know what they have," Palamas suggested.

Tainler was now panicking. "Might they fear that we've made it into a weapon?"

"Their intensive scans were probably checking to see if you *had* weaponized the *na'hubis*." Kirk nodded toward the display on the console.

"But we haven't. They know we haven't, don't they? Does that mean they will leave us in peace?" Pippenge asked.

"Unlikely." Spock toggled a switch, and the view returned to the basic data on the compound. "Considering their actions, the Kenisians may want to continue the experiments they were conducting thousands of years ago."

Kirk stepped away from them, studying the consoles and the hatchways. "It's more urgent than that." The captain wasn't sure if he was getting that feeling from having talked to Zhatan and the personalities within her or from when she force mind-melded with him. Somehow it must have come from her. Otherwise why would he know that the Kenisians were on a timetable?

"They want these containers."

"Mines," McCoy corrected.

"*Why* do they need them?" Kirk asked. "How many other installations are there like this? How much of this compound has been stored elsewhere?"

Spock checked the computer again, scrolling through a series of reports in the Kenisian language. "If I interpret this correctly—I can only surmise—"

Kirk didn't care about the qualification. "How many, Spock?"

"I believe this was a unique installation. It is possible the Kenisians hoped this weapon would end their war, but did not have time to complete it."

"If they had, how would they have even used it? They'd destroy their own planet just to keep invaders out? 'If I can't have it, no one can'?" McCoy's tone was thoroughly irritated, as if the Kenisians who designed the weapon were in the room.

"It is not a rational plan. But if they're Vulcan—" Palamas began.

McCoy cut her off. "A modern Vulcan wouldn't. But one without logic?"

Spock agreed. "We were brutal and heartless before embracing Surak's teachings. My world was devastated by war after war." He paused. "It was not rational, but savage and vicious."

"They obviously don't have the means to re-create the *na'hubis*." Kirk turned directly to Pippenge. "We need to get rid of it. The *Enterprise* isn't back yet. When Mister Scott returns, I can have a team beamed down to remove it all. With your permission."

"I— I don't know," Pippenge stammered. He was an ambassador, not a head of state. "I'd have to consult the Court. President Moberte would have to authorize—"

"We may not have time for that." Kirk pulled out his communicator and flipped it open. "Kirk to *Enterprise*." He nodded toward Pippenge. "The ship may be in range. I'll need you to contact your President and get clearance for us to beam down the proper equipment."

"I will do so now." The ambassador looked away, nervously making his call.

"Kirk to *Enterprise*." The captain fussed with his communicator's dials. "Kirk to *Enterprise*." Even without the ship in orbit, there should be some kind of response signal showing a channel was open. There wasn't. "Spock."

Instantly, Spock drew his tricorder from the lip of the console where he'd set it down. He began scanning and pulled his own communicator out to watch what happened when it tried to open a frequency. "Jammed."

Kirk knew it, but needed the science officer to confirm. "Try to find the source, Spock. We have very little time." He turned to Pippenge. "I need to see those containers."

The ambassador nervously stroked his hair. "Tainler can escort you."

"I have the plans to the site." Tainler moved toward one of the hatchways. "Follow me, please."

Kirk ordered Palamas, "Recall the elevator. Let Kaalburg and Ottenbrite know to be on their guard."

"Aye, sir." She walked toward the elevator.

The captain turned to follow Tainler.

McCoy called after him. "Jim, what's going on?"

His useless communicator held tightly in his right hand, the captain looked solemnly at his friend. "A fable is coming true."

"Captain Kirk, wait." Pippenge ran after him. "Please explain. A fable?"

On his way through the hatch Tainler had opened, Kirk stopped to meet the ambassador's eyes. "The demons are coming, Mister Ambassador."

THE CAPTAIN AND TAINLER returned to the central control room after only two minutes. They found Pippenge nervously pacing, shedding hair into his hand and onto his robes: loose strands of both dark and white had fallen and were laying oddly across his breast.

A bit out of breath, Kirk huffed to Spock, "What about the jamming? Can you tell where it's coming from?"

"From here."

They all looked toward the elevator, its doors now open. Zhatan stood inside, flanked by two heavily armed soldiers. A third hulking soldier held a squirming Palamas. He pointed a weapon to the A&A officer's head. It looked like a cross between a Romulan disruptor and an ancient Vulcan laser pistol, which suggested some cultural designs were deep-seeded.

"My men." Kirk instantly thought of Kaalburg and Ottenbrite.

"You might say they, too, are 'jammed.'" Zhatan didn't smile. She didn't seem to be enjoying this as much as her words might suggest.

Kirk hoped his men weren't dead. Perhaps there was a Kenisian neck pinch. They had a weapon to Palamas's head but hadn't shot her. So there was a chance.

"I knew you weren't gone." Kirk wouldn't play games by asking Zhatan what she wanted. They all knew. He only hoped to delay her long enough that Scott would return, get no answer to his hails, and beam down a security team.

"You're an insightful commander," Zhatan said. She motioned in a way that encompassed them all. "Remove your weapons and communications devices, please."

With Kirk's nod, the landing party removed their equipment and placed everything on the lip of the console. As the captain lay down his phaser, he pulled Palamas away from the Kenisians and moved her behind him.

"As proficient as you are," Zhatan continued, "we are better. Collectively we have hundreds of years more experience than you."

"Experience, but not wisdom," Kirk said, hoping to engage her in debate now that Palamas was out of direct danger. "Why do this to the Maabas? You could have a home here. With them. In peace."

"Peace," Zhatan said bitterly, "no longer interests us."

SIX

Ordering them to lead the way, the Kenisian commander directed the *Enterprise* officers and the Maabas to move through the hatchway that led to the ancient facility. For reasons she didn't care to divulge, Zhatan needed the original computer banks.

In an attempt to stall until the *Enterprise* returned, Kirk was happy enough to go along.

"How did you manage to return to the system without my ship detecting you?" he asked her.

"We're more clever than you may credit us, Captain."

"Oh, I credit you quite a lot."

"We sense some disdain in your tone."

"Do you?" Kirk tried to slacken his pace so he could hang back and get closer to Zhatan, but the guard who'd threatened Palamas—a large cross between a Vulcan and a Neanderthal—pushed him forward. Of the three guards, he was the biggest and seemed focused on Kirk. The other two held their weapons on Spock and the lieutenant, and McCoy, Pippenge, and Tainler respectively.

"If we were as vile as you think us," Zhatan said,

"would we not kill you where you stand? We do not *need* you."

Kirk thought that sounded like she was trying to convince herself she was acting justly. Or at least not foolishly.

"You're looking for a weapon of uncontrollable destruction."

"It can be controlled. It will be," she said. "We are sure it can be done."

Can be, Kirk thought. "So you've never used it."

"It has been beyond us," Zhatan admitted sadly. "We have held the plans within us for so long."

"But you needed the prototype. You don't remember it all." Like some ancient game of telephone, Kirk surmised, their memory of the plans had become too divergent from the original.

"As I said, Captain, you're quite astute." Was that respect in her tone? How many of the consciousnesses within Zhatan admired Kirk, and how many wanted him dead?

That was something he might have to test.

"We have a modern version of the devices you found," she continued. "But we do not have all the details on the original. Some things," she said quietly, "are lost to time."

"And," Kirk pressed on, "you don't have the *nu'hubis*."

"*Na'hubis*," she corrected him. "But you are right. Re-creation and refinement has always eluded us."

Spock spoke quietly from his position near the front. "We accessed Maabas copies of your data. If your antiquated computers no longer function, would it not be best to use more modern equipment?" Kirk knew he, too, was looking for a way to slow down the Kenisians until the *Enterprise* returned. If they decided to go back, rather than forge ahead, it would waste significant time.

"Did you find details on how to create *na'hubis*, Mister Spock?" Zhatan asked. "Or meticulous plans on the prototype?"

"No."

"Because such information would be hidden, nontransferable. And incorruptible."

"You didn't have time to take the plans or the compound when you fled," Kirk realized.

Zhatan softened, as if remembering far back—part of her likely was—and her voice was heavy with emotion. "We tried. There was great debate about what the weapon might do to our planet, and some were very much against its use without further testing." As if pivoting on a mental heel, Zhatan became bitter. "Others were sure it would work, and we were denied the chance to save ourselves from exile."

Differing factions, Kirk thought. *How many are still alive within her that remember the exodus?* The captain stopped and waited for Zhatan to catch up with him. It was all so natural that the guards stopped, eating away more time.

"Zhatan, you can have your planet back. You can share it with the Maabas. We can even find a new world for you." Kirk held out his arms, half pleading with her, half welcoming her in peace. "There doesn't need to be violence."

She sighed. "Captain, we are well aware that your ship is due to arrive soon. You Starfleeters seem to be ones of habit and schedules. We applaud it." She motioned him forward with her weapon. "But we shan't be fooled by your tactics."

"Keep walking," the guard next to him said, pressing the point of the weapon into Kirk's back. Reluctantly, the prisoners started down the corridor again.

When they entered a stairway that led down—to where, Kirk couldn't see—he thought this should be where he made his move.

Mock-tripping, Kirk stumbled down three stairs and into Pippenge as well as McCoy's and Tainler's guard, which caused Spock and Palamas's guards to falter.

Spock quickly recovered and attempted to subdue his sentry with a neck pinch, but the move was anticipated and blocked.

By the time Kirk had gotten two blows into the jaw of his immovable guard, Zhatan fired a warning shot of bright green energy that smashed into the stairwell ceiling above them and sent sparks showering down. "Enough!"

Knuckles stinging, Kirk straightened from the

awkward crouch he'd been in. He'd planned to spring from his legs to strengthen the next punch—a difficult move to perform while on stairs—but he never got the chance.

Foolish. The space was too confined for that to have worked. As he panted stale air in and out of his lungs, Kirk remembered that the atmosphere was thinner and the tri-ox was wearing off. And his strength waned with it.

They continued down the stairway. "We know you had to try," Zhatan said. "But you needn't worry about yourselves or what happens t—"

At the bottom of the stairway, they moved into a large room. There was a computer kiosk to the left, and opposite that were the containers Spock had shown them.

The *na'hubis.*

Once they were all inside, Kirk turned to watch Zhatan. *What had she been about to say?* If Kirk needn't worry, was it because they'd be dead?

No, he thought. Using the weapon on the planet would defeat the purpose of their return. Kirk couldn't believe they'd be so irrational that they would destroy their adopted homeworld just because someone else had colonized in their absence.

The tone of Zhatan's voice, the feeling he got when she was in his mind—

"You want revenge," Kirk said. "Not against the Maabas, but whoever pushed you from this world."

Zhatan stared at him for a long, uncomfortable moment. *What was she thinking?* And how many minds inside her were debating what she should tell him?

"Not revenge," she said finally. "Justice. For the lives upended by a war of aggression."

"Justice?" Kirk asked. "Or punishment?"

"Do you not have a system which penalizes wrongdoing, Captain?"

Kirk nodded. "We do. Only when someone is found guilty is a punishment carried out."

"Conquerors, by their actions, are guilty of many crimes."

Kirk could feel the anger radiating from her, like waves of emotional heat. Again he wondered if it was something left over—some tenuous link—from the forced mind-meld. If so, he felt no influence, just a thread of understanding.

Instinctively, the captain knew not to ask her who she was to try, convict, and carry out a sentence for past crimes. The consciousnesses within Zhatan probably remembered the atrocities they suffered. To her—to all of them—this was not something from a school lesson. It was their personal history.

Pulling a device from her pocket, Zhatan placed the small semicircle-shaped object on the computer kiosk. The unit hummed to life, and a series of holographic images rapidly sliced through the air above the kiosk.

The blur was too quick for Kirk to read, but he noticed Spock registered what—for a Vulcan—passed as surprise, perhaps even shock.

The captain was poised to finally ask why, but Spock was already stepping forward.

"This weapon must not be used."

The Vulcan's Kenisian guard tried to pull him back but they were of relatively equal strength and the thin air did not hamper Spock.

"Be silent," Zhatan snapped. She moved to fire her weapon at him, but then she pulled her arm back a bit.

"I cannot," Spock said.

"Mister Spock, don't," Palamas whispered.

"The Maabas archive did not have complete data. The true purpose of this weapon"—he nodded toward the kiosk's holographic display that continued to flash by—"is to vibrate subatomic particles in such a way that energy and matter break down irrevocably."

"Hardly," Zhatan said. "The process can be limited. We now know exactly how to regulate the effect." She sounded like a scientist giving a lecture.

"Captain," Spock said, turning to Kirk, "the Kenisians mustn't be allowed to detonate one of these mines. Humans feared there might be a chain reaction from splitting the atom, that it would destroy the atmosphere. The database showed Kenisian scientists debated the same quandary. They did not finish the experiment." He looked at Zhatan. "They'd decided the risk was too high."

"They were wrong," she said. "*We* were right."

Kirk had his answer about the Kenisian factions. The cooler heads that prevailed and lost a war to save their planet were gone. Those who would risk everything were perhaps all that remained.

"The fabric of space itself is in peril," Spock said, and hearing that from someone not given to hyperbole sent a shudder down Kirk's spine. "You will destroy far more than your foe."

"Listen to him!" McCoy pulled forward but was held back by his guard.

Zhatan pulled the object from the kiosk and returned it to her pocket, then regripped her weapon and changed its setting.

"There is no telling the extent of such an event," Spock said. "This arm of the galaxy could simply cease to exist. Energy and matter would collapse, creating a void of nonexistence."

"You're wrong," she told him, "and I shall prove it to you."

Zhatan pulled the trigger, as did all her guards. A green flash was followed quickly by darkness.

WHEN SPOCK REGAINED consciousness, he was neither on the planet, nor back aboard the *Enterprise*.

He *was* on a space vessel. He could feel the vibration of engines through the deck plates and the oddly undefinable quality of artificial gravity that differed slightly from the natural pull of a planetary body.

The Vulcan opened his eyes, and they quickly adjusted to the light. He had been placed on a bunk attached to a bulkhead. Having been unconscious, the position was uncomfortable and he stirred. This awakened Pippenge, who was lying next to him. The rest of the landing party were not present.

The walls were an unremarkable gray. The bunk was sturdy and seemed to be part of the wall rather than attached, as he previously assumed. The room was otherwise bare. There was illumination wherever the overhead met the bulkheads, but there didn't appear to be a door or other path of egress. Clearly they were in some sort of holding cell.

"Are you well?" Spock stood and helped the ambassador to his feet, steadying him by lending support at his elbow and the small of his back.

"I—I think so. I ache all over. And itch. I itch for some reason." He began scratching his arms and then his legs, thumbs pinching at the skin through his robes. He finally scratched the length of his body in an attempt to stimulate the feeling away.

Spock also noticed a mild sensation on his skin. Pulling his tunic sleeve up, he looked down at his arm. His skin held a darker green tinge than usual, as if he'd been slapped—everywhere.

The wall across from them parted, as if the bulkhead was slit by an invisible knife. Zhatan and two guards stepped through, then the aperture closed again, resuming its smooth appearance.

"Forgive me." The Kenisian woman's own skin was also greener than its usual pallor. "The flush you feel is the result of our matter-energy teleportation system. We don't generally use it for living matter, and it is far harsher than your system."

Spock had experienced harsh transporters before. The Klingons, for example, did not ameliorate their process for comfort.

Zhatan didn't hold a weapon, but her two guards carried sidearms and daggers. Spock had seen the same type of knives at certain rites and ceremonies that harkened back to the pre-Surak era. The guards were also helmeted, which was another echo of ancient times.

"Why are we aboard your ship?" Spock asked.

"A direct question," she said. "We shall offer as direct an answer." Moving to the wall where she'd entered, Zhatan touched it with her palm. A table and three chairs transported in front of them. In moments they were fully formed, and Zhatan moved to one of the chairs. "Please sit."

Intraship transporting, but only of inanimate objects. "Fascinating," Spock said as he lowered himself onto one of the chairs. It was comfortable and instantly conformed to his shape.

Only recently familiar with advanced transporter technology, Pippenge reacted more slowly. Continuing to pick at his itching skin, he cautiously examined the chair before sitting down.

"Creating furniture and even temporary bulkheads is quite easy," Zhatan explained. She knocked a knuckle on the slab that spread out between them. "We can even put cushions on the seats, though we've never found them comfortable texturally."

"An interesting and useful technology." Spock admired the innovation, but discussing it didn't answer his question. "Why are we your prisoners?"

Zhatan, to her credit, acknowledged her crime without obfuscation. "We have need of your skills."

Pippenge looked to Spock, then back to Zhatan, probably wondering what skills a politician might have that could be useful to her.

Spock merely waited for her to explain.

"You impressed us," she said, looking directly at the *Enterprise*'s first officer. "You comprehended much of the science you saw in only brief flashes. You were able to predict—albeit incorrectly—some outcomes our own scientists projected. With further study we believe you can be useful to our goal." Zhatan paused, and Spock sensed that some internal debate was transpiring. Her eyes flicked a bit from one side to the other, as if figuratively watching an argument between two opposing cliques.

"Despite our disagreement," she finally said, "your help will be instrumental in preventing the outcome you fear."

"You have your own scientists." Spock's tone was even, but he thought a note of distrust might have slipped into his voice.

"We do," she agreed. "But your mind is similar to ours and you have a different scientific base than we."

"Then why am *I* here?" Pippenge asked nervously.

"You," Zhatan said matter-of-factly, "are here to decrypt, if necessary, the Maabas archives we have acquired."

"Which archives?"

"All data relating to our installations that your people have pillaged for their own gain."

Pippenge looked confused, his pale brows furrowed. "We were studying ruins. Archaeological sites long abandoned and grown over. We pillaged nothing."

While her words were very accusatory, there was nothing in her voice to suggest Zhatan was angry with Pippenge. "Your technological progress has been bolstered by studying ours, has it not?"

"But I am no scientist." In trying to persuade her, and despite its being true, Pippenge's lament made him sound unconvincing. "I know nothing about the ruins."

"Scans show your computer systems difficult to access without a Maabas interface." She leaned back in her chair, seeming almost bored talking to the ambassador.

"Yes, we use a gene-based system. But if given proper access—"

"We stole your archives, Ambassador," she said flatly. "No access was granted."

Pippenge frowned deeply. He surely did not wish to be involved in these machinations. "I don't know how to aid you. I know nothing about the computer systems—"

"You know enough to be helpful, we assure you."

It was possible that the Kenisians merely required the ambassador's DNA to design a cipher, or they intended to use his high-level access to assist them in another way.

"You will be taken to a location," Zhatan told Pippenge, "where you will be asked to advise our computer technicians. We assure you no harm will come to you, or your people, if you cooperate freely."

"The threat, of course," Spock said, "is that should he choose not to 'cooperate freely,' his safety and that of the Maabas people cannot be assured."

Zhatan nodded. "Correct." She motioned to a guard who pulled Pippenge from his chair, which immediately dematerialized, either because it was no longer needed, or because Zhatan had it removed in an attempt at posturing.

"Wait," he called back to Spock, then looked to Zhatan. "Please!"

The wall slid apart for the ambassador and his escort, then fluidly sealed itself again. Spock saw no mechanism to open the doorway, but sensed it was controlled telepathically. Later, he would explore the possibility of his being able to manipulate the apparatus.

"After we show you to your quarters, will you join us in our laboratory, Commander Spock?"

Cocking his head to one side, the Vulcan kept himself from expressing his surprise, but he had to admit that he was taken aback. "Am I not to be treated like a prisoner?"

"How is a prisoner treated?" she asked. "You cannot leave this vessel or access unauthorized sections. You will assist us in completing the *na'hubis* refinements proving that your concerns about its overreach are unjustified."

Spock nodded slowly. Her argument had an internal logic, but reason demanded one's premises to be noncontradictory as well. "And if the destruction cannot be limited to the extent you expect?"

"It can," she said. "It will."

There was a slight threat in her voice, but the danger which concerned Spock was the very real possibility that the Kenisians would use their weapon to the detriment of trillions upon trillions of lives.

"You cannot bend science to follow your will," he told her. "That is an axiom everyone must understand, no matter their philosophy. To be commanded, nature must also be obeyed."

She smiled, and Spock couldn't help but wonder which of her personalities was behind the expression. Or was it *she*—the one named Zhatan? He could not imagine she wasn't, at some time in her life, an individual.

"We don't coerce science, Mister Spock, but we do master it."

"With my help?"

Zhatan shook her head. "We will use the weapon with or without your assistance." She shrugged in a manner very humanlike, something a Vulcan would not do. "Is it not *logical* to work with us to attain a goal we both seek: limiting the destructive power of the *na'hubis*?"

Discouragingly, she applied reason to her argument, but not to the entire situation.

"You can limit the destruction entirely," he pointed out, "by not employing the weapon at all."

"That," she said coolly, her dark eyes like two chunks of coal, "is not an option."

SEVEN

"Sir? Are ya all right?" The voice was familiar.

Kirk tried to move, and on the third attempt he believed he met with success. His elbow was in someone's hand, and he felt himself sit up as he blinked into the light. How many times would he be knocked unconscious on this mission?

"Fine," he told Scott. It was Scotty, wasn't it? He looked up at the man to make sure. Indeed it was his chief engineer. The captain looked around groggily. "Everyone else?"

"Lieutenant Palamas, Doctor McCoy, and Tainler are fine, sir. And Ottenbrite and Kaalburg are embarrassed that they let the Kenisians get the drop on them."

Suddenly Kirk was more alert, and he pushed himself to his feet with Scott's help. "Spock? Ambassador Pippenge?"

"Unaccounted for. I have the landing party searching for them."

Where could they be? He looked hastily around and noted the Kenisian mines, as well as the computer kiosk, were gone. He'd spun around so quickly that he nearly lost his balance.

Hand back on the captain's arm, Scott helped him maintain his footing.

"What happened, sir?"

The captain rubbed his temple and steadied himself both physically and mentally. "A Kenisian disruptor," Kirk said. "Set to heavy stun."

"Aye," Scott said through a grimace. "I assumed that much, sir."

"Where are they?"

"I don't know, sir. We patrolled the edges of the star system, as ordered. When the increased sensor range didn't show anything, I took us to the Kenisians' last known position. Nothing. We tried to track their ion trail . . ."

Scott walked with Kirk as he checked on McCoy, who was sitting, back against the wall and knees up.

"I'm fine, Jim." McCoy, still recovering, gestured for the captain to check on the others.

Tainler was already up and bowing over Lieutenant Palamas. Unlike the humans, the ambassador's aide was accustomed to the atmosphere, and the stun hadn't affected her as badly.

"Tracked it where?" Kirk asked.

"That's the thing," Scott said. "Sensors . . . well, they reported the Kenisian ship all over the system and beyond. There's no way they could have traveled that distance in that time."

Swallowing roughly over a dry throat, Kirk searched for an answer as to how that was possible. He couldn't imagine a way, but his thoughts were likely still muddled from the disruptor stun.

"Recall the landing party, Mister Scott." The captain pulled in a deep, unsatisfying breath and turned to face Tainler. "May I ask that your people continue the search, just in case."

"Just in case, sir?" Scott asked.

"I doubt either Spock or Pippenge is here."

Tainler looked around as if they were hidden somewhere in the room. "Then where are they?"

"The Kenisian vessel," Kirk said.

"But where is that?" Tainler asked.

"I don't know," Kirk admitted. "But I'm going to find it." He flipped open his communicator, and with a quick chirp it found its frequency. "Kirk to *Enterprise*."

"Enterprise. *Uhura here, sir.*"

"Stand by, transporter room. We're beaming up."

JAMES KIRK MARCHED onto the bridge. Experienced *Enterprise* officers knew from his stride that the captain was not happy. Sulu was already vacating the command chair for his station before Kirk was two steps out the lift, but instead of heading to the center seat, the captain went straight to the science station.

"Report."

Ensign Chekov turned away from the scanner cowl. "No luck, sir." He flipped a switch on the console, and a display above them became a map of the star system. A small globe showed the planet's position, and a smaller blip indicated the *Enterprise*. When the ensign hit two buttons and toggled a switch, the screen populated with several hundred dots that cut paths this way and that across the system.

"That's the Kenisian ship's reported activity?"

"Yes, sir. It's impossible. They'd have to be traveling in the system for months, not the hours they had."

Impossible wasn't what Kirk wanted to hear. "I need answers, mister." He ground his teeth tightly until his jaw began to ache.

"I know, sir." The young man shook his head, struggling to find a solution that wasn't apparent to either of them.

Kirk rubbed his eyes and looked up at the display again. Searching for a pattern, he saw several possibilities, but all were improbable.

Also searching the display, Chekov mumbled, "It's no wonder we couldn't find them *anywhere*— this suggests they were *everywhere*."

That's it, isn't it? Kirk thought, and he was reminded of an instance where a cloaked ship had been found by using their proximity to a star with a strong flow of plasma. "They were everywhere and nowhere," he whispered. "Overlay the local stellar wind pattern."

Leaning into the console, Chekov worked the controls. When he tapped a last button, the display changed, and a layer of color rolled out from the star like galactic arms. The strongest points of Kenisian ion concentration coincided with the plasma currents.

Chekov gasped lightly. "Sir, what did they do?"

"They seeded the star, Mister Chekov." Kirk pressed his lips into a thin line. "They used the stellar wind to disperse their own trail, and mask their true comings and goings." It was genius, in its way, and on a certain level Kirk had to admire it. Still, frustration tensed his muscles and balled his fists at his sides. "We can't track them."

"Then how do we find them, sir?" Chekov asked.

"Spock will contact us." He turned to Uhura. "Monitor all subspace frequencies."

"Aye, sir," Uhura said. As the captain passed her station, the communications officer whispered, "Can we be sure he'll be able to?"

Stepping to the command chair, Kirk watched Maaba S'Ja spin below them. The truth was there was no way to know.

He swiveled toward the engineering station. "Operational status, Mister Scott?"

"All systems repaired and functioning, sir."

Good. Kirk nodded his approval. *But where to go?*

And, once the *Enterprise* found the Kenisian vessel, what could they do? If this weapon was as bad as Spock said—and the captain was sure it was—what was his next step?

That would have to wait. First, find them.

"Ready a series of probes, Mister Chekov." Scratching a slight itch on his palm by running it against his pant leg, Kirk began formulating a plan. "The weaker the stellar wind becomes, the more their real ion trail may show itself. Let's take a look."

A STARSHIP'S CREW QUARTERS were not luxurious, nor were they meant to be. They were utilitarian, relatively spartan, and spoke to no particular culture. This was intentional by Starfleet, as the crews were a collection of myriad civilizations, all with very different tastes in décor. The Kenisian cabin offered to Spock was quite different.

The more time he spent aboard Zhatan's vessel, the clearer it became that culturally they were closely related to Vulcans. The fabric on the bed was similar to one he'd seen at his father's sister's house when he was five. She had many antiquities, and much of the decoration in that cabin looked akin to what he now saw. Not identical, but from similar roots.

Zhatan noticed he was examining things with great focus. "It is pleasing?"

"It is . . ." Spock traced his finger along a small figurine that sat on a shelf. The sculpture was a bird not native to Vulcan. Perhaps it could be found on the world the Maabas now called home. Regardless of origin, the artistic style was reminiscent of the early Vulcan masters. ". . . familiar."

"One of us fashioned that," Zhatan said. "Centuries ago. It's called a *h'roole* and sings a sweet song just before dusk."

That, Spock thought, was a significant piece of information. While the Kenisian commander referred to herself as "us," she also modified it with the phrase "one of." That suggested individuality heretofore unseen. Who was Zhatan as a singular being? Assuming the process of *shautish-keem* was as the Vulcan myth described, the distinct personalities housed within the being should be able to assert themselves *as* individuals. And with practice, the original mind should be able to hold sway over the others.

Who is she now? Which one, Spock wondered, *of a multitude?*

"You admire the workmanship?" Zhatan asked, indicating the bird sculpture.

"Very well crafted." He nodded. "Similar to the Heta'ar period on Vulcan." He picked it up, examined it again, and put it back on the shelf, slightly askew from where it had been. "Where was this created?"

"In a different lifetime." She reached over and adjusted the figure, "fixing" the position that Spock had deliberately misaligned.

A penchant for artistic endeavor did not soften his view of her. Earth's Hitler painted. Kodos of Tarsus IV was a thespian. That Zhatan of Kenis Prime crafted decorative figurines did not mitigate her desire for mass murder.

"So not *these* fingers?" He reached out to touch her, but she pulled away. "Those are not the hands of someone hundreds of years old."

Zhatan smiled. "We cannot be seduced, Commander."

He clasped his hands behind his back. "I assure you, that was not my intent." And in fact, it was not. But he *was* trying to make some sort of connection with her. Not mental, as that presented certain dangers. But there may come a time, Spock knew, when it might be necessary.

"You plot against us." Zhatan pointed to herself, and a rather antagonistic smile played on her lips. Or was it arrogance? She sat in one of the more plush chairs within the living area of the cabin, and motioned for him to take the other.

Nodding toward her, Spock sat. "I consider all alternatives."

"Including helping us?"

"Affirmative." Spock placed his clasped hands in his lap. "That *is* one of the options offered."

Almost mimicking his body language, Zhatan sat similarly to the Vulcan—hands also in her lap, her elbows at the same angle against the arms of the chair. He thought this was a subterfuge, as there wasn't anything particularly Vulcan about the way in which he sat. She was trying to give him a false confidence that Kenisians and Vulcans were so similar that little dissimilarities didn't matter. It was a tactic that suggested she knew very little of modern Vulcans.

"May we be involved in your thought process?"

Spock raised a brow at the invitation. Was it an appeal to meld? After the attack on Captain Kirk, such a request would be forcefully denied.

"Forgive us," Zhatan said, seeming to appreciate his caution. "We were not suggesting anything more than verbal discourse." Again she smiled, and had she truly been trying to seem more Vulcan than Kenisian, that was an expression she should have hidden.

"Discourse is always preferred to violence."

"We would not attempt violence against you."

"Indeed?" Spock had recently been stunned to unconsciousness at Zhatan's command, but he decided not to remind her of that fact.

"Violence would not work to sway us against *our* will," she explained. "We don't believe it would influence you, either."

"Yet you took forceful action against Captain Kirk."

She replied in an ancient form of Vulcan, in a phrase that translated more or less to, "He is of a different tribe from thee."

Racism, Spock thought, *was not unusual in the ancient Vulcans.* Fear—the root of racism—is one of the most base humanoid emotions. If Zhatan were trying to show how similar she and Spock were, she had just demonstrated how untrue it was. She was a throwback to the time before Surak, when their homeworld was fractured and violent.

"I will not," Spock said slowly, "assist in the construction of a weapon which would bring death to billions or perhaps even trillions of life-forms."

Zhatan frowned.

"However," he added, "it would be immoral to not attempt to limit the destruction you seem determined to inflict."

She smiled deeply.

There would be no likelihood, Spock decided, that he would be able to dissuade Zhatan from her perilous course. Given that, he would need to proceed with slowing her efforts while attempting to alert the *Enterprise* to whatever he could ascertain about her plans. "You shall have my assistance."

Standing, Zhatan motioned toward the doorway. "Then let us begin."

————

THE KENISIAN scientific facilities were admirable. More robust than the *Enterprise*'s labs, Spock equated the quality to a starbase level.

The expanse was nearly double that of *Enterprise*'s cargo bay. Individually enclosed labs lined the walls to either side. Three areas used for testing or simulations were open, and much of the equipment Spock could see looked familiar enough for him to deduce a Federation analog. Others looked downright Vulcan in style, and the remainder were completely alien to him.

In the very center of the complex was what appeared to be a staging area. On a dais—with cables and monitors attached—was a larger, more modern version of the ancient mines they'd found at the abandoned Kenisian installation. To one side were what appeared to be the fourteen original mines filled with the *na'hubis* compound.

Just past that area, toward the right, was a small complex of computer consoles. Nearby was the ancient Kenisian kiosk taken from the installation, as well as a Maabas terminal, presumably also transported up from the site. At the Maabas console sat Ambassador Pippenge.

There were no guards near the ambassador, Spock noted. The only security were the two armed Kenisians just outside the door they'd entered.

"Impressive, is it not?" Zhatan asked.

Was she looking for Spock's approval? Despite

the risk he might offend her, he was noncommittal. "It should be adequate."

If a frown pulled at her lips, he had to admit it was rather slight. "We don't desire the destruction of the galaxy. That's why you're here."

His lips a thin line, Spock was cautious in reply. "How much destruction do you desire?"

"H-how much? Th-there . . ." Zhatan stammered, and he turned to meet her eyes.

Calmly, Spock pressed further. "Which of those within you decides the parameters, and what are their limits?"

"Parameters of what?" Her voice was suddenly soft, and she seemed to be confused.

"The purpose of the weapon you hope to employ is annihilation." Spock spoke evenly, hoping to keep Zhatan off-balance. "You don't wish too much destruction, therefore you must have a value-based formula defining how much devastation you will require."

"One star system," she said, seeming to regain her composure.

Which star system? Spock wondered. "And if you obliterate two in the process?"

"That would be pitiable," she said, "but the fault would lie with those who initiated this conflict, not with we who would end it."

"How pitiable would it be," Spock asked, "if we

can only limit the weapon to ruining three systems? Or four? Or ten?"

She was silent, so Spock continued.

"How many innocent lives are to be deemed forfeit to your plans?"

At this, Zhatan said nothing. After a long moment, she walked away and motioned him to join her. "You will have access to all the data and material you need related to our designs and research."

Spock considered his options. Zhatan was moving the conversation past his questions, and therefore he thought it best to do the same. "I will need computer access to do additional scientific investigation. If you allow me to communicate, covertly, with Federation databases, I should be able to—"

Zhatan cut him off with a wave of her hand. "Commander Spock, do not insult us. There will be no access to our main computers, nor communication links to your Federation. We are not fools."

She showed him to the console next to the Maabas ambassador. "We expect reports on your progress every two hours. Do not disappoint us." As she turned away, Zhatan said to Pippenge, "That includes you, Ambassador."

The ambassador was dumbstruck. Immobile, he watched Zhatan cross the lab. It took two minutes, twelve seconds for her to exit as she kept stopping to talk to various scientists, and then and only then did the ambassador allow himself to shudder.

When he'd composed himself, Pippenge rose to embrace the Vulcan. "Mister Spock, I am *so* glad to see you."

Arms pinned to his sides, Spock uncomfortably attempted to reassure the ambassador. "Thank you, sir. Please disengage, and I will explain our options."

There were several Kenisian scientists within earshot. Given the acute hearing which Vulcanoids possessed, Spock knew covert communication with the ambassador would be difficult.

Pippenge backed away, patting Spock's arms and smoothing his uniform tunic as he did. "I'm sorry, I'm sorry, Commander."

"An apology is unnecessary." Spock motioned toward the chair in which Pippenge had been sitting. "Please."

The ambassador sat, and Spock took the seat next to him. "I have informed Zhatan," he began, "that I've agreed to aid the Kenisians toward their end of limiting the destructive properties of their *na'hubis* mines."

As a political animal who dealt with words on a daily basis, Spock hoped Pippenge could read between the lines and see the more tacit message he was trying to send. Later, if they could discuss things in detail, the Vulcan trusted he could fashion a jamming device which would give them privacy from the covert monitoring that was surely in place.

"You have agreed . . ." Pippenge repeated, and then his eyes widened in understanding. "I see, Mister Spock." He turned back toward his computer console. "Then I shall endeavor to cooperate in the same manner."

"I assume," Spock said, turning to his own console, "that the task they wish you to accomplish is taking more time than either you or the Kenisians anticipated."

Again, the unspoken message was one he hoped Pippenge would understand.

"I'm afraid it is," the ambassador said, and Spock wasn't quite certain if Pippenge was playing along with the subterfuge or was merely confounded by his assignment. "I am not, as I explained to them, any kind of computer expert."

"I believed they were going to harvest your DNA to assist them in their pursuit."

"They did," Pippenge said, rubbing his arm. "Relatively painless. But I believe they are having difficulties attaining the results they desire."

That, the Vulcan thought, *is fortuitous.*

As he initiated his computer access, Spock decided that trying to inspect the ancient mines would be seen as suspicious. Instead, he called up the design specifications of their newer prototype. Once he gathered enough information, he could reasonably request to examine the older mines for comparison.

The Kenisian plans were detailed, and in a language Spock mostly understood, or could at least decipher with minimal effort. Setting up an algorithm to translate it into modern Vulcan would be his first delaying tactic, but that would come later. For now, he knew he must investigate as much as possible before claiming he wasn't fluent enough in the Kenisian language to be immediately helpful.

As he spun through schematics and test results, Spock grew increasingly concerned. The Kenisians' latest prototype was further along than even Zhatan might have realized. There was very little work to be done to make the mine into one of the most powerful weapons the galaxy had ever seen, and if Spock's calculations were correct, it could very well destroy the fabric of space for thousands of parsecs.

He could not allow the device to be used. Even if it meant destroying the Kenisian ship to ensure that outcome. However, that path might be as dangerous. If he could find a way to destroy the vessel, the resulting explosion—because the *na'hubis* compound was on board—could turn Zhatan's ship into a giant mine.

To accomplish his end, Spock would need to tread carefully.

Switching his field of study from the newer prototype to schematics on the testing equipment, the Vulcan found that there was a strong similar-

ity with Maabas technology. Since a great deal of
Mabba S'Ja's advancement was based on the discoveries found in the Kenisian ruins, the ambassador
might be of more help than Spock had previously
surmised.

Using his console to create a secure connection
between his station's computer and Pippenge's communications implant, Spock attempted to send the
ambassador a private, uncompromised message. "*If
you read this, please indicate so covertly.*"

Seeing Pippenge's reaction, which Spock thought
was somewhere between a quiet nervous collapse
and what Doctor McCoy once referred to as a "con-
niption waiting to happen," it was clear the ambassador saw the communication.

If anyone else did, Spock knew his next message
would bring the Kenisian guards down on them.
"*We may need to destroy this vessel.*"

The Vulcan could see Pippenge visually gulp.
Then, in a reaction that very nearly astonished
Spock, the ambassador turned slightly and ex-
pressed his agreement: a pursing of his lips, a Maabas's nod.

Spock had offered Pippenge no way to otherwise reply securely, so he sent another message.
"*Please wait, Ambassador. We may yet be able to
take more positive action.*"

When no guards came crashing down on them,
and there was no overt difference in the manner of

the Kenisian staff, Spock believed the communications he'd sent had, in fact, been protected.

He sent another. "*To further my efforts, I will need your help at the proper time.*"

Again, Pippenge pursed his lips. There was, Spock surmised, a great strength under the ambassador's nervous demeanor.

The computer systems to which Spock and Pippenge had access were isolated, and there was no transceiver with which Spock could send his secure messages to anyone outside the lab. That was likely why he was able to covertly communicate with the ambassador. Monitoring an internal network from the outside would open a hole in security, and the Kenisians obviously wanted no possible breaches.

"I am not sure what to do," Pippenge said aloud, feigning frustration with his task and in actuality sending Spock a message via his own method.

Replying via his secure system to the ambassador's internal system, Spock reiterated, "*Wait.*"

WAITING WAS the worst part. And yet, as a starship captain, it often seemed to be Kirk's primary duty.

Probes had been sent out in all likely directions and even in a few unlikely ones. Telemetry from their scans would paint a more complete picture of the Maabas star system. The captain hoped the probes would find a clue to the course Zhatan's ship had taken. They didn't know where the Kenisian home-world was or if the ship had come from a base.

Unless Kirk heard from his missing first officer—and there was no guarantee he would—this was their only chance to track the Kenisians and stop them. With luck, they would also retrieve Spock and the Maabas ambassador.

McCoy had joined the captain on the bridge. As he stepped into the command well, he asked the question on everyone's mind. "Any news?"

Kirk shook his head.

"How're you holding up?" the doctor asked quietly.

"Are you asking about my recovery from the Kenisian disruptor stun, Doctor?" Kirk's tone was harsher than he intended, but the last thing he wanted was being coddled on the bridge of his ship.

"Sure," McCoy said unfazed.

Of course Kirk had Spock on his mind. But there was more going on than just the abduction of his first officer and the ambassador.

As McCoy stood there anxiously spinning the ring on his pinky finger, Kirk frowned at his own overreaction.

"Sorry, Bones."

Simultaneously shaking his head and half shrugging, the doctor merely grunted his acceptance. "They're fine," the doctor assured Kirk and probably himself as well. "They wouldn't take them just to kill them."

"Why take them at all?" That was the part Kirk didn't understand. When he was Zhatan's captive, Kirk considered forcing her to take him with her—or at the very least finding a way aboard her vessel. But he didn't think Spock would be taken in his stead, and certainly not Ambassador Pippenge.

"I don't know," McCoy said. It was at times like this his friendship with his frequent Vulcan foil was most evident. "But if anyone can figure a way to send us a message, it's Spock."

Kirk nodded in agreement. It wasn't so much Spock having a method of communication that the captain worried about, but the opportunity to use it.

After a few more words of consultation, McCoy retreated from the bridge. Every so often Kirk would ask Uhura if she was picking up anything. Answers ranged from "No, sir," to "Not yet, Captain," and finally she just grimly shook her head.

Tedium weighed down for another hour and a half before Chekov called from the science station. "Sir, I think I have something."

Kirk spun his chair toward the ensign and launched himself to the upper bridge. "You *think*, or you *do*, Mister Chekov?"

"Here, sir." Chekov flipped a switch to enable the display above them. He was either uncertain of just what he'd found, or more likely was unwilling to risk being wrong in front of his captain. "This looks like a heavier concentration of plasma. Perhaps it was their course into and out of the system."

With careful study, Kirk concluded the same as his navigator. It felt right—a course away from the normal shipping lanes and the Federation. A course one might take to avoid notice.

Kirk gave the navigator a satisfied smile. "Good eye, Mister Chekov." He nodded the ensign toward the navigation console. "Set a course based on that trajectory."

Moving quickly, Chekov stepped back to his station. Ensign Jolma moved to the science station from his post at environmental control.

The *Enterprise* crew knew their duties well and performed with great efficiency. His confidence in them gave Kirk comfort, but he was still unsettled that Jolma was at Spock's station. Not that Jolma wasn't a competent officer—he was. But Spock should be there.

Moving back to the command well, Kirk refused to sit. Tension continued to kink his neck and back, and he watched intently as Chekov plotted the new course.

"Laid in, sir," the ensign told him.

"Mister Sulu." Kirk finally lowered himself into the command chair with some measure of relief that he was at the very least doing something. "Maximum warp."

"Maximum warp, aye."

EIGHT

Zhatan pulled the arms of her command chair toward her, as if it were a protective cocoon.

"Nidal, how goes the ship?" This was her customary informal greeting to her first. Whether Zhatan had left Nidal in command or not, the younger Kenisian woman never took Zhatan's seat. She always stayed at her helm.

The commander knew her first had several former helmsmen within her, and preferred her navigation and piloting duties to being left in charge.

"Unabated," was Nidal's traditional reply. "Ever unabated."

That hadn't always been true, but by judging the tone of Nidal's voice, Zhatan could infer the level of calm or danger.

Today there was a pensive calm in her tone.

"What troubles you?" Zhatan asked.

Pecking at the controls of her console, Nidal shrugged noncommittally.

"We know better," the commander said with a tired smile.

Nidal merely grunted. Their breakup had been

a bad one, but they both knew they would, eventually, work out their short-term differences.

They had been coupled at an early age, mainly because many of the consciousnesses within each had known some of those within the other from time immemorial. Zhatan alone had several dozen *ka'atrehs* that had been betrothed to at least as many as those in Nidal.

Despite that, their relationship had often been uneasy. Unfortunately, that was how things were sometimes. Many of the personalities within a physical form might be compatible with those within someone else's corporeal host. But if the two hosts were not fond of one another, strife reigned.

The problem could have been political. Many of those within Zhatan did not like Nidal's more pacifist leanings. They were certain that many within Nidal were equally repulsed by Zhatan's ideologies.

"We are still on course?" Zhatan asked.

Twisting around to glare at Zhatan, Nidal looked hurt. "We may not agree with the course, Commander, but we stay it nonetheless."

Zhatan sighed. "We want you to agree. Many of you do. Why do you fight us so?"

Tapping in a command to her board that allowed her to turn her attention away, Nidal spun fully toward her commander and former consort. "Define 'fight.'"

Standing, Zhatan gestured toward her quarters. "Speak with us privately."

With a nod, Nidal rose and exited, Zhatan following her.

Once alone, her first's expression turned angry. "We have *never* fought you," Nidal said. "We have encouraged you. We have debated you. We have occasionally questioned you. But we have *never once* fought you." An insulted glow brushed her cheekbones.

"What you call debate, many would consider a fight."

"You will know it when we decide to fight you, Zhatan." Nidal's eyes were green with anger and ready to tear.

"Are you threatening us?"

"Ugh!" Nidal turned away. "How can you be so insipid? Why would we threaten you? How could you even question our loyalty? We may not be with you any longer, but we have *always* loved you."

"Always?" the commander spat. "When Alkinth moved to stop this mission, you testified in *his* favor. Not ours."

Nidal buried her face in her hands. "We have apologized tenfold for that transgression. Will our penance ever end?" When she looked up, tears had been covertly wiped away. "When do you learn to move on from the past? Ever? Must all wrongs be forever remembered?" Throwing herself into the chair in front of Zhatan's desk, her first composed herself. "No one has supported you more than we. It wasn't our decision to end things. Our pride in you, no matter your decisions in this mission, has never waned." She reached out with one hand. "We would still have you back."

Within her own heart, Zhatan—*just* Zhatan— knew Nidal was right. Tibis may disagree, but no one had been more loyal than Nidal. And no one knew her better.

Taking Nidal's hand and embracing her would have been a warm feeling that she needed right now. But that part of her was quickly silenced.

The more conglomerate entity in Zhatan's form reasserted itself, and the room emotionally chilled.

Turning on a heel, the commander retreated to her bridge and to her chair.

Quietly, and still shaken, Nidal followed.

Pulling her earpiece from its storage on the side of the chair, Zhatan tapped a button and placed the receiver near her ear. "Lab progress report," she ordered.

Sciver, her chief scientist, answered quickly, "*The Vul-kuhn complains of difficulty reading our language. He says it is archaic and he is uncertain of several glyphs.*"

"Does he now?" she asked coldly.

"*Yes, Commander. We are allowing him to build a translation matrix which can be applied to all files. He believes it will save a great deal of time.*"

"We see." Zhatan frowned. "Is this warranted?" Owing to the fact that he had far fewer consciousnesses within, Sciver had less rank than Zhatan. Still, she trusted his judgment. Often more than she trusted Nidal's.

"*It is likely unavoidable. He attempted to explain the Vul-kuhn language to us, but we've neither the patience nor the time. None among us is a linguist.*" Sciver sounded tired, Zhatan thought. She sympathized.

"Very well. Explain to him that we expect actual progress at the next report interval."

"*Yes, Commander, we will do so.*"

"Thank you, Sciver. Bridge out."

Returning the earpiece to its station, Zhatan sighed.

"*He delays us,*" Tibis thought.

"*Yes, he stalls.*"

"*Do not trust him.*"

"*Don't trust.*"

"*He is purposely dilatory.*"

"*Perhaps.*" Zhatan rubbed at her neck and tried to will away her exhaustion. But she didn't wish to sleep. "*We will know for certain in a day's time.*"

"*A day is too late.*"

"*Kill him now. He cannot help.*"

"*He will not help.*"

"*Nidal may disagree, but Sciver does not.*"

"*Sciver knows Spock may still be of use.*"

"*Sciver gave evidence against Alkinth. He believes in our goals.*"

"*The Vul-kuhn does not respect us,*" Tibis said.

"*He is honorable. We are of the same blood.*"

"*No, he does not agree.*"

"*Kill him. And the Maabas fool.*"

"*No, do not kill them. They are useful. They will help.*"

"*We have time,*" Zhatan thought. "*We are two days' travel away from the destroyer's homeworld.*"

"*The Vul-kuhn must solve the equations we cannot—before we use the na'hubis.*"

"*He will perfect our weapon.*"

"*He will delay. He cannot be trusted.*"

"*He wants to limit the destruction.*"

"*He wants to hamper our efforts.*"

"*He will work for us against his will.*"

"*He will betray us,*" Tibis said.

"*Enough,*" Zhatan snapped. "*He will do as we need.*"

"*He will.*"

"*Vul-kuhn are of our blood.*"

"*He will not betray us.*"

"*He will betray us!*"

"*He will not.*"

"*Trust in us.*"

"*No, listen to us.*"

"*Silence. We will rest.*" Zhatan rose and moved toward the door to her quarters. "Nidal, wake us in an hour."

Nidal nodded. "Yes, Commander."

"We will rest," Zhatan said again as the bridge doors closed silently behind her.

OF THE FOURTEEN ancient *na'hubis*-filled Kenisian mines, it was difficult to know which Spock should investigate closely. He was interested in only one in particular.

Unfortunately, Sciver, the Kenisian scientist who'd given him access, did not understand why Spock needed to examine all the barrels. "Is not one much the same as another?"

With the best skeptical expression he could gather, Spock sought the man's gaze. "You have schematics on these, but no designers' notes," he explained. "I need to compare the actual artifact with the archival plans if I am to understand what, if anything, was changed in the production of your latest prototype."

Pausing in thought a long moment, Sciver finally clenched his jaw and nodded. Presumably, the internal debate that attempted to weigh whether Spock's explanation was a proper one had ended in the Vulcan's favor.

Left to his own, Spock was able to closely examine the containers with a Kenisian tricorder. Before he switched it on, Spock inspected each visually. He did not want the unit's memory to record the presence of the item he wished to recover.

On the fifth mine, Spock found what he sought. The captain had hidden his communicator within a ventilation panel that ran vertically along the left side of the container. When he and Tainler left for the vaults with his communicator, and returned without it, Spock knew that had been Kirk's plan. To help avoid detection, the power source had been disengaged.

Covertly, Spock spirited the unit away, concealing it in his palm and then smoothly slipping it into the top of his boot. The bulk would show if one were looking for it, but to a cursory glance it would go unnoticed.

Continuing his ruse, Spock examined the other nine mines as closely as he had the first five. He took readings, and when he was finished, he handed the Kenisian tricorder back to Sciver, who barely looked up from his work.

"I will need these results for further study," Spock said. "Can they be transferred to my console?"

Busy with his own simulations and study, Sciver handed the tricorder back to him. "You have access to do that yourself. Simply place the unit close to the console and the transfer will begin."

Spock took the tricorder back. "I shall return it when the transfer is complete."

"You needn't," Sciver said. "You may have need of it again."

Nodding, Spock walked toward Pippenge and the computer consoles to which they were assigned. *I shall indeed have need of it*, he thought.

Once the tricorder transferred the data he'd scanned, Spock contacted the ambassador through his computer implant. *"I require your help to communicate with the* Enterprise.*"*

Initially stunned by what Spock was proposing, Pippenge quickly recovered and feigned confusion at the task assigned to him by the Kenisians. "I am not at all sure what to do," he mumbled. Spock hoped this wouldn't become so rote a response that it would be noticed by those watching them.

Spock sent another message. *"I will guide you. I need to link the transceiver in your implant with a communicator Captain Kirk concealed in one of the* na'hubis *mines."* It was his hope that the Maabas technology, similar enough to Kenisian, would be less likely to be detected when in use.

The ambassador turned to Spock, blinked at him in shock a few times, then turned back and pretended to work at his console.

Raising a brow, Spock was unsure if Pippenge was more surprised at the captain's subterfuge or that it was possible to link a Starfleet communicator to his implant. Perhaps he thought it would cause injury.

"No harm will come to you in this process, I as-

sure you," Spock sent. Engineering the transmission between the communicator and the implant was an easier task than the next step, which was to find a way to boost the signal in a manner that would go undetected to the Kenisians. That would be a more difficult maneuver.

"Hmmmm," Pippenge said to himself again. "How . . . I wonder . . . does this work?" He tapped at his console, but what showed on his display was unrelated to his true intent.

Spock was concerned that this attempt to clandestinely communicate might be overheard and understood, but no Kenisian technicians or scientists showed any interest.

Daring to send the ambassador a longer message, Spock attempted to explain as much as time allowed. *"I will route messages to and from your implant. Using the transceiver in my communicator, I hope to enhance the signal with some of the equipment in this lab. Much of the Kenisian equipment looks similar to Maabas technology. I may need your assistance to quickly understand it. Time is, and will continue to be, of the essence."*

Without looking directly at Spock, Pippenge flattened his lips, expressing his understanding.

Explicitly not acknowledging the ambassador, silently or otherwise, Spock took the Kenisian tricorder, double-checked that its data had been transferred to his console, and rose to make his way to one of the nearby labs.

Once there, tools were readily available that met his needs. The communicator was opened with ease, and the transceivers—the main and the backup unit—were removed. The unneeded housing was returned to Spock's boot, so that it would not be found.

The tricorder was a more difficult matter. Opening it wasn't his concern. But how could he discern the purpose of the components without testing them?

Here was the first instance in which the Vulcan would need Pippenge's aid.

Returning to the computer console, Spock related to the ambassador, in great detail, the components he found in the tricorder. When he'd given that overview, he asked Pippenge his thoughts on their respective functions.

After twenty-three point two minutes, the ambassador looked exhausted, but progress had been made. Spock returned to the lab and introduced his communicator's transceivers into the tricorder.

When that was complete, he now had a unit to test, but no way to do so, except in use. Once again, he returned to his work station. Initiating a simple message from the tricorder to Pippenge's implant via the communicator's circuits was the first step.

Spock sent, *"Ambassador. This is a test. If you are aware of this message, please indicate receipt in some overt way."*

Before Pippenge could react, Sciver was upon them.

"Why have you done it?" the Kenisian demanded, his cheeks flush green with anger. "Can we not trust you in even the smallest way?"

Pippenge sprang from his seat so fast that Sciver was startled. "Forgive us! We did not know it was wrong!"

Brows furrowed in confusion, the Kenisian looked at Pippenge as if he was mentally unbalanced. "Sit down. We are not addressing you."

"I—oh." The ambassador took his seat, still looking like a bundle of nerves, but at least quiet for now.

Sciver turned his attention only to Spock. "Explain your actions."

"Which actions in particular?" Spock asked coyly.

"Toolkit thirty-three."

Maintaining a rather blank look, Spock nodded, accepting that the topic was toolkit thirty-three despite being offered no context. "What of it?"

"You used it, but did not put it away," Sciver explained, his complexion still blushed with pique. "That is unacceptable to us. Some of these instruments are powered. It is neither safe nor wise to leave them unattended."

Bowing his head, Spock acted properly chastised. "You have my most sincere apology."

After a single curt nod, Sciver turned away. Before Spock and Pippenge could even share a glance, however, the Kenisian twisted back.

"What were you using it for?"

"Pardon?"

"The toolkit," Sciver pressed. "Why were you in need of it?"

Without hesitation, Spock presented an earnest façade. "Uncertain of the tools available to me, should the need to use them present itself, I thought I should familiarize myself with the lab as best I can."

Sciver looked uncertain as to the honesty of that answer.

"Occasionally, knowing one's options in advance can hasten solutions when problems present," the Vulcan added.

Seeming satisfied, Sciver nodded and turned away a final time, leaving them relatively to themselves.

Glancing at Pippenge, Spock found the ambassador looking quite shocked. There were anecdotes that suggested Vulcans were incapable of lying, and the Maabas may have heard those tales.

Many had misinterpreted the Vulcan disdain for mendacity to mean that they would never speak falsely. Such a tenet, however, would be illogical on its face, as there were times when telling a fiction was the most moral act one might take. Knowing the widespread acceptance of this fable, Spock had bent the truth on a number of occasions.

Explaining this would be an interesting discussion to have with Ambassador Pippenge later.

For now, Spock sent the following to the ambassador's implant: *"We must amplify this signal in a method that will not be noticed."*

Spock had an inkling about how to achieve that, but with the opportunity would come great risk.

WHEN THE *ENTERPRISE* tilled uncharted space, there was an exhilaration to it that spoke to Kirk's soul. It was contained excitement, always promising something new, something interesting just ahead.

Now, as they headed into the unknown, following a thin thread of plasma radiation that might, or might not, lead to Zhatan's ship, the exhilaration had been replaced with anxiety.

It wasn't merely that a Kenisian fleet might be waiting for them. There was no telling whose territory they were invading. There could be a hostile reaction to their pursuit, by one or more powers. It wasn't the way the Federation liked to make first contacts.

The most frustrating part was that there was no way to know if they were on the right track. Events had moved so quickly that the path Chekov found could have been where the Kenisian came from as much as where she'd gone. If it wasn't to the same location, and they were now tracking back to her point of origin, there would be little time to pick up her trail again.

The captain still wasn't sure how he knew Zhat-an's task was so urgent, but he did.

Had Spock been present, he might have pointed out how illogical it was to trust such a feeling. Although, after some years serving together, the captain knew there was more to his Vulcan friend than just logic.

What if he's dead? Kirk wondered for a quick moment, then caught himself and scuttled the negative thought.

He looked down at his right hand and found it curled into a fist. Rather than releasing it, he brought it to his chin and bounced it there a few times. *Spock will find a way to communicate. He'll find a way.*

"Captain?"

Uhura's voice drew Kirk from his darker thoughts.

"Yes?" Coiled with tension, the captain sprang toward her station, just as the lift doors opened and McCoy stepped onto the bridge.

"Jim?"

The captain waved him off and looked at Uhura.

"I have a signal on subspace four-oh-seven, sir," she said.

"Jolma," Kirk called to the ensign at the science station. "Track it." Excitedly, he motioned to the speaker on Uhura's console. "Let's hear it."

"Spock?" McCoy asked.

Ignoring the doctor, Kirk gestured to her speaker again.

She shook her head, one bright green earring waggling against her earpiece. "It's character based and encoded, sir."

He nodded. "Decode and translate to audio, Lieutenant."

After Uhura flipped a series of switches, the computer read the message aloud: "Enterprise, *this is Spock, authentication Victor nine-six-five-six Eta Nu. Please respond in like code.*"

McCoy grinned at Kirk, who quickly motioned to Uhura. "Respond."

Having already configured the computer to translate the code and character, Uhura spoke, "*Enterprise receives. Authentication Baker seven-three-one-two Omega.*"

Throat dry with anticipation, Kirk bounced slightly on the balls of his feet.

McCoy smiled, but Kirk couldn't. There were too many unknowns. Where was the message from? Was there a delayed send? Was Spock able to reply? Kirk trusted his first officer to overcome such scenarios, but until they heard back, the captain would worry.

Come on, Spock. Be there.

The captain twisted toward Jolma, who was peering into the sensor cowl. "Ensign?"

"Not enough to go on, sir."

Adjusting her earpiece, Uhura smiled. "Reply incoming, Captain." She tapped at her board to put the message through.

"The ambassador and I were abducted to assist Kenisians in use of na'hubis weapon. Current location and course unknown."

"Uhura, send this: Continue contact as long as possible. Tracking signal to source. Report status."

She sent the message.

They waited. Kirk looked from Jolma to Uhura for a sign that something had changed. The captain paced between the science and communication stations.

McCoy stood just beyond Uhura, leaning close into her station, chewing softly on his thumb.

"Was he caught?" the doctor asked.

Kirk shook his head. Perhaps the message merely came from farther away than they imagined? Tracking the signal would tell them distance soon enough—*if* they could get a lock on it.

Although the captain hadn't envisioned the Maabas ambassador would be swept up, his plan was mostly working as he intended. Kirk thought *he* would be in Spock's place, but considering the circumstances, this way was probably better. It didn't mean that the captain liked it.

"Receiving," Uhura called, and Kirk was instantly by her side.

"Sending full report burst."

"Well," McCoy said, "he's all business."

That, Kirk thought, *would be Spock.*

Uhura's slender fingers swiftly worked at the controls. "Capturing report, sir."

"Send this," Kirk ordered. "How close are Kenisians to testing prototype weapon?" Doubtless that information was in Spock's missive, but Kirk didn't have the time to skim through it now.

As they waited for the response, Kirk stalked back over to Jolma at the science station.

"We are on the right course, Captain."

"Location?" Kirk asked.

"Not yet, sir," Jolma said.

"It's in line with the course we've taken?"

"Yes, sir. Definitely."

"Good," McCoy said. "That's good, right?"

The captain huffed out a semirelieved breath. "It isn't bad, Bones."

"Getting another message, sir."

Kirk turned back to Uhura's station.

"Kenisians will test weapon in battle against their ancient conquerors. Situation grave. Destruction could reach Beta Quadrant."

"Beta Quadrant," Kirk mouthed silently.

Uhura drew in a sharp breath, not quite a gasp, but she, too, was shocked.

"What the devil?" McCoy's eyes met Kirk's.

"Worse than we thought," the captain said, more to himself than McCoy. He looked toward the main viewscreen, past the points of light which appeared to speed away and outward. In the abyss of black beyond the visible stars, trillions and trillions of life-forms lived.

One act might end them all. One insane act of rage.

That wasn't really what Zhatan wanted, Kirk knew. Once again, he wasn't sure *how* he discerned that, but he was certain of it.

Wasn't he? Could that be a side effect of a Kenisian meld? Did he *feel* that he knew her and was that a weakness she'd passed to him purposely?

Kirk didn't have any answers. He hoped that his willingness to ask meant that he wasn't under any outside influence.

"Send to Spock." Kirk turned back to Uhura and placed his hand on the back of her chair. "We are on intercept course—"

Jolma interrupted, "Sir, I haven't pinpointed—"

The captain continued, silencing the ensign with a glare. "We are on an intercept course. Will need consistent contact to pursue from a distance. If we are unable to reach you in time, you must take sole action to keep the *na'hubis* weapon from being used. Up to and including General Order 23."

Kirk noticed that every head on the bridge snapped up for a second, but only for a second. Starfleet General Order 23 mandated the destruction of an enemy vessel at any cost, including personal. It was issued only in the most dire of occasions. This was surely one of them.

Working the *Enterprise*'s scanners, Jolma hurried to make sure the captain was able to keep his promise.

Kirk knew they were on the right track and that any location pinpointed *now* wouldn't be useful when *Enterprise* arrived at those coordinates. If the Kenisians were planning an attack, they wouldn't be heading in the most direct course.

And just in case the Kenisians were eavesdropping, Kirk wanted them to know that the *Enterprise* was on her way.

The captain knew if the *Enterprise* couldn't arrive in time, Spock would have to destroy the Kenisian vessel. If he could.

Continuing his attempts to find the first officer, Jolma was frustrated. "I need one more contact, Captain. Just one more."

Kirk nodded, appreciating the ensign's dedication.

They waited for Spock's acknowledgment—two minutes, then five, then seven, then ten.

"He's fine," McCoy told Uhura as the captain left them for the command chair. "Just delayed. Someone walked in or . . ."

It sounded to Kirk as if McCoy was reassuring himself as much as the lieutenant.

When he looked at the chronometer for the

sixth time in as many minutes, the captain noticed seventeen minutes had passed since Spock's last contact.

Would Zhatan kill them if they were found to be acting against her?

Was she really a murderer? If so, why not kill Kaalburg and Ottenbrite on the planet? Why not leave Tainler and the *Enterprise* landing party for dead?

By definition of her Kenisian condition, there was more to Zhatan than met the eye. Kirk hoped the depth he'd seen within her wasn't an illusion she'd implanted to confound him.

Somewhere deep in his gut, the captain felt he was missing something. He rubbed his chin and tried to imagine where the lost puzzle piece could be.

"Uhura," he said suddenly, spinning about, "get me in touch with Ambassador Pippenge's assistant, Tainler."

She nodded and set to work as McCoy stepped down toward Kirk.

The doctor motioned toward the chronometer that sat between Sulu and Chekov. "Been a long time."

Too long, Kirk thought.

NINE

"You are taking too long, Mister Spock." Zhatan's demeanor was that of an impatient proctor to her student, as if she'd asked her captive to solve a simple equation for the class, and he was purposely dawdling.

He was. But that made the equation no easier to unravel.

"I am unsure what exactly you expect." Hands clasped behind him, Spock stood as Zhatan strode around him, perhaps in a manner she thought intimidating. Certainly Pippenge, still sitting at his computer console, was sufficiently unsettled.

"We expected a new approach. Sciver has reviewed your notes, and all we see are diligent appraisals of what we already know." Zhatan stopped, stood in front of him, and mimicked his posture. "We are not looking for evaluations. We need breakthroughs."

"Scientific innovations do not occur on a timetable," Spock said.

Frustrated, Zhatan stamped a foot in a childlike manner. "They can! Did you not—with only minutes to perform the task—once formulate a matter/antimatter intermix procedure that saved your vessel from a decaying orbit after her engines had been in cold shutdown?"

Resisting the urge to show shock, Spock merely raised a curious brow. "Interesting." There was no way to have that information unless the Kenisians were far more familiar with the Federation—and Starfleet—than they had let on. "I must now assume the timing of your arrival within the Maabas system was not happenstance."

He hadn't framed that as question, because the answer was obvious.

At first Zhatan hesitated as if caught in a lie. After that, she simply nodded.

However, Sciver looked quite taken aback. Eyes narrow, he sought the commander's gaze. "Is this true?"

She silenced him with a sharp glare, and he bowed his head in recognition of her authority.

"I don't understand," Pippenge said.

Turning to face the ambassador, Spock explained. "Commander Zhatan has just revealed that she has classified Starfleet intelligence. Either she sought out this information previous to the *Enterprise*'s arrival in the Maabas system—"

"The Kenisian system," Sciver corrected.

Spock tilted his head toward Sciver and nodded. "As you wish." Turning back to Pippenge, the Vulcan continued. "Either the Kenisians surveilled the *Enterprise* and researched its crew, or they sought out an individual of specific scientific abilities who is assigned to the *Enterprise*, and it was serendipity that we were dispatched for this mission." He turned to Zhatan, hoping she would indicate which was true.

"We have been monitoring the Maabas for some time," she admitted, her voice now softer, but her posture straightened with pride. "When the Federation ventured within the system, we began to investigate Starfleet as well." She shrugged. "Your ship frequents this sector. It was important to learn about your captain, you . . . all those who could be in command and might stand against us."

"And within my past accomplishments you saw an opportunity to help you meet your ends."

Zhatan nodded.

"Within you reside four hundred thirteen minds?" Spock asked. "How many of those have worked on the very weapon you seek to re-create?"

"There is a degradation—"

"Commander!" Sciver snapped. Whatever Zhatan was about to reveal, he obviously considered it inappropriate to do so.

Zhatan didn't care. "You're dismissed, Sciver."

"Commander—"

"Dismissed," she said through gritted teeth.

Sullen, the Kenisian scientist skulked away toward one of the labs.

Zhatan took a deep breath and continued, "I give you truth, Spock, but we want truth in return."

An interesting mixed usage of "I" and then "we." Was the individual that was at Zhatan's core promising him honesty, and the collective of her different personalities asking for his reciprocation as payment?

Spock nodded his agreement and waited patiently.

Zhatan looked at Pippenge, perhaps deciding whether he should be present for whatever admission she was going to make. Turning away from the ambassador, Zhatan had obviously decided he could stay.

"We are not," she said slowly, "always . . ." Her sentence trailed off unexpectedly, and she sighed.

"Honesty can be disquieting," Spock told her, releasing his hands from behind his back and allowing them to hang effortlessly at his sides. "But it is often preferable to falsehood, nonetheless."

Clearing her throat, Zhatan hesitated.

She is, Spock thought, *so very young, despite all the ancient minds within her.*

"The whole is not *always* greater," she said finally, "than the sum of the parts."

"I understand." Spock nodded, and he may have allowed a bit of pity to seep into his voice.

She looked calmed, he noted. Relieved that she need not relate to him all she intended.

However, Pippenge was confused. He looked from Spock to Zhatan. "Forgive me, Commanders . . . but *I* do not understand. Please explain."

"Any mind, even a highly ordered and resilient Vulcan mind, can be taxed to its limits," Spock said. "The life essence of an individual normally resides within a single physical brain. There have been instances where one's consciousness was stored in another, or even in an inorganic vault of sorts. But there is no record of someone acquiring several such consciousnesses—let alone hundreds—without going mad."

"We are not mad," Zhatan protested, but she sought Spock's eyes only a second before looking away.

"No," Spock agreed, "but you are troubled."

She shook her head. "You don't understand as much as you thought."

"Then by all means, clarify."

Fingers to her temples, Zhatan massaged them a long moment before speaking. She shifted her weight anxiously from one foot to the other, then began. "As I tried to explain, there is a degradation of faculties. Even with the support of archives and prototypes . . . we lack . . . certain . . ."

"You lack total comprehension," Spock concluded, noticing that she again used the word "I" rather than "we."

Zhatan nodded. "Among us are the scientists

who worked on the original weapon. But the science is lost to us," she lamented. "We know it *is* possible to limit the destruction. But we do not understand enough of the physics to re-create it." She looked at Spock, meeting his eyes for the first time since she'd revealed her truth to him. "You *must* help us."

"You want his help to destroy us?" Pippenge asked.

Zhatan had been so intent on Spock, she seemed startled by the ambassador's question, if not his presence altogether.

"Our only interest in Kenis Prime was the *na'hubis*. We would not seek to remove you from the planet."

Pippenge didn't believe her. "Then why threaten us?"

Half sighing, half shrugging, Zhatan seemed to offer an honest answer. "After much reconnaissance, we thought you weak and easy to manipulate. Threatening you was a means to an end, not the end in itself."

Covering his mouth with a fist clenched so tightly that it began to shake, Pippenge cried. Within seconds his entire body quaked with sobs. Tears of anger, or tears of relief? Spock could not decipher which.

Nevertheless, having lived his entire life with emotional beings within his orbit, Spock could understand the ambassador's pain. He reached out his left hand and placed it on Pippenge's right shoulder, steadying him.

"You will excuse me," the ambassador said, clearing his throat. "But I thought my people would die in the tens of millions." He looked up at Zhatan, a bitter expression tightening his face. "My people still believe that. You have terrorized, abducted, absconded—"

"Immaterial." She waved off his concern and his emotional torrent. As if a switch had flipped, her heart was again hardened, and she turned to address only Spock. "Now, it is time for your truth."

"What truth do you seek?"

"We believe you've been purposely dilatory in your efforts to control the *na'hubis* compound. Will you work with haste toward our end, or are you dooming us to the great unknown?"

Spock opened his mouth to reply, but Zhatan interrupted.

"Not using the weapon is an unacceptable choice to us." Straightening her tunic and standing taller, as if suddenly emotionally bolstered from within, she stared him down. "Your only alternatives are to assist us, and lower the risk of the outcome none of us desire, or deny us, and doom yourself and the galaxy to uncertainty and possible death."

"*Probable* death," Spock corrected.

Zhatan nodded. "Then you know what you must do."

———

"WHAT NEWS of Ambassador Pippenge, Captain?" A small line of static bisected Tainler's image on the main viewer, but despite the distance, the picture was amazingly clear. Maabas subspace communication was more advanced than the Federation's, and there was only minimal delay between locations. "And of Commander Spock as well," she added guiltily.

"They're alive," Kirk said. "But not out of the woods."

Her lips puckering in confusion, the translation of that idiom was clearly awkward. "They have been taken to a forest?"

"They're still in danger," Kirk corrected. "But with your help we may find a solution."

Pursing her lips with exaggerated emphasis, Tainler was eager to oblige. "I'll help in any way I can, Captain. Any way I can."

Like Pippenge, his assistant was equally ready to help. This was the Maabas hospitality Palamas had written of in her report. "We need access to whatever historical archives you have, going back as far as Maabas history goes."

"The material on the ruins which Pippenge granted Mister Spock?"

Kirk thought on that a moment. "No, everything you have. The ruins, your time on the planet, even how you came to find it. Everything the Maabas have documented and recorded."

Again, Tainler flattened her lips. *"I shall see to it. Please stand by."* She rose from her desk and walked out of frame.

"MADAME PRESIDENT?" Tainler flashed the door light again. "Are you present?"

After a long pause, the door to President Moberte's office slid open revealing her ornate fixtures and baroque desk. She stood, pacing, talking, and put up a hand for Tainler to wait until she was done. Representative Lodi sat next to the window, drinking from a tall glass and looking out at the cityscape.

"Yes, I understand your point, Prefect Tyms. And I hope you appreciate mine. These are certainly troubled times, but I trust we shall be able to meet the challenges together." She paused, listening to his end of the conversation, and then said, "Thank you. Please wish joy to your family for me. Yes. Good night."

Tainler felt her face flush. Had officials as far down as the Prefects heard about the situation with the Kenisians? Secrets *were* hard to keep.

"My apology," Moberte said, turning to greet Pippenge's assistant. "Tyms, once again, is having his preelection palpitations."

"Oh," Tainler said, relieved. "Then he doesn't know about—everything."

Moberte chuckled at the thought. "I shudder to think how that conversation would go. No. There have been no leaks."

"Yet," Lodi added, still looking out the window.

"How may I be of service to you, Tainler?"

"Captain Kirk is requesting full access to our data archives. More than the information previously granted. He wants access to all our historical data, even previous to the migration."

The president looked at Lodi, studying her. "Indeed?"

"An interesting request," Representative Lodi said. "For what purpose?"

Hesitating, Tainler was unsure how to answer. She hadn't even asked. Was she going to be in trouble for not getting full information? "I don't know," she told Lodi, then looked at Moberte. "I assumed it would not be a problem. Was I mistaken?"

Swallowing hard, the president exchanged a long glance with the representative.

"It may not present a problem," Lodi said.

Why were they so concerned? Tainler searched their expressions for some clue, but they were politicians and skilled at hiding their true intent.

"Problem?" she asked, a bit more indignantly than she intended.

"No problem," Moberte said. "Give them the access."

Tainler pursed her lips. "There is more going

on here than it seems," she said. "Ambassador Pippenge's life is at stake. What secrets are you keeping?"

Pinching the bridge of her nose for a quick moment, Moberte moved to her desk chair and settled into it.

I am to be relieved of my duties, Tainler thought.

But then Lodi rose to stand behind the president. "Reveal it," she whispered.

Reveal what?

"It could jeopardize our relationship with the Federation," Moberte snapped. "Now is not the time."

"If they're looking for it, they already suspect," Lodi said calmly. "If they're not, they likely won't find it." She folded her arms, grasping each elbow between her thumbs. "If they truly are our friends, why keep this secret?"

"Because it shows subterfuge," the president said guiltily.

"Did we lie to them?" Tainler asked incredulously as she stepped toward them. "Is that what this would reveal?"

Moberte pursed her lips. "In a sense, yes."

"They'll understand," Lodi said. "Give them the access they desire, and we shall endure the consequences."

Moving closer toward them, Tainler was determined to know what it was they feared. "What is this about? This situation is too serious to play such political games. Tell me."

The president hesitated, but Lodi did not. "Long-range sensors detected the Kenisians some months ago. The Science Directorate was able to ascertain that their technology was similar to that found in the ruins."

Stunned, Tainler backed away instinctively. "This is why we suddenly embraced the Federation."

Pressing her lips into a thin line, Moberte admitted it tacitly.

"We thought we might need their protection," Lodi explained. "Obviously we were prescient."

"Who?" Tainler demanded. "You? And you?" She accused them both.

"I and the Court knew," the president said.

"Ambassador Pippenge didn't know," Tainler realized, and Lodi confirmed it with a pucker of her lips.

"We thought it best the delegation act in isolation from our intentions," Moberte said.

"Except for Skent? Is that why he was snooping around?"

Lodi sighed. "He isn't that clever and was merely curious. No one asked him to steal Federation secrets."

That much Tainler believed. Skent always had been a bit of a fool, and what he'd done had been harmless enough.

"They will not abandon us," Lodi said as she moved toward Tainler and took the woman by the shoulders. "Have faith in the Federation. We believe them to be of good character. They will overlook our misstep, should they learn of it."

Tainler scoffed. "They're of good character. What are we?"

"Desperate," Moberte said. "And even after all these years, still afraid of genocide."

Lodi released Tainler and motioned her out of the room. "Go. Give them the access they request."

Tainler looked to the president, who pressed her lips together in agreement. "Worry not," she said. "I don't think it's what they're looking for."

"WHAT EXACTLY are you looking for, Jim?" McCoy asked.

"I'm not sure." Kirk offered the doctor a half shrug. "I'm hoping I'll know it when I find it."

The doctor was unsatisfied by the captain's reply.

Just then Tainler returned. *"Captain? I have authority from President Moberte to open our planetary databanks to you. I will send your communications officer the proper security protocols."*

Kirk glanced back at Uhura, who nodded in acknowledgment.

"This is unprecedented access for an offworlder," Tainler continued.

Of course, Kirk thought. The Maabas had been xenophobic before finally embracing what the Federation had to offer. And yet, they'd opened their arms warmly once they'd chosen their path. "Please extend the president my deepest gratitude, as well as my assurance that your databanks are safe with us."

Her expression wrought with emotion, Tainler's voice was thick with held-back tears. *"Never mind the data, Captain. Whatever you search for and no matter what you find . . . just bring Ambassador Pippenge back and save our world."*

The only response to that plea that Kirk could manage was a nod. *"Enterprise,* out," he said softly. The main viewscreen returned to a starscape at warp.

Save our world? If the Kenisians used that weapon, there was a lot more at stake than one planet.

Twisting around, Kirk pushed himself up and toward Uhura. "Lieutenant?"

"Yes, sir," she said softly, one hand gliding smoothly across her console. "I have full access to the Maabas records."

"Set up an instantaneous gateway," Kirk ordered. "I want our computer to be able to search and interpret the entirety of their archive."

"Aye, sir."

Were Spock available, Kirk would ask him to take lead on the task of searching the Maabas records for relevant information. But the captain had done some of that as a young lieutenant, and he knew another officer who had the kind of mind that could sift large amounts of data quickly. "As soon as that's ready, please join me in the briefing room, Uhura." He stepped toward the lift. "Have Lieutenant Palamas meet us there."

"Sir?" Still working her controls, Uhura turned and looked after him curiously.

"We're going on a fishing expedition."

McCoy stepped up from the lower bridge. "Jim, you don't know what you're fishing for."

"I'm casting a wide net," Kirk said, continuing the metaphor as he stepped into the lift.

"*COMMANDER?*" To be roused by Nidal's voice was an unexpected comfort, and Zhatan reached across the bed toward her. But Nidal wasn't there. "*Commander?*" It was the intercom.

Groggily, Zhatan tapped the comm button above her bed. "What is wrong?"

"*Nothing, Commander. You were expected back at the beginning of the watch. Are you well?*"

We are not well, Zhatan thought, but she didn't want to have that argument again. "We are fine," she lied.

She hadn't meant to fall asleep. She had only intended to meditate, but slumber had come too quickly to avoid.

Once on the bridge, Zhatan felt more herself, and comfort returned as she took her command chair. At least her ship was a constant, forgiving companion.

"Engineers are complaining that maintaining our present velocity is becoming difficult." Nidal handed her a palm screen with the report. "They suggest cutting speed by one third."

Zhatan skimmed the recommendation. "So we see."

"Shall we reduce to level eight?"

Hesitating, the commander was awash in internal input.

"We must not slow."

"Maintain speed."

"We cannot be delayed."

"Stay strong."

"Listen to us."

"Kirk is following. We know he is."

"Maintain speed."

"If we reduce to eight," Zhatan told Nidal, "Kirk will intercept us."

"We've had no indication the *Enterprise* pursues us." Nidal shrugged. "We tainted the heliosphere as you ordered. Our path is well masked."

"Well masked." Zhatan shook her head. "But not perfectly so." She handed back the palm screen.

Nidal took it, glanced at the report again, and sighed slightly. "Commander, we *cannot* maintain this speed. Reducing to level eight is more than a suggestion."

Zhatan looked away. "We are the commander here. Only our own wishes are more than suggestions."

"How do you know Kirk pursues us?" Nidal was clearly frustrated, but there was a reason she was only the first and not the commander.

"We know," Zhatan said. "We touched his mind. We know his soul."

Nidal seemed to let that sit for a while. She nearly turned away, then said, "*Enterprise*'s pursuit does not improve our engines. We must limit our speed."

"*Do not,*" warned Tibis, and the others stirred.

"*Mustn't.*"

"*Maintain.*"

"*Maintain.*"

"*Reduce.*"

"*Listen to us.*"

"*Listen.*"

"*Maintain.*"

"*Reduce.*"

"*Stay vigilant.*"

"*Kirk pursues,*" Tibis cautioned.

"*Counter him.*"

"*Confound him!*"

"*Maintain speed.*"

"*Reduce speed!*"

"Deal with Kirk now."

"Cripple Kirk."

"Maintain!"

"Stop Kirk," Tibis ordered. *"He must be stopped."*

"Stop him."

"Stop him."

"Yes, stop him."

Zhatan nodded to them. "Stand by to reduce speed to level eight," she told Nidal. "We will delay Kirk. Or, with luck, stop him."

SWISHING THE COFFEE around the cup by rolling it in circles, Kirk watched as a lick of steam rose from the black liquid.

It was his second cup. Uhura was still on her first. Palamas had tea but she'd left it untouched.

At the center of the briefing room's long table, the tri-viewer showed a rolling list of data that at this point had become a blur to the captain.

"Here's something interesting," the communications officer said, looking up from the data slate she'd been monitoring.

"What?" Kirk stood and reached out a hand as she brought him the slate.

"I'm not sure it's pertinent," Uhura said, "but it explains a lot."

The captain scanned the data, smiled, then handed it back to her and sat down. "It does, yes."

Palamas cleared her throat. "Want to share with the class?"

"The Maabas aren't babes in the woods," Kirk said, bemused. "They knew the Kenisians were around—or suspected it, at least. Which is why a treaty with the Federation became so important."

"And you're not surprised, sir?" Palamas said.

With a chuckle, the captain explained, "Why would they all of a sudden change their minds and push for an expedited agreement? I don't believe in coincidence."

"They must have known we might find this," Uhura pointed out. "But they gave us full access to their records. They could have deleted that part of the archive."

"We would be left with a data hole that they would have to explain," Kirk said. "It was a brave move."

"They need us," Palamas said empathetically.

Kirk nodded and took a sip from his coffee cup, then set it on the table and began again. "Let's try a different tack."

Seated in front of the computer console, Uhura looked up. "I'm certainly ready for a new approach. I don't feel we've learned much."

"I'm still not sure what we're looking for, sir," Palamas said.

"As I told the doctor, I'm hoping," Kirk said tiredly, "we'll know it when we see it."

"We know," Uhura began, "the Maabas found the planet twenty-four hundred years ago."

"Twenty-four hundred thirty-three years," Palamas corrected.

"Thank you," Kirk said with a smile.

"Forgive me, Captain." Palamas cradled her tea in both hands and took a small sip. "Historians and dates," she explained.

Kirk nodded his understanding. "*Over* two thousand years ago the Maabas landed on this planet. They migrated to the same locations where the Kenisians had built their civilization," the captain said.

"Temperate areas, land which could be cultivated, near resources, potable water sources," Uhura added.

"Which is how they found the Kenisian ruins," Palamas said, taking another sip from her tea.

"Correct." Kirk rose and began to slowly pace the room. "They find the ruins—most of them aren't hard to find—and, being a highly technological people, they wanted to study them, learn from them."

"But they don't," Palamas chimed in, "at least not at first."

"You're right," the captain agreed. "They're war weary."

"They cannibalized what technology they could find," Palamas added. "The earliest histories are personal diaries and private archival footage."

Kirk nodded. "A society in survival mode."

"In some ways the personal is a more interesting history," Palamas said. "Unfiltered by official historians. Unedited." She turned toward Uhura. "Lieutenant, can you find the archive labeled one-four-three-four *indok*?"

Uhura nodded toward the tri-viewer as a shaky recording taken thousands of years ago began to play. A mother sat cradling her crying baby as the wind kicked up and people ran for shelter.

The baby was long dead. Her great-great-great-great-great-grandchild was long dead too. But her progeny *had* survived and thrived, and now were being threatened along with a large swath of the galaxy.

"Who is that?" Kirk asked of the vid.

Uhura checked. "Archive recorded by Arublis Pa'atar Maalganq." She looked up. "No information on the mother or her child."

"They're long since dust," Kirk said quietly.

"The Kenisians aren't," Palamas said. "From what you have told us, sir, some of the same ones who lived then are alive in other people's minds."

"Whoever attempted to conquer them got more than they bargained for," Uhura said. "They created an eternal enemy."

"They did," Kirk agreed. *But who were they?* He stalked back toward Uhura and flipped a switch. "Computer."

"*Ready*," the computer replied in a voice that was a cross between respectful and bored.

"Access all Maabas databanks and cross-reference against Federation historical records."

"*Working*." There was a short pause. "*Ready*."

"According to the archaeological investigation conducted by the Maabas, how long was the planet uninhabited before they arrived?"

"*Working*."

Kirk felt a smile tug at his lips. He knew he was on to something. He wasn't sure what, and maybe it was just the excitement of posing a question they'd not asked before. But if the answer spurred on another question, and another after that . . .

A few chirps and the computer continued. "*Maabas Archaeological Institute estimates between two hundred fifty and three hundred years.*"

"That would mean Zhatan's people lived there about three thousand years ago," Palamas pointed out, but the computer disagreed.

"*Incorrect.*"

"Explain," Kirk demanded of the computer.

"*Archaeological evidence suggests third race between Kenisian and Maabas habitation.*"

"Damn." Kirk slapped the back of his right hand into the palm of his left loudly enough that Uhura, startled by the sound, blinked her eyes. "Conquerors conquer for a reason."

"Resources," Palamas told Kirk. "Computer, extrapolate from sensor data and archives. Has Maaba S'Ja been stripped of natural resources?"

"Working. Negative."

Kirk shook his head and began pacing again. "If you can manage warp speed, the resources you need move from basic elements to dilithium and rodinium."

"The planet isn't rich in either and never was," Uhura pointed out.

The captain nodded and bit his lip thoughtfully. "What if . . . what if the Maabas and the Kenisians are somehow connected?"

"How?" Palamas asked.

Kirk motioned to Uhura. "Star charts—show me where the Maabas came from, in relation to their current system."

Uhura nodded toward the tri-viewer. "Onscreen, Captain."

A graphic of the sector displayed. One area was labeled "Maaba S'Ja system" and another was tagged "Former Maabas system." They were relatively far apart and seemingly unrelated.

"Cross-reference, Starfleet survey reports, all planets in this sector with signs of previous but not *current* civilization, or . . ."—Kirk paused, searching for the right phrase—"or current civilizations that have undergone interstellar war within the last six thousand years."

"Working."

Slowly the graphic was populated with flashes, red dots appearing first over one system, then another, and another, until there was a wide line of indicators which cut a path across the sector.

A cold shiver danced down Kirk's spine. He heard Uhura's intake of breath, and when he glanced at Palamas, she looked ill.

"How many lives," she asked quietly, "across how many worlds, do you suppose?"

The captain shook his head and slumped down into the seat next to Uhura. He didn't want to give voice to a number. Too many zeros, too much death.

"The Maabas and the Kenisians were displaced by the same conquerors," Palamas concluded.

A guess, Kirk thought. *But an educated one.*

"Why?" Uhura's question was pertinent, but unanswerable.

"The powerful often crave more power." The captain shrugged, looked at his coffee cup across the table, and decided against reaching for it.

Despite the sour feeling about what they'd learned, Kirk knew they were on to something. What answers it might give them he wasn't sure, but the more information they had, the better. "What *did* they want?" the captain asked himself quietly.

"Perhaps the same thing Zhatan wants," Uhura offered. "Revenge?"

"Zhatan didn't want revenge against the Maabas," Palamas said. "Even if it seemed like it at first."

"That's it, Lieutenant. That's *exactly* it," Kirk said.

"Sir?" Palamas looked to Uhura for a clue but she just shrugged.

"What if," Kirk began, and his face flushed with the exhilaration that he finally had a grasp of the situation, "*na'hubis* was not developed by the Kenisians. Or maybe it was. Maybe this conquering race learned about it, decided to steal it." He was all over the place, and so he paused, took in a breath, and slowly released it. "Whatever the case, the Kenisians didn't care about the planet as much as the *nu'hubis*."

"*Na'hubis*," Uhura corrected, always the linguist.

Kirk nodded. "The *na'hubis* represents horrific power."

"If you're looking to destroy an entire space sector," Palamas said, "what good is it to anyone who wants to live in it?"

"A bargaining chip," Kirk said, placing his hand out as if an actual item sat on it. "Zhatan said they thought *na'hubis* could be harnessed, if properly controlled." He closed his hand quickly as if grasping something before it fell.

"The destroyers look for it," Uhura picked up a stylus from the table and tapped it on her lips absentmindedly, "and when they don't find it—because the Kenisians have hidden it—they search other worlds in this sector."

"They took what they wanted, and destroyed

what they didn't," Palamas whispered sadly. Repulsed by the thought, she shuddered.

"Maybe they considered themselves naturally superior. Maybe they're different enough they don't respect life-forms like us." Kirk paused, setting that thought aside. "Whatever the reason, something changed, because we've never heard of them. For whatever reason, they retreated at some point, or returned home."

"But now," Uhura said, "the Kenisians have found them."

"*We* need to find them." Kirk stood. "And get there before the Kenisians do."

As Kirk started for the door, the red alert lights began to flash and the bosun's whistle sounded. "*Bridge to Captain Kirk.*" Sulu's voice sounded urgent.

The captain spun toward the nearest table comm and mashed the button with his fist. "Kirk, here."

"*Sir, sensors detect incoming attack.*"

"How many contacts?"

"*Hundreds, sir. Hundreds.*"

TEN

"Platforms three and four in that section are empty, Commander."

Zhatan nodded. "Thank you, Nidal."

"There were a few still loaded in platform two, I sent those as well."

Acknowledging that with only a sigh, Zhatan steepled her fingers in thought. In *thoughts*.

"*Feel no guilt.*"

"*He was against us.*"

"*Against us.*"

"*He would stop us.*"

"*Kirk would end us if he could.*"

"*No, he is a good man.*"

"*We have not killed him. Just delayed.*"

"*He may yet survive.*"

"*When he pursues again it will be too late.*"

"*He could die.*"

"*They should die.*"

"*They shouldn't.*"

"*If Kirk is gone, Spock may not help us.*"

"*He will because it is logical.*"

"*He will not if he is aggrieved.*"

"Enterprise *should be destroyed for our safety,*" Tibis counseled.

"*No. They are of good character. We touched Kirk's mind.*"

"*He would stop us.*"

"*He is a fool.*"

"*We should hope for his death.*"

"*We could have made sure of it.*"

"*No! That is not our place. He has not sinned against us.*"

"*Stopping us is sin.*"

"*He will not stop us.*"

"*He cannot! We must prevail,*" Tibis said.

"*We will.*"

"*We will prevail.*"

"*We will.*"

Sighing again, Zhatan turned away from Nidal when she saw her first glancing back at her.

"What troubles you, Commander?"

"Nothing," Zhatan said. "There is simply much to consider."

Leaving her station, the first came up to the command chair. "Please," she whispered. "Confide in us as you once did. We see you are torn, and we can help."

Flicking a look at the bridge crew at their stations, then back to Nidal, the commander shook her head. "We should debate our decisions with you, here, on our bridge?"

"We aren't asking you for debate," her first said quietly. "We ask that you use us to help order your thoughts. You are so closed now. You never used to be this circumspect. Not with us."

That was true. In all the years they'd known one another in their current physical forms, even before their relationship had blossomed, Zhatan had used her first as a sounding board. That was why she'd named her as first. But when Nidal testified alongside Alkinth, and used personal, private conversations against Zhatan at the hearing, things had changed.

Yes, Nidal had apologized. Yes, Zhatan had forgiven her, in word if not in deed. But the pain of that time remained. How could she now confide in one who had betrayed her?

How could the commander also keep from confiding in her first?

"We *are* torn," Zhatan admitted. "As we're sure you are also."

Pleased at the confession, Nidal smiled. "Less so than you, we think, but yes. We can see it both ways. Kirk is a hindrance, and the *Enterprise* is a powerful vessel."

"We don't wish him dead. Most of us do not," the commander said.

"We know that." Nidal touched the arm of the command chair rather than reaching out for Zhatan's hand. "You *have* given him a chance at life, and that is something."

Eyes cast sadly down, the commander shook her head. "And yet those in us who wish him ill are pleased at the prospect he shall not survive."

"We all bear such a burden," Nidal reminded her.

"Which of those in your heart," Zhatan said, looking up, "were conflicted about your past wrongs?"

Sighing, her first turned away. "Always back to that."

As Nidal returned to her station, Zhatan regretted picking at the scab just as they seemed to have moved past it, if even for just a moment.

We're sorry, she thought, but didn't let the words pass her lips.

"BATTLE STATIONS. Battle stations. All hands, battle stations."

As quick as the tubolift was, to the captain it wasn't fast enough. He burst onto the bridge and was at the command chair in four steps. Uhura had been behind him but by the time he turned to look, she was at her station.

"Hail them, Lieutenant. Warn them off."

"Aye, sir."

Sulu was already at the helm when Kirk stepped off the lift, and he'd likely been there since calling red alert.

"No reply on any channel, sir," Uhura told him.

He didn't think there would be. "Tactical," Kirk

ordered, and the main viewscreen switched to a graphical view of their relative position and the hostiles around them.

Hundreds of hostiles. Incoming.

At the center of the screen was an icon indicating the *Enterprise*. Spread out before them, hundreds of small dots, maneuvering wildly closer.

"Identification?"

"None," Jolma said, his voice just this side of panic. "I mean, unknown, sir."

"Evasive, Sulu?"

"Unsuccessful. They blocked our path—accelerating toward us."

"How many exactly?" the captain asked.

"Sensors indicate," Jolma paused to check, "two hundred and seven, sir. Power signatures similar to the Kenisian vessel."

That was not a surprise. Kirk looked back to the young man at the first officer's usual station. He considered replacing the ensign with Chekov, but wanted to keep his best navigator in place. Every officer was once a raw bundle of nerves. Jolma's training would compensate.

"Life-signs?" Kirk asked.

Peering deep into the sensor cowl, Jolma shook his head. "No readings. Could be shielded. Would be cramped, though. Each is spheroid, just over three meters in diameter. Mass is twenty-five thousand, two hundred kilograms."

A lot of mass in a small package.

"They're highly energized," Sulu added, subtly reminding Jolma that the captain didn't hear the ensign's first report because he wasn't on the bridge.

"And very fast," Chekov said.

"I don't read weapons." Jolma turned and looked to Kirk, who shook his head.

"They *are* the weapons, Ensign."

Silently, Jolma gulped.

The captain didn't blame him. They were bullets—warp powered instead of gunpowder propelled, but with enough apparent and actual mass to tear the *Enterprise* to shreds. "How shielded are they?"

"Class three, sir."

Lovely, Kirk thought. "Time to intercept?"

"Three minutes ten seconds," Chekov replied.

"Let's back off, Mister Sulu." Kirk crooked a thumb aft. "Alter course. Come about to two-one-two, mark seventeen."

Nimble fingers worked the helm, and Sulu nodded. "Aye, sir."

Enterprise turned and sped away, but the hostiles continued in pursuit.

"They have increased speed, sir, and are maintaining course." A bit of shock tinted Chekov's voice as he kept his eyes glued to his readout. "Time to intercept, three minutes."

"What we need," Jolma said, "is a place to hide. A gas giant, maybe?"

"Not to hide, Mister Jolma, but a gas giant is an excellent idea." Kirk turned to him with a smile. "Find us one, and if it has some rings we could use them."

Jolma twisted back to the science station. "One point seven parsecs away." He turned toward Kirk and grinned. "It's ringed, sir."

"Other planets?"

"Seven in all. Two are rocky. None have life-signs."

"Good." *That just might do*, Kirk thought. "Mister Chekov, lay in a course." He thumbed the comm button on the right arm of his chair. "Kirk to engineering."

"Scott here, sir."

"We're about to get hot, Mister Scott."

"Aye, sir. How hot?"

"Jovian hot."

There was a slight hesitation before Scott offered a disquieted, *"Aye, aye, sir."*

"Kirk out."

"Course laid in, Captain." Chekov gave an extra push to the last button in the sequence, and his hands hovered at the ready.

"Mister Sulu, take us in. As close and as fast as we can."

Under the helmsman's guidance, *Enterprise* thrust itself toward the ringed Jovian planet.

"Hostiles in pursuit," Chekov said.

On the main viewscreen, the tactical display was

awash in dots, twisting this way and that, spiraling madly toward the *Enterprise* as it drove toward the planet.

"Put her just outside the rings."

"Aye, sir," Sulu said, but glanced anxiously at Chekov, who seemed equally uncertain.

"Intercept in one minute ten seconds, sir." Controls at the ready, the navigator prepared to fire both phasers and photon torpedoes.

But the captain knew the weapons weren't enough. Two hundred and seven intelligent missiles. It was overkill. The *Enterprise* could outrun them, eventually. But they would have to retreat, losing precious time.

The attack was interesting. Zhatan was walking a line between not trying to destroy the *Enterprise*, but not caring if it was destroyed. Perhaps being a multividual was more a disorder than the Kenisians would care to admit. If Zhatan had this kind of weaponry at her disposal, wouldn't ridding herself of the *Enterprise* be the wiser path?

The hidden message in this attack was that Kenisians were aware they were being pursued. Zhatan could have been privy to their coded communication with Spock, or she might have assumed the *Enterprise* was following. Worse yet, this could be Kenisian space and their surveillance equipment recognized the *Enterprise* as an invader and alerted Zhatan automatically.

Chekov nervously called out, "Twenty-three seconds to contact with first of hostiles."

"Push her, Mister Sulu." Kirk could see the tension in his helmsman's shoulders.

Sulu leaned over his console as if he could physically push the ship along. "Aye, aye, sir."

The thrust of the engines could be felt through the deck plates.

Kirk considered transferring power to the aft shields, but the fore shields were needed as they plunged toward the gas giant.

"Captain?" Jolma's voice was an overexcited squeak. "Hostiles are increasing speed. Using the planet's pull to accelerate."

Kirk could see on the tactical display that hundreds of dots were plummeting toward his ship as she dove toward the planet.

"Fifteen seconds."

"Alter course on my mark, Sulu. Ninety degrees port." The captain leaned forward in the command chair, his eyes locked on the tactical display and the indicator that showed the first of the missiles bearing down on them.

"Impact imminent," Chekov reported.

"Ten seconds," Sulu said.

"Mark, Sulu!" Kirk gripped onto the arms of his chair and held tight. "Full-power turn."

Enterprise whined, bulkheads and inertial dampers creaking under the strain.

The first three spheres flew past, unable to break away from the pull of the planet. They were struck by the larger pieces in the ring. Crushed and crumpled, they fell into the gas giant's atmosphere.

On the tactical display, Kirk watched as the rest of the missiles turned with them, still in close pursuit.

And then one took the lead.

"Aft torpedoes, full spread," Kirk ordered over the howling engines. "Fire!"

Red orbs of power launched behind *Enterprise* and crashed into the nearest missile.

A white-hot bubble of explosive energy crackled forward.

Kirk was pitched from the command chair and groaned as he rammed a knee into the lip of the console between Chekov and Sulu.

Lights flickered and dimmed, with only sparks illuminating the billows of smoke that poured from overloading circuits. Loose cabling crackled above, and Kirk blinked as particles of insulation rained down as a support strut clattered to the deck to his left.

Emergency lights clicked on as the crew found footing and stumbled back to their stations.

Then another explosion rocked the ship and inertial dampers shut down, hurling the crew in every direction.

Darkness blotted all and refused to wane.

———

"SOMETHING IS WRONG, Commander Spock."
The ambassador was again pretending they were
discussing the Maabas computer console, but what
actually concerned Pippenge was that Spock had
sent three new coded messages to the *Enterprise*
without response.

Spock couldn't be sure what had gone wrong.
"*They are unable to respond, or they are not receiving the messages,*" he told Pippenge covertly via his
implant.

When the ambassador saw the message, he
pursed his lips in way of acknowledgment.

"*There are several possibilities,*" Spock continued.
"*But one theory does not have more evidence to support it over others.*" He didn't care to get into the
specifics of the countless potentialities. The *Enterprise* could have sustained damage to the communications equipment or it could be out of range. They
could have encountered external forces that made
communication silence necessary or unavoidable.
More grimly, the ship could have been destroyed.

Turning back, Spock knew, would not have been
an option, not for James Kirk. If it were at all possible, the captain would still be in pursuit.

However, it may not have been possible. Spock
would need to strategize for that contingency.

To stop the Kenisian plan, Spock would now
have to be more proactive rather than playing along
with the Kenisians' desire to limit the *na'hubis*

weapon. In fact, the Vulcan thought, he might need to perfect it.

Spock sent to Pippenge, *"It is time to succeed at the task which you've been delaying. I will need full access to the Maabas archive."*

The ambassador's jaw gaped open. "I—I have feigned nothing," he said in a low voice. "I truly don't know how to do it."

Spock pulled in a long breath and released it slowly. Speaking in an equally hushed tone, he said, "That, Mister Ambassador, is a problem."

DNA-based computers were known to Federation science, but when the Vulcan attempted to help the ambassador in his task, solutions did not immediately present themselves.

As he investigated, Spock was acutely reminded why the Federation saw a benefit in scientific exchange with the Maabas. The computer they had designed was straightforward, but after attempting to compromise its security, a program was triggered which modified its genetic code. Now, it could not be accessed, except by a particular Maabas individual. Ambassador Pippenge was indeed unable to unlock the console. The only individual who could was likely the technician who originally set up the computer.

"We need," Spock told Pippenge, "for you to be a different person."

Eyes wide, the ambassador seemed very unsure what to make of his statement. "I beg your pardon?"

"A person's genetic code is much the same as that of anyone else of their race. Genetically speaking, most differences between individuals are on a superficial level."

Pippenge flattened his lips. "Yes, this I know. On our native homeworld, a small tree-dwelling creature no bigger than your hand is an evolutionary precursor to Maabas. Genetically, I believe it is a ninety-three percent match to any living Maabasian."

"You," Spock said, tilting his head toward the ambassador, "are better than a ninety-nine percent match to whomever established the baseline for this computer."

"But it takes one hundred percent, does it not?"

"Yes," Spock replied. "But computers only do as they are told. Without access, we cannot instruct it to work differently, but we might use its own strict adherence to protocol against it."

"How?" Pippenge was truly interested, and in his excitement, his anxiety faded.

"By masking the discordant portion of your DNA from the scanning instrument of the computer." Using the Kenisian tricorder for its intended purpose, rather than covert coded messages, Spock scanned the ambassador. "What will remain, as far as the computer is concerned, will be a one hundred percent match."

After recording Pippenge's genetic code, Spock

then scanned the Maabas computer console. Another problem presented itself. Apparently, despite his default attempt to not express such disappointment visually, the ambassador knew they'd encountered a problem. "What troubles you now?"

"There is no DNA sample within the computer itself. It's likely an encoded file."

"Which we cannot access."

Spock nodded. "Correct." Working the tricorder again, the science officer set up a connection to the Maabas computer. "However, we can attempt to feed versions of your genetic code into the system. When one matches, we shall be alerted."

"Will that not take a great deal of time, Mister Spock?"

"It may." Setting the Kenisian tricorder to its task, Spock lowered it carefully to the corner of the console.

At their next progress report, Sciver listened quietly to Spock's explanation of what he was doing to help Pippenge, then without comment had a guard escort the Vulcan to the room where Commander Zhatan was waiting.

Presumably, this was her office, but it showed no signs of decoration other than benign and neutral walls. *Perhaps*, Spock thought, *it was a common area used for impersonal interviews and one-on-one discussions.*

Spock sat in the only chair available, which was

directly in front of the desk behind which Zhatan was seated. Like the chair in the cell, this too shaped itself to meet his contours.

Without prompting, Spock explained to her exactly what he'd told Sciver.

When he was finished, she nodded her approval. "Our medical team was working on a gene-therapy to change his genetic code," she said, amused.

"Unnecessary," Spock said. "One can more easily block a scan than alter what is being scanned."

She smiled again, but mirthlessly. "Yes, of course."

"You are troubled?" Spock took his hands off the arms of the chair and placed them elegantly on his lap. He hoped to suggest a more open demeanor.

Studying his visage for a long moment, Zhatan tilted her head in curiosity. "What would you know about the realm of feelings?"

Raising a brow, Spock demurred. "I?" He shook his head. "Only that—as a Vulcan—I deal with very strong emotions which by necessity must be kept in check. I may be more informed on the topic of feelings than you assume."

A trace of understanding touched her expression, and either she lost her tenuous grasp on it, or one of Zhatan's many personalities thrust it away.

What had the captain seen and felt when melded with her? Spock couldn't help but wonder. Having been connected to a collective consciousness before, he'd known the telepathic touch of more than one mind. But that instance was unique, where a single will dominated those linked to it. Zhatan's situation was drastically different, with fewer personalities, but perhaps none truly in control.

Spock had chosen the path of the ill-considered mind-meld before. He didn't wish to repeat past mistakes. But he was admittedly curious.

He pressed, "What specifically troubles you?"

For a few seconds, Zhatan seemed to be on the cusp of a reply. Looking away, she merely asked her next question, "How long do you expect before you have access to the Maabas archives?"

"Unknown," Spock said. "The process ends when the correct combination of genes is blocked. I haven't enough data to make a prediction."

"How long *could* it take?" she asked.

Spock was only as frank as necessary. "Given the number of protein-coding genes within Maabas DNA, the process of elimination could take years." Technically, that was correct, but didn't account for that fact that Spock had programmed the tricorder to try only viable combinations. In actuality, the sequencer could run its course in four days.

"We don't have years," Zhatan told him.

"Would it be inappropriate to ask why?"

Once again she hesitated, and the machinations within were obvious. "The situation is . . . multifaceted," she said finally, and very quietly, as if nervous that she might hear herself.

"Most situations seem complex from within. An external, impartial view can offer clarity."

"Is that what you are?" Zhatan laughed. "Impartial?"

"I am not your enemy." Spock was careful to say "I" and not "we." He would not speak for the Federation, or even Starfleet, because aligning himself with others would not gain her trust.

"And we are not yours," Zhatan said, but the answer was more perfunctory than meaningful.

"You seek to harm your conquerors," Spock said. "Clearly, whatever war you fought with them was, at some point, won. Why pursue retribution in such haste?" Thinking it futile to convince her against revenge, he hoped first to hear why the Kenisian had a stringent timetable.

"Haste?" she scoffed. "This has been hundreds of years in the planning."

"Would hundreds of years *and a day* be too long?"

A sneer curling her lips, Zhatan was roused to anger. "It would!"

Spock maintained his Vulcan calm, which he knew could be a risk. "Why?"

The commander answered without hesitation. "Because they rouse! We beat them back to the point where they had *no* ships, *no* cities! We crushed them back to the stone age, and in seven hundred years they have pulled themselves back to the warp age."

"You did not commit genocide," Spock said. "That was an admirable choice."

"It was our 'admirable' *mistake*!" She mashed her fist hard onto the desk in front of her. "We watched, oh we watched." Zhatan launched to her feet and began to pace the room, pent-up tension venting itself through her gait. "After the war, to save their lives, and those of their children, we sentenced them to technological oblivion. They agreed. But within two generations they'd broken the pact. Ignored it! But we were watching." She wagged a finger at Spock, as if she were lecturing him. "There was a time when, like you, we were a peaceful people. We decided not to obliterate them. So we merely destroyed their industrial base—again—and went on our way."

Deducing the next part, Spock nodded. "But they rebuilt a third time."

"Every fifty or sixty years," she said, exasperated. "We would monitor from afar, and make visits when we had to . . . but we grew complacent. Their homeworld is far from where we settled, and we were swayed by their pleas. With time, we allowed basic technology."

"But one innovation led to the next."

"Yes. Now, they are ready to touch the stars again. Our probes show a highly active warp travel. A large fleet—and the building of a starbase."

"And you believe they will use this base to launch an attack on you."

"Why wouldn't they?" She leaned down, palms flat against the tabletop, and looked him in the eye. "Wouldn't you?"

"No," Spock said.

"Of course, *you* wouldn't," she sneered. "But any being who understood fear *would*."

Pulling his hands across his chest, Spock interlocked his fingers and made his posture as impassive as he could. However, what he said he meant to sting. "I know fear, Commander. I've experienced it, and its negative ramifications. I've seen it force others to either condone or commit horrific acts. It is *your* fear, in fact, that would ask me to be complicit in a holocaust."

He expected her to rage at him. Instead, Zhatan straightened and then dropped herself back into the chair. "I *am* afraid." Eyes closed, she sounded exhausted. "There is no way back from this course."

"I" again. There was most surely an individual within, even if it were in constant conflict with her other selves.

"There are alternatives to fear," Spock told her quietly. "One can have an emotion without acting on it. One can use it to inform their feelings, but nothing more."

"But we, Commander Spock, are not *merely* one," Zhatan said. Her eyes opened suddenly, and once more they had grown cold.

ELEVEN

The sound of impact was a slow-motion crunch, as if someone had put the vessel in a vise and tightened it.

Dust and debris shook from overhead. Cables fell, insulation dropped, consoles spasmed.

Lights crackled off, and the red glare of backup lighting flicked on, then off again.

"*Coolant leak, deck seven, section ten.*"

"*Circuit overloads, propulsion baker-one, alpha; linear section five-nine. Repeat, Circ-O-L, P-B-one-A, L-five-nine.*"

"*Auxiliary engaged.*"

"*Responding.*"

"*System status?*"

"*Null.*"

"*Intercooler?*"

"*Stand by.*"

"*Fail-overs in tolerance.*"

"*Phaser systems?*"

"*Active.*"

"*Photon control?*"

"*Nominal.*"

The din of a starship during damage control. Training takes over, duty becomes paramount, and a captain hears and distinguishes it all.

The engines still whined, so Kirk knew they were moving. The sizzle of sparks from above had decreased, and the fans worked to pump out the acrid smoke. The lights were on, if a bit dimmer. *Enterprise* was alive and kicking.

The captain helped Sulu return to his seat at the helm, then noticed Chekov was already back at navigation. Behind them, Uhura stood, working her console, her chair tipped onto the deck at her side.

"Could be worse," Kirk heard Chekov murmur.

Sulu shook his head. "Really?"

An engineering tech had fallen from the upper bridge onto the steps. She was bleeding from the top of her head, and Kirk called to Uhura as he helped the woman up. "Medical team to the bridge."

"Th-thank you, sir."

Her elbow shaking in his hand, Kirk sat her on the upper deck and looked at the gash that ran across her hairline. "That doesn't look too bad."

"I'm fine, Captain, it's just a scalp cut."

Returning to the command chair, the captain studied the tactical display on the main viewer. It confirmed what he knew—they weren't out of danger.

"Multiple shockwaves overloaded our shields," Jolma yelled to be heard over the din.

"Systems stabilizing," Forbes said from the engineering station. "Shields holding at sixty-eight percent."

Not enough.

"Hostile missiles still in pursuit," Chekov said.

Retaking the center seat, Kirk scanned the tactical situation more closely. Several of the spheres had fallen into the planet, just as the captain had hoped. Too many were following them. Those they'd torpedoed had not only damaged the *Enterprise*, but sent some of their brethren to their demise.

The captain leaned forward toward navigation to make sure he was heard. "Mister Chekov, I need a torpedo spread as far back as you can. Try to thin the herd." Kirk looked to the helm next. "Sulu, orbit close as possible."

Enterprise dove down again, and the missiles followed. Shields sizzled against the thickening planetary atmosphere.

"External view," Kirk ordered, and the main viewer tactical display disappeared, while the image of the gas giant filled the rest of the screen. It roiled beneath them, an inhospitable place for a vacation home.

The captain moved to the edge of the command chair. "See that moonlet, Sulu?"

The helmsman looked up and nodded. "Aye, sir."

"Use it," Kirk ordered.

That was all Sulu needed to hear. Under his

hands, *Enterprise* looped up and around the moonlet. His fingers pressed harshly at the controls, and yet moved elegantly at the same time. At his touch, the ship dove sharklike through a turn around the rock. The pilot-fish missiles followed. When Sulu pulled the ship harshly away, several more of the spheres slammed into the moonlet and other ring debris.

"Phasers, fire!" Kirk ordered. *Enterprise* connected blue threads to the closest, weakest targets.

One pursuer lost its engine and swiftly succumbed to the planet's gravity. Another's navigation sensors were scrambled, and it spiraled out of control until it hit three others and they all exploded into a massive ball of energy.

"Shockwave," Jolma called, and they braced for the impact.

Sheets of energy slammed into *Enterprise*'s shields, rattling the ship. More dust fell from above, but nothing collapsed, and sparks didn't fill the air as they had before. No one was tossed from their seats, only shaken in them.

On the main viewscreen, despite having turned away from the planet, an orange glow diffused across the screen from the starboard side.

Sulu glared down into his tactical display. "Another set of missiles struck the surface of the planet, sir."

"They're fast, but not that smart," Kirk said.

As if to punish the captain for his brief moment of celebration, the engines complained with a whine which suggested the ship was losing power.

He glanced to Forbes at the engineering station.

"Structural integrity fields are down sixty percent, sir."

The captain jammed the end of his fist onto the comm button. "Kirk to Scott."

"Scott here." The engineer was out of breath and sounding haggard. *"Between the gravimetric pull of the planet and the force of the shockwaves, structural integrity field generators are overloaded."*

Kirk had known the engineer long enough not to haggle with him. "How long?"

"Keep her on an even keel for ten minutes," Scott said. *"And by ten, I wish I meant five, but I mean ten, sir."*

"Understood, Mister Scott. Ten minutes, but not a minute more. Kirk out." He thumbed the button to close the channel and wondered how he would carve that long of a lull into an ongoing battle.

"Sulu, continue evasive. Move around the rings for now, in and out. Lose as many as possible, but keep us steady as you can."

"Aye, aye, sir."

Alert lights still flashing, but the klaxons thankfully muted, Kirk moved toward the science station. "Jolma."

The captain noticed that the ensign instantly tensed when he said the young man's name.

"Sir, one moment."

The captain motioned to the screen above the station. "At ease, Jolma. Punch up the data on this star system."

With a nod, Jolma worked quickly and diligently. He tried to stifle a cough, his lungs probably still smarting from the smoke.

Kirk realized his own throat stung and turned for a moment to Uhura. "Lieutenant, have someone bring us all some water."

"Aye, sir."

"I have it, Captain." Jolma gestured to the screen and wiped the sweat from his forehead with his uniform cuff, all in one awkward movement.

On one screen scrolled the relevant data. On the other, a graph of the system, an orange circle representing the K-type star and its planets.

Kirk leaned over and hit a few buttons, changing the scope of the data. "What about an Oort cloud?"

On the screen above them, the graphic of the system zoomed out until a multicolored, hazy ovoid shape appeared, encapsulating the star.

"There is a lot of mass out there, sir," Jolma said.

"Yes. And just waiting for us." Kirk strode back down to the command chair, briefly taking notice of Chekov's confused expression as the navigator turned from his station.

"Waiting for us?" Chekov asked.

"Waiting for us, Mister Chekov." The captain returned to the center seat.

"Make for the Oort cloud. Gentlemen, find us the biggest comets, rocks, or other planetesimals you can, and plot a circuitous route."

"Aye, sir."

"Yes, Captain."

Come along for the ride, the captain thought as his ship sped away. The tactical display showed the missiles tracking and trailing her. "That's it," he said quietly. "Follow us down the rabbit hole."

At maximum impulse, the travel time to the system's Oort cloud was less than what Scott needed. The *Enterprise* tacked back and forth, forging a path of zigs and zags. The structural integrity fields were needed to supplement the ship's structure, but the stress Kirk had placed on those systems when in close orbit around a gas giant and dodging missiles was far greater than what was needed for the simple maneuvers they used now. It would give the engineers a chance to make their repairs.

Damage control teams fanned out across the ship to clear debris, reroute power where possible, and replace circuits when needed. Support teams also came with small bars of nourishment and thermoses of water. The captain waved off the protein supplement but was grateful for the drink. "Thank you, yeoman," he told the man who handed him a cup.

The bridge continued to be a hub of activity as Sulu and Chekov worked to keep the *Enterprise* on an "even keel" and the missiles at bay.

As one closed on them, a twist starboard or port and a well-aimed phaser shot would knock the sphere off course. They didn't need to destroy the missiles—disabling them was enough.

Three more closed, and all were dispatched with a mixture of phasers and torpedoes.

"They are very stubborn, sir," Chekov said.

"So are we," Kirk assured him, but the captain was as frustrated as the navigator. Every moment they spent in this system was one they lost in their pursuit of the Kenisian vessel.

After nine and a half minutes, Kirk called down to his engineer.

"Mister Scott, give me the good word."

"We're just finishing, sir." Scott sounded restored, refreshed—as if making repairs to his engines caused a similar rejuvenation in the engineer. *"We've replaced the primaries and bolstered the shielding on the secondary."*

"As usual, Mister Scott, you've earned your pay. Kirk out." He hit the arm of the chair, closing the channel, and inched forward in his chair. "Now, Mister Sulu, we pull them into the cloud."

The helmsman smiled. "Aye, aye, sir."

An Oort cloud wasn't a tight asteroid field, although this one had more mass than Kirk had seen in any other planetary system. Piloting between icy planetesimals wasn't difficult, and none of them would have enough gravity to be a problem for either the *Enterprise* or her pursuers.

"A nice big rock, Mister Chekov." The captain smiled, reveling in the fresh idea. "We're going to play some billiards."

Kirk could tell the navigator was grinning. "Yes, sir."

The ship swerved toward the first rock within range. The Kenisian missiles followed. Chekov and Sulu worked in concert, meticulously operating their consoles.

Nodding at the small planetoid on the main viewer, Kirk twisted toward Jolma. "Ensign, plot fissure points on that planetoid and feed information to the targeting sensors."

"Aye, sir." His voice steady, Jolma seemed pleased there was something proactive he could do.

Certainly the captain was.

The object wasn't as large as many Kirk had seen or even landed on with a shuttle. But that was good. He needed a smaller body—one that could be cleaved.

"Get it between us and them, Sulu."

The captain didn't have to worry about turning it into rubble and the possible ramifications to planetary life. Debris was exactly what he wanted.

Sliding over and then in front of the huge rock, *Enterprise* spat torpedoes at very specific points.

Chemical flame and plasma fire erupted as they sped away.

"Reverse angle on viewer," Kirk ordered. As the small planetesimal shrank away from them, molten rock burst in all directions. One missile after another spiraled off course. Some exploded upon impact with the white-hot ejecta, causing shockwaves which disabled or destroyed others behind them. But many were agile enough to avoid the destruction and continue pursuit.

The captain watched for changes on the tactical display. The number of hostile contacts had dropped, but not enough.

"On to the next one, gentlemen," Kirk said, releasing a long pull of breath.

And the next one went much the same, and more enemy missiles were destroyed.

Enterprise rounded yet another planetoid, this one much larger than the first two.

Was it too large to break up easily? The captain didn't think so, just a little more.

"Give this one a little extra, Mister Chekov."

"Aye, sir."

Jolma did his part, feeding the targeting computer with the best locations to strike the mass to cause it to fracture. Chekov and Sulu handled their tasks as well, maneuvering the ship and firing on the mega-asteroid. The captain thought the extra salvo would be enough.

He was wrong.

PIPPENGE WAS AFRAID. He rocked nervously back and forth, and Spock assumed it was a Maabas custom to ameliorate anxiety. It did not seem to be working.

"Ambassador." When Pippenge didn't reply, Spock leaned over and gently whispered again. "Ambassador?"

While continuing to rock, he angled his head toward the Vulcan and seemed attentive enough.

"I understand your apprehension," Spock said. "But we must acquit ourselves as rationally as possible if we're to achieve our goals."

Pippenge nodded, but did not cease his movement.

James Kirk excelled in at least one area Spock did not: the ability to act impulsively—based on what the captain called his "gut"—and somehow attain his sought-after goal.

If rash action was called for, Spock was at a loss on how to determine just what act that should be.

Was it possible to dispose of the prototype mines before they could be used? Unlikely. At least not in a way that they could not be easily regained.

And the consequences could be severe enough that he'd be helpless to act further.

Could he destroy the Kenisian vessel? Perhaps. But Spock's access to essential systems was severely limited, and should he manage it, the *na'hubis* could be catalyzed, rendering the reason for his sabotage moot.

Might he be able to slow the vessel's progress? *That* was a distinct possibility. How? Would he be able to protect himself and the ambassador from retribution should his sabotage be discovered? That option needed considerable thought.

Turning to his console, he sent another message to Pippenge's computer implant. "*I shall attempt to contact the* Enterprise *again.*"

Apparently stunned by receipt of the communication, the ambassador froze in place for an instant, then turned and looked at Spock hopefully.

There was no reply to his first message. Spock sent another, and after an appropriate amount of time passed, another.

With each attempt that went unanswered, Pippenge appeared more distraught.

Anticipating what the ambassador might ask him, Spock attempted to comfort his companion. "*They're likely out of range.*"

Pippenge was visually displeased with that answer.

"*Or,*" Spock added, "*they are maintaining communication silence for a specific purpose.*"

The ambassador's eyes widened, and Spock inferred he was being asked why Captain Kirk would do that.

"There are many possibilities."

Some of them, Spock thought, *are unappealing.*

Hearing the Kenisian tricorder chime, Spock lifted the unit from his console and examined the readout on its small screen.

"A change?" Pippenge asked.

Spock pursed his lips a moment, both instinctively and because that was the accepted Maabas mannerism indicating the affirmative. "A genetic code match has been formulated. We now have access to your people's computer archive."

The ambassador was unsure how to process that news. "This is a good thing? Or not?"

"That remains to be seen."

Calling up the data Maabas scientists had gathered on the Kenisian installation and the *na'hubis* compound, Spock got to work.

After a minute or two, Pippenge leaned toward the Vulcan and asked in a hushed tone, "Is there anything I might do to help?"

Spock sensed the question was of the type often asked by those who wanted to offer their assistance but hoped such aid would not be accepted. "Not at the moment."

The ambassador nodded and pinched the bridge of his nose with the thumbs of his left hand. "If you do need me, please let me know." His head lolled to one side, as if suddenly asleep.

"Ambassador?" Snapping his fingers twice, the Vulcan tried to rouse Pippenge, but there was no reply. Apparently he'd entered some sort of self-induced meditative state.

Appreciative, Spock continued his work.

The Maabas scientists, he found, were very thorough in their study of the *na'hubis* compound. They didn't call it that, merely referred to it by exhibit number and date code, which catalogued when it was found and by whom. There was something refreshing about the tone of the documentation. It was logical, well-ordered, and as complete as possible.

Still, they did not grasp the destructive power of the material. Had they, their tests would have been performed off-planet—or not at all.

While absorbing all the material he could find regarding the *na'hubis*, Spock contemplated his plan to slow down the Kenisian vessel. Sabotage was not a tack he wished to take just yet, for several reasons, including it might end in their deaths. A hostage was only valuable to a certain point, and his and Pippenge's value would be severely compromised if he acted so covertly against Zhatan.

No, his version of a "rash" act would be to talk. And in this case, to lie.

———

"YOU ASKED to see us." As Zhatan strode across the laboratory toward them, she noted Pippenge's meditation, shook her head with some disdain, then focused solely on Spock.

"I did." Spock leaned to one side and showed her his computer console's monitor. "We have had access to the Maabas scientific archive for the last seventy-six minutes."

"We?" Her eyes darted to Pippenge.

"The ambassador is in a meditative state which assists him in coping with the twin stresses of abduction and overt physical threat."

Zhatan's lips thinned into a genuine smile. "You have a sense of humor, Mister Spock."

Choosing not to reply, he gestured to the console again. "You will be interested in my findings."

Her smile evaporated. "Proceed."

Spock called up a forged Maabas findings document he'd created just minutes before. He felt assured that should Kenisian experts check, they'd deem it legitimate. Computer records could be forged with some ease, at least for one with his experience. "The Maabas scientists were puzzled by the *na'hubis* and its properties. However, they did manage to initiate a partial catalyzation for three hundredths of a second."

Incredulity slackened Zhatan's jaw, and her eyes widened. "And they never pursued it?"

"They were not aware of it." Keying the console,

Spock displayed a data chart on the screen. "The event was hidden in their data, but having studied your simulations, I recognized it."

She scanned the screen with intent interest, doubtless allowing the former physicists within her a chance for a close study of the fabricated experiment. "You found this, in only seventy-six minutes."

"Negative. I found it in forty-three minutes. The remainder of the time, I searched for verification of the findings. Unfortunately, this was the only example of catalyzation I found."

Stunned, Zhatan took a step back. "We need to verify it."

Spock stood and clasped his hands nonchalantly behind his back. "I concur. But experimentation cannot occur within an active warp field without significant risk of uncontrollable chain reaction." There may have been some truth to his statement. Spock could not be certain. But he needed the "fact" to be believed.

"Simulations—" she began to protest, but Spock shook his head, cutting her off.

"Would be inadequate."

Zhatan frowned and opened her mouth to speak, but again Spock interrupted.

"If you truly desire to contain the destruction, and only seek to injure a specific target, this is a course you must take."

"You want me to stop this vessel. Here? Now?"

"Stopping forward motion is unnecessary. Sub-light speed can be maintained. The experiments only require there is no active warp field in proximity. Necessarily, the engines must be taken offline to a cold state."

She shook her head. "Impossible."

"If my suggestion is unsatisfactory, I am open to hearing yours. A satellite lab, perhaps, to which we can transfer the *na'hubis* mines?"

"No. There must be another alternative," she protested. "We cannot delay."

"Your alternative is to use the mines as they are," Spock said matter-of-factly. "You will destroy your enemy, yourselves, and possibly this arm of the galaxy." He met her eyes as earnestly as possible. "Or, you can shut down your warp engines and allow testing to begin at once." He did not add his usual reminder that she could decide against the attack entirely.

Zhatan stared at him silently for a while before finally turning on her heel and walking toward the doorway. "We must give this some thought," she said. "I will let you know."

At that, Spock raised a curious brow.

"COME IN," Zhatan greeted her first. "We need your help."

Nidal stood before the commander's desk and waited. "Yes?"

"We must contact the Assembly."

Eyes wide, Nidal lowered herself awkwardly into a chair. "Now?"

Zhatan nodded. "We've not the strength to do it alone. If you are by our side, we can endure it."

Eyes moist, Nidal nodded as the commander raised the screen and initiated the call. They both turned and steadied themselves.

"Assembly Vital, this is Zhatan and Nidal aboard the warship *Pride*. We would seek your counsel."

At this extreme distance, there was a delay before they were met with a simple audio reply. "*Pride, this is Vital. Do you request a joint session?*"

"We do."

"*Stand by.*"

They waited. Zhatan knew the time of day would mean a joint session wouldn't take long to call to order.

When the screen came to life, the Assembly chamber spread across it. Even at the wide angle, it was impossible to view the entire chamber. Thousands of seats were available under the glass canopy, though only three hundred were currently filled. At the forefront were the elders, including the emperor.

Alkinth was, of course, just to his right. Zhatan could guess what his advice would be. Still, the majority had voted for this course, and they were unlikely to have changed their minds while she was away, Emperor Kand especially.

"The Vulcan has been superficially helpful," the commander explained. "But he is of our blood, and he suggests the *na'hubis* can be controlled."

"*That is excellent, Zhatan,*" Kand said, and those around him nodded their agreement. "*We know many had their doubts about this plan. We did not.*"

Alkinth did.

"We would have to stop dead where we are to perform the necessary tests," she explained. "This would delay our arrival in the conqueror's system."

The emperor frowned. Alkinth's expression was difficult to discern across the distance, despite the quality of the image. Even if this wasn't the kind of delay he'd be against, he could use it against her and so Zhatan imagined he was inwardly smiling.

"*You said this was so urgent there could be no delay,*" her adversary charged. "*Has your opinion changed?*"

Most in Zhatan despised Alkinth. Tibis especially thought him a coward. Within him were the majority of the ancient physicists who worked on the *na'hubis*. If any could have helped her, they were within Alkinth. But he'd refused, and even a request from the emperor had proven futile.

"*Challenge him,*" Tibis prodded.

"*Embarrass him.*"

"*Explain ourselves.*"

"*Counter him.*"

"*Debate him.*"

"*Silence him.*"

"*Insult him.*"

"As an experienced battle commander," Zhatan said, focusing on Alkinth, "our skill is to modify our strategies as needed to ensure victory. Urgency has not abated, but success demands we alter our plans temporarily."

Someone leaned close to Emperor Kand. The commander couldn't tell who it was, but probably his loyal advisor, S'toas.

One of Zhatan's childhood friends, S'toas had come far in life. He had chosen a political life, while she'd followed a military one. They'd both dreamed of one day leading people in different ways. Now, she had a ship, and he had an emperor.

As much as Alkinth had acted against her, S'toas had operated in her favor.

"*This is your mission, Zhatan,*" the emperor said. "*We think all are in agreement that you should determine the particulars.*" He waited to see if anyone disagreed.

Only Alkinth raised his palm. "*Before we decide, we would hear Nidal on this topic, as the commander's trusted first.*"

This is why Zhatan had asked Nidal to be present. Here was her chance to staunchly defend her commander's position.

Unexpectedly, Nidal didn't hesitate. "We agree

with the emperor," she said. "This is Commander Zhatan's operation. We defer to her wisdom."

Alkinth looked highly disappointed. That alone was worth the discomfort of asking Nidal to participate.

"*Let us know of your decision, Commander,*" Kand said. "*We shall await your word.*"

Zhatan nodded, and the transmission ended.

Turning to her first, she smiled. "Thank you."

Nidal sighed and demurred.

"What is wrong?" Zhatan asked. "Are you embarrassed to support us in front of Alkinth?"

"We've never cared about him."

"Then what is wrong?"

"Nothing. We played our part in your game," Nidal said as she stood to leave, "just as you wished."

"No," Zhatan snapped, rising and pulling her back. "We sincerely asked for your counsel—in front of the Assembly, no less! You should have given it honestly or not at all. We order you to always speak truth to us."

Unable to smother her laughter, Nidal pulled her arm free and lowered herself onto the cushioned bench near the doorway to the bridge. "There have been times when that was certainly *not* your desire, let alone your command."

Zhatan couldn't help but smile, though she quickly regained her composure. "We want to know what you truly believe," she said more softly.

"How much weight will you give our opinion?" her first asked.

The commander considered that a moment. She respected Nidal, loved her, and believed her counsel was of value. It was only on the topic of their mission that they had so vehemently disagreed. Like Alkinth, most of those in Nidal believed their enemy had been punished long enough and it was time to meet on neutral ground and come to a more long-lasting peace. Most in Zhatan did not. The Kenisian people were also divided and had debated what action they should take for many months. Zhatan's side had won, and Nidal had accepted it, but those wounds, at least on the commander's part, were still raw. Despite her political victory.

"We will consider your opinion as we always have."

Her first smiled again. "We were hoping for better than that." Both laughed, and when the serious tone returned, Nidal leaned forward and spoke frankly. "You're conflicted. We know this. You seek our opinion to bolster what you truly want to do."

"Stop," the commander ordered. "We told you we were not playing games."

"We shouldn't have called it a game," Nidal admitted in a grumble. "Our point is . . . our *wish* is, that for once you examine your true desires and let them sway you."

Zhatan wasn't sure what those were anymore.

She wanted too many conflicting alternatives. She wanted Nidal, but didn't. She wanted her enemies dead, but parts of her just wanted them left alone.

Tibis, though . . . Tibis wanted every last enemy to perish. And she wanted full control of it all—the *na'hubis*, the Vulcan, the *Pride* . . . Zhatan could feel it. Tibis wanted to be the commander, rather than one of many voices whispering in her ear.

Never. This was Zhatan's life.

The commander sat down next to her first. "You have always been our first desire," Zhatan said, taking her hand.

"Don't," Nidal protested, pulling away. "That's true for some of you, but not all." She stood abruptly. "Drop out of warp and do the tests, Commander. That is our opinion. We cannot be known as extinguishers of the galaxy."

Waving her off, Zhatan dismissed that notion. "We've never believed that's possible, no matter what the Vulcan says."

"And yet you trust him." Nidal stood. "Why ask his expertise and then not accept it?"

Did she trust Spock?

"We do not!" Tibis raged.

"We must not."

"We do."

"He would not lie."

"Trust him."

"We trust him."

"*We cannot.*"

"*We do.*"

"Yes," Zhatan said finally. "We believe Spock is trustworthy." She stood and returned to her chair. "Reduce to sublight and prepare to shut down all warp engines."

"*No!*" Tibis protested, but her voice was quickly lost amongst the others.

Nidal asked a parting question. "What of Kirk? If *Enterprise* is still in pursuit, will he not be able to intercept us?"

Zhatan shook her head. "By now, Kirk is likely dead."

"And has *that* been your desire?"

The commander hesitated. She had touched Kirk's mind. Tried to manipulate it and found that task exceedingly difficult. Part of her was still with him, in a way, because what she'd attempted, though unscrupulous, was nevertheless intimate.

"Whether I wish it or not," Zhatan said, "it is his fate."

TWELVE

The first missiles hit the planetoid hard, then exploded into it, thrusting the mass forward. On the viewscreen, what should have been the shrinking image of a hunk of space rock grew larger, enveloped by the energy of an exploding engine.

On impact, several Kenisian mines were destroyed, but the planetoid turned to shrapnel which flung itself toward the *Enterprise*.

She lurched forward under the force—first from the energy wave, then from spikes of stone and globs of molten rock.

The *Enterprise* shields were struck hard, closer and faster than what they were designed for. The shrapnel *was* slowed, and that was the only reason the vessel wasn't torn to shreds.

But like heavy hail on a thin tin roof, shards of rock and debris hit the ship with a seemingly endless torrent of loud thuds.

Kirk looked to a display above the engineering station and watched as multiple pinpoints of damage appeared. Red marks dotted his ship; the *Enterprise* bleeding.

He spun to Uhura, ordering, "Damage control teams, all decks. Engage emergency bulkheads where the fields have failed."

"Yes, sir."

My fault, Kirk chastised himself as the ship creaked around him. But there wasn't time to indulge in guilt. His anger turned to the mass of automated missiles.

"Chekov, find us a comet."

Quickly, the navigator answered, "Course laid in, sir."

"Sulu, engage." Kirk could feel tension spread from his neck down to his shoulders. An icy comet appeared and grew slowly at the center of the viewscreen. Tactical readings showed seven hundred Kenisian missiles still in pursuit.

Tail pointing away from the K-type star, the comet appeared typical: a chunk of ice and rock orbiting a distant star, the solar wind pushing its tail away like a pennant.

"Tractor beam," he ordered. "Stand by."

"Tractor beam, aye," responded Forbes at the engineering station.

Watching the range to comet intercept tick ever closer, Kirk also kept an eye on the incoming missiles. For this to work, the timing would need to be perfect.

"Are you familiar with the game of baseball, Mister Forbes?"

"Uh . . ." The engineer met his captain's gaze with uncertainty. "I've heard of it, sir." He shrugged, his fingers still hovering just over the tractor controls. "I'm from North Yorkshire, sir. I'd know cricket better." He frowned. "But I don't. Never really cared for sport, sir."

Kirk smiled at the nervous engineer. "On my mark, tractor the comet." He nodded toward the helm. "Sulu, once we have it, swing it around—right into the nearest mass of hostiles." He turned back toward engineering. "Transfer tractor control to the helm."

The bridge was eerily quiet as the crew waited for *Enterprise* to get into range.

"Tractor beam, now!"

Forbes activated the console.

Slender tendrils of energy connected with the comet and jolted it off its course.

Sulu spun the ship, pulled the icy rock around, and then released it when the angle was right.

As *Enterprise* sped away, the comet crashed directly into the lead Kenisian missile. At the speeds at which they traveled, the icy rock tore through the first sphere, splitting it in two before the resulting explosion pressed outward in a bubble of destruction that expanded in all directions, destroying several other ballista around it.

"Ride it out, Sulu."

The helmsman grunted through gritted teeth. "Aye, sir."

As the first shockwave hit, Kirk felt the deck plates tremble up through his boots, then the arms of his chair.

The viewscreen crackled with interference, static disrupting the forward view of the K-type star in the distance. Tactical data disappeared as sensors were hampered by the wave's radiation.

Slowly, the convulsions became tremors and then weaker shudders as the shockwave dwindled and the ship stopped clattering.

The sensors unscrambled, Kirk eyed the tactical readout with cautious optimism. In all, now one hundred fifty-three missiles had been destroyed or disabled. The rest—fifty-four in total—were scrambling around the shockwave, trying to recover their target.

"Nicely swung, Mister Sulu." Kirk gave the lieutenant a grateful nod and a proud smile.

"I know baseball," the helmsman told Chekov, just loud enough for Forbes to hear and react with a shrug.

"We're not done yet," Kirk told the bridge crew, his own exuberance bubbling up and loosening his knots of tension. But their success had inspired the captain. "Let's try something a bit different. Mister Sulu, take us to the system's star."

"Sir?" Sulu turned to confirm his order, and the look on the captain's face was all the confirmation he needed. "Aye, aye, sir."

Speeding toward the K-type star, Kirk readied his ship for one final push to rid them of their deadly shadows.

"Mister Forbes, stand by on the tractor beam again." The captain absentmindedly ran his fingers along the wooden part of his command chair. Real wood—something organic on a ship whose bones were from materials not seen in nature. Humans had been in space for so long it seemed natural. James Kirk knew there was nothing natural about it. Starships harnessed unnatural energies, and they took the crew to the most unnatural place of all: deep space. Touching the wood on the arm of the *Enterprise*'s captain's chair connected him with home.

"Come in as low as possible, Sulu." Kirk motioned to the tactical display of the fifty-four missiles that had managed to make it out of the Oort cloud. "Burn off as many as you can."

By now, the Kenisian missiles that remained had been damaged, but not enough to give up their pursuit.

Kirk thumbed a button on the arm of his chair. "Kirk to engineering."

"*Scott here, sir.*" The engineer's voice was all business, and he sounded extraordinarily busy.

"Scotty, I need all available power to the shields and the tractor beam."

"*The tractor beam?*" Scott sounded like he'd been

asked to hand someone a pineapple instead of a probe.

"Tractor beam, Mister Scott. I need it in twenty seconds."

"Aye, sir." The engineer wasn't sure of the exact purpose.

"Kirk out."

Watching the orange globe expand across the viewer as they neared the star, the captain flushed. It wasn't tension or anticipation, but his ship having trouble compensating for the heat.

"Hull temperature rising, sir," Jolma called out.

"Nearing tolerance," Forbes added.

Enterprise continued nonetheless. "Stand by on that tractor beam, Forbes."

"Aye, sir. What am I grabbing?"

One side of Kirk's lips curled up. "The star."

Slowly, Forbes turned his head to meet the captain's gaze. Kirk could feel Jolma and a few others watching him.

"Captain?" Forbes finally asked, his expression a mix of confusion and skepticism.

"Reach as low as you can into the stellar atmosphere," the captain told him, then looked to the helm. "Sulu, you'll help him. Push in as far as she'll take it and then reverse at max impulse, plotting a tight spiral at Z plus zero-one-zero degrees."

A bead of sweat slid down Sulu's cheek as he punched the commands into the controls. "Yes, sir."

The captain noticed the back of his own neck was wet. The bridge felt like a sauna. The K-type star now filled the main viewer in its entirety. "Reverse angle. Zero magnification."

As *Enterprise* pressed farther into the corona, Kirk watched the missiles behind them spinning and tumbling against the friction of the stellar atmosphere. A few lost their navigation systems and spiraled off, burning as they fell into the chromosphere.

"Reduce speed, Mister Sulu. One tenth."

Sulu nodded and the Kenisian spheres grew closer on the main viewscreen. They were catching up.

"Hull temperature rising. It's at ninety-two percent of tolerance, sir," Forbes reported.

"Internal temps thirty-three degrees and rising, Captain," Jolma complained.

"Stand by." Kirk slowly inched forward in the command chair. As the spheres wobbled on the viewscreen, the captain wasn't sure if the missiles were quivering from their own structural difficulties or if it was because the *Enterprise* was experiencing turbulence.

"Tractor beam now, Forbes. Sulu, go!"

Fingers of energy reached down, gripped a giant swath of solar atmosphere and pulled it back toward them.

Under Sulu's control, *Enterprise* twisted, curled upward, then gathered itself and sped away. The tractor beam hadn't the range to continue, but the streamer of fire and plasma it had pulled up coiled into a funnel that engulfed the missiles.

The coronal tornado whipped several bright prominences into the pursuing missiles. A peppering of explosions dotted the orange disk that filled the screen. Kirk watched the explosions expand and disappear as the *Enterprise* sped away. The tactical display confirmed it; the threat was gone.

"Hull temperature dropping," Jolma reported with an exhausted chuckle. "No hostiles in pursuit."

"No casualties, Captain," Uhura said. "Crew cooling down." She smiled and waved a hand in front of her own face.

Kirk returned the smile, wiped his brow with his tunic sleeve, and though he felt a tug of unease even after their victory, he told the bridge crew, "Good work." He turned fully toward Uhura. "Secure from red alert. All hands to repair stations as needed."

"Aye, sir."

"Course, Captain?" Chekov asked, and that bit of unease grew in Kirk's gut again.

"That, Mister Chekov," he said as he leaned forward, "is a very good question."

"IMPOSSIBLE." Sciver closed the panel and twisted a magnetic lock. "There are systems we shall not allow you to access."

"Understandable." It was not in Spock's best interest to actively antagonize the Kenisian scientist. Which didn't mean he could not do so passively. "If you will be kind enough to present a list of all restricted systems, I'll be delighted to redesign my experiments to conform to your limitations. Please inform your commander I'll have a revised time estimate within two days."

"No," Sciver huffed quickly, clearly irritated. "We . . ." Whatever he planned to say, he stopped himself and paused to consider his next words carefully. "*You* will make a list of the systems you'll need to access, and we will seek Zhatan's approval."

As if the Kenisian had just uttered the wisdom of Surak himself, Spock nodded diffidently. "Of course."

Dithering as he turned, Sciver twisted right back. "Zhatan trusts you."

There was no question, so Spock merely gazed at him.

"If you seek to join her thoughts to yours, we warn you, she's incorruptible."

Spock nodded. "I've no doubt."

Curtly nodding back, Sciver spun and walked away.

Returning to his console, the Vulcan considered Sciver's statement and attitude.

Pippenge, whose brief meditation had refreshed him significantly, watched from his chair.

"What is wrong, Mister Spock?" the ambassador asked.

Articulating that list, Spock thought, *would take a great deal of time.* But he knew Pippenge had referred to whatever incident had surely left some sign on his face. "An interesting conversation with Mister Sciver."

"Was it a useful discussion?" Pippenge asked.

"I am not certain."

"WE DON'T LIKE HIM." Sciver stood before his commander, arms held tensely behind his back.

"'Don't like,'" Zhatan said with a sneer. "We don't remember asking for a list of your likes and dislikes."

Opening his mouth to speak, Sciver instantly reconsidered, perhaps remembering to whom he spoke. "Commander, forgive us—"

"Stop." Zhatan put up a hand. "You are not insubordinate for expressing this opinion. Many hold the same."

He relaxed a bit, his stance softening, but his hands remaining behind his back. "He is too polite. Too genial. We feel he still delays us purposely."

"Of course he does." She looked out her office port into the dark, unmoving starscape. "But he is of Vulcan. He understands us better than an alien. We are of like blood."

"Blood, yes. But are we of like goals? We think not."

Zhatan nodded. "We agree, of course. Our goals are not the same, but his needs merge with ours rather nicely, would you not agree?"

"Hmmm," Sciver grunted, presumably considering that notion. But his next question was unrelated. "If he cannot limit the destructive radius of the *na'hubis*, will we still use it?"

The query shattered across her desk like a piece of jagged glass.

"Of course not."

"Of course."

"We can't."

"We must," Tibis said.

"Horrible."

"Necessary."

"Insanity."

"Vengeance!"

"We should."

"We cannot."

"Mustn't."

"We will," Tibis assured them.

Zhatan stared hard at Sciver, but said nothing for a very long time. Finally, she turned away and again looked out into the coolness of space. "Give Spock what he needs."

————

"AGAINST OUR BETTER JUDGMENT, you have been granted the access you requested." Sciver's expression was twisted into what Spock believed was thinly veiled scorn.

Did "our better judgment" mean those consciousnesses within Sciver or Zhatan as well? If anyone's judgment was in question, it was all the Kenisians. Wanting to deploy this powerful weapon was a poor decision. Spock suspected all Kenisians suffered from the same mental disorder.

Attempting to reason with such individuals—multividuals—was not an easy task.

"Thank you," Spock said simply, and he waited for Sciver to hand him the magnetic lock.

When the Kenisian held it out, Spock took it with a grateful nod and turned nonchalantly toward the panel he'd previously wanted to access.

Sciver left, seemingly uninterested in monitoring the Vulcan. Or perhaps merely satisfied with the electronic surveillance already in place. Spock understood such limited observation when working at a computer, but now he had access to the vessel's power systems. He couldn't help but wonder if some of the consciousnesses within the crew were trying to covertly help him avert the weapon's completion. Was Sciver's apparent disdain a reaction to those within that urged him to trust or help Spock? It was a possibility Spock might be able to use.

Opening the panel, Spock considered if the better option was to meld with one of the Kenisians. Sciver's warning that Zhatan could not be corrupted by such a joining indicated to Spock that it was possible.

Forcing someone to mind-meld was highly unethical. Zhatan did it to Captain Kirk, and had Spock allowed himself to have a feeling about the incident, it would have been rage. He could assume that a high number of the consciousnesses held within either Sciver or Zhatan would be equally irate should Spock attempt such a violation. It was possible the combined mental strength of the Kenisian might overwhelm him and cause permanent damage.

For now, Spock needed to focus on the task at hand. Within the access panel was a power conduit. With the warp power offline, he would be able to route power to the lab testing equipment he'd requested. The first of these tests would allow him to manipulate the smallest possible amount of the *na'hubis* compound with high-energy plasma. When contained properly, it would not develop a chain reaction.

Was there a way to successfully attain the experiment's data without stopping the Kenisian vessel? Yes. But because neither Zhatan nor Sciver knew an alternative test, they had to agree to his recommendations.

Calling the ambassador to assist him, Spock began his work. Pippenge walked over, seemingly happy for the distraction. Spock had been sure to inform the ambassador that considerable effort had been made to avoid the Kenisians blaming Pippenge for any of the Vulcan's actions.

"How may I help, Mister Spock?" Since his self-induced meditative rest, Pippenge had embraced a remarkable calm. He even sounded mildly cheerful. Doctor McCoy would be interested to study the physiological part of the process. Spock was curious himself.

"I will need the instrument displays monitored and certain tools handed to me."

"I am gratefully at your service, Commander." The ambassador bowed slightly.

Reaching into the panel, Spock worked while Pippenge talked.

"You know, I never thought—even as the ambassador to alien worlds—I would be on a journey such as this. Our ancestors, of course, were deep-space travelers, but no Maabas has left our current home system for many years. Centuries, at least. Not until our negotiations with the Federation began in earnest. And now look where I am."

Pippenge was just talking, and Spock had tasks to perform, so therefore he did not reply.

The ambassador continued unprompted. "We search within rather than without, you see. That's why we have more deep-sea vessels than orbital ones. Did I tell you my niece was fourth in command of a ship? An ocean vessel. I speak to her at least twice a week." His voice began to waver a bit. "Though I have not since we . . . left, and she is likely quite worried by now."

"Will your government have informed her of your disposition?" Spock asked.

Pippenge puckered his lips. "Doubtful. How could they? If they told her the truth, it could spread and panic would ensue."

Handing the ambassador one tool and asking for another, Spock continued to work as Pippenge chattered on.

"I must tell you, despite the façade, I am quite frightened."

Pulling his arm out of the access panel and turning to face the ambassador, Spock was uncertain how to reply.

While humans seemed to like baseless assurances at such a time, and he had even indulged in that with Pippenge to some degree, the Vulcan didn't wish to lie to the ambassador. He would rather be forthright. As always, Spock had to walk in a middle-ground.

"Fear need not be an irrational emotion," Spock said. "Under the circumstances, your anxiety is warranted."

From the ambassador's expression, the Vulcan

could tell he had not ameliorated his dread. What had McCoy once told him? *Pep talks aren't your strong suit, Mister Spock.*

What would Captain Kirk say in such a circumstance? How would he hearten Pippenge's mood? Perhaps a reasonably upbeat comment might spare the ambassador some angst.

"You can use fear to prepare yourself for useful action, or you can allow it to cripple you into inaction. Having spent time with you, I believe you are prepared for the former."

His flattened lips becoming a smile, Pippenge grabbed Spock's hand to shake it heartily, then dropped it and quickly changed to the Vulcan salute. "Of course, you are right. Thank you, Commander. I trust we will both prosper long and live happily."

The Vulcan returned the obligatory salute and set out to continue his work.

They toiled silently for some time. When Spock was done rerouting the power, he made sure to disable certain fail-safes he thought might prove useful. One of his alterations would cause the vessel to slowly vent plasma that could be identified by the *Enterprise*'s sensors.

If they knew where to look.

THIRTEEN

The captain's plan had been to backtrack through history and study all records on whoever had gone to war with the same foe as had attacked both the Maabas and the Kenisians. There were a dozen worlds who'd seen conflict with the same aggressor. Now Kirk had to pinpoint their origin. He believed Zhatan was taking Spock and Pippenge to that location, so that was where the *Enterprise* needed to be.

"Anything, Lieutenant?" Kirk asked Uhura. He'd tasked her with contacting all the systems they'd known to have been previously attacked. Most had replied, but two had refused once the topic was explained. The captain had hoped he could send a message that both assured them and implored them for help sufficiently.

Uhura was sure they were receiving Kirk's personal message, but he had not persuaded them. "I'm sorry, sir. The two remaining worlds refuse to reply."

The ten other civilizations that had survived this foe's attacks and still existed had been more open. Some had offered access to their historical archives for Palamas and Jolma to pore over. A few had said no record existed from that time. But the data the *Enterprise had* been given access to led to their first lead: a name.

The conquerors who worked their way across the sector during the time period the Kenisians were displaced had been called many things—the marauders, desolaters, decimators—all very dark and horrible as they likely were. They all had records suggesting it was the same race: archives showing the same vessel types, the same weaponry, and the same methods. But most never named the attackers. Only two had mentioned "the Sahntiek."

Whether that was a race name, or a cultural designation, no one knew.

"It could be their word for warrior," Uhura offered.

"Or a political designation," Palamas said from the alternate science station where she'd been reviewing records. "On Rigel IV, inhabitants of the Argus valley call themselves *J'fren,* which is the name of an ancient political party that seceded from the hill society."

It didn't much matter to the captain. He wanted to call them something other than "those who conquered the Kenisians."

"Sir, none of these archives talk about a planet of origin for the Sahntiek." Frustrated, Jolma pinched the bridge of his nose tightly then mopped his brow with a tunic sleeve. The bridge hadn't been warm for quite some time, but the young ensign was being asked to perform beyond his experience.

"Take a break, Jolma." Kirk nodded toward the turbolift.

"Oh, no, sir."

The captain cut him off, his tone somewhere between concerned father and commanding officer. "How long has it been since you slept? You stayed on an extra watch already. You're no good to me tired, Ensign. Rest. That's an order."

Looking defeated and more than a bit dejected, Jolma trudged to the lift.

"Nice bedside manner," McCoy muttered. Kirk hadn't noticed the doctor enter the bridge.

The captain motioned to Uhura. "Lieutenant, take over for Mister Jolma."

Gliding easily from her seat to the science station, she winked at McCoy. "*I'm* on my *third* watch. But I'm not annoying the captain with my youth and inexperience."

That stung a bit, because Kirk didn't want to discourage Jolma, but experience did matter, and Uhura had more than the ensign.

The doctor replied with a wink, "I manage to annoy the captain without the benefit of youth."

"Let's assume," Kirk began, "that the Sahntiek attacked planets in the order they found them. Where would that place their point of origin?"

"Hmmm. Let's see." Uhura ran the calculations. Her hands glided as gracefully over the science station console as they did her communications controls. Eventually she motioned to the screen above her. "Here we go, sir."

The captain stepped over to the rail. The display showed a series of planetary systems in this sector and listed the dates of conflict. A curved line charted a backward trajectory to three possible star systems of origin.

"That narrows it down," Kirk said, thoughtfully running a finger on his lower lip. "But we don't have time to investigate each system."

"We're going in the right direction." Uhura's encouraging smile was still vibrant after all they'd been through. She had the confidence of an experienced officer. The young ensign would get there, but not everything could be learned in a double watch. Some things had to be lived.

"Probes, sir?" Chekov asked. "One in each possible direction."

Kirk turned toward the ensign. "We need to pick directions to go in, and by the time we get telemetry back that indicates we're on the wrong track, we'll have wasted too much time. Maybe more than we have."

"So what now?" McCoy asked. "Eeny meeny miney moe?"

Kirk responded quietly. "No." He stepped up to

his chair. "Spock knows we're looking for him. Even if we're not in communications range, he'd leave us a trail to follow."

"I'm sure he will if he has the means, sir," Palamas said. "But how do we know he does?"

"He's Spock," Kirk said matter-of-factly as he twisted toward Uhura. "You're still trying to make contact?"

She nodded. "Yes, sir. An automated message is repeating on his last known frequency. We'll know if he responds."

"*When* he responds," McCoy said.

The captain nodded and motioned toward Uhura. "Continue a full long-range sensor sweep."

Sliding into place behind the sensor cowl, she nodded. "Aye, sir. What am I looking for?"

"A sign."

If Spock were alive, he *would* signal the *Enterprise*. The captain was certain of it. No matter the odds, Kirk wouldn't allow himself to believe his first officer and friend was dead.

CHRIS JOLMA FELT DEAD. But exhaustion shouldn't matter. He'd joined Starfleet to see what was out there, not the overhead above his bunk. *Sleep*, he tried to convince himself. *The captain ordered you to sleep*. But that wasn't how such things worked.

His mind raced; mostly about the actions he might have taken that wouldn't have suggested to the captain that he rest.

"Stupid," he told himself, and he slammed a fist harshly against the bed frame.

Filling Commander Spock's shoes was an impossible task. Rationally Jolma understood that the captain wasn't expecting him to offer the same expertise or skill that someone more experienced could bring to bear. Emotionally, that didn't matter.

Jolma hadn't joined Starfleet just because he was curious and wanted to explore. His grandparents had been a big influence in his life and both had been in Starfleet.

His father had left when he was young and hadn't been there for him. He wasn't a bad man, just not a great father. His mother died when he was eight, and he had gone to live with his maternal grandparents.

They'd passed some years ago, before he'd left for the Academy. They knew it was his goal and had always supported it. His grandmother was concerned about him pulling duty on a ship and told him stories about her time on a starbase. But Jolma wanted only one thing: to serve on a starship.

Without his parents, without his gran and gramps, Starfleet became Jolma's new family. Since his transferring to *Enterprise*, James Kirk had become a father figure. Not that the captain knew or even suspected. To him, Chris Jolma was just another ensign.

He does remind me of my grandfather, the ensign thought. Neither man would raise their voice. They chastised someone by being disappointed, rather than angry.

At Starfleet Academy, one of his roommates had been reprimanded by an instructor, not for a failure of procedure, but one of character.

Cadet Bleda was one of those "fake-it-until-you-make-it" types. It didn't engender confidence among his peers or superiors. He didn't break many rules, but neither did he respect them or consider the reason why they existed.

It was one thing to read about Starfleet legends like Jonathan Archer, Robert April, or Kelvar Garth, and another to try to emulate them.

When Bleda failed a psycho-simulator test, not for indecision but for his judgment, he wasn't dismissed but held back.

Resentful and worrying about his career, Bleda had complained that his shot at a captaincy had been ruined.

Jolma remembered telling him, "It's that kind of thinking that got you where you are."

Bleda accused him of being a robot and doing whatever his instructors said.

"Of course," Jolma had retorted. "That's why it's called training."

Not all people who enter the Academy graduated. His roommate hadn't.

Jolma had. He was on the *United Starship Enterprise*, the finest ship in Starfleet.

Sleep, he told himself. *And when you wake up, get back to work and show the captain what you can do.*

"WHAT DO YOU THINK has happened, Commander? Could they be dead?" Pippenge whispered.

Spock hesitated to answer. The *Enterprise might* have been destroyed—that was but one of any number of outcomes they needed to consider. However, dwelling on it was illogical. But it was also what could be expected when dealing with beings who allowed their emotions to run unchecked.

"I choose not to assert a conclusion without conclusive evidence," Spock said finally. He'd crafted that sentence with care, trying to impress upon the ambassador that his current emotional state was his choice. "It would be best," he added, "if we remained focused on the task at hand."

Spock continued sending covert messages to the *Enterprise* via his hybrid of Starfleet, Maabassian, and Kenisian technology.

When Sciver came to check on their progress, the only overt task which Spock seemed to be immersed in was monitoring an ongoing test with the *na'hubis* compound.

"State your progress."

Swiveling toward the Kenisian scientist, Spock was guarded. "Assessments are continuing." He motioned to the console display as data scrolled by.

"We want to know what you've learned," Sciver prodded.

Spock raised one brow. "I cannot factually say I've learned anything until all experiments are complete. That is the reason for the tests, to confirm or refute my hypotheses. As a scientist yourself, I am sure you'd concur."

Screwing his lips into a tense frown, Sciver glared at Spock.

Eyes wide, the Vulcan waited, head tilted slightly to one side.

"We wish to review your data," Sciver said. "You will forward your readings to our console immediately."

"Of course." Spock bowed his head respectfully. As the Kenisian turned to leave, Spock added, "Should you need further assistance, please ask. I'd be happy to explain."

Sciver stormed off, his face green with rage.

"Is it wise," Pippenge whispered, "to provoke him?"

Responding directly to the ambassador's implant, Spock was forthright about his plan to, in his own way, act as James Kirk might. "*I'd previously thought not, but there is an instability within him.*

If it moves him to anger, that may be to our benefit. Acts of fury are not often thoughtful, and they are easier to outwit."

Pursing his lips, Pippenge agreed.

"YOU'VE REVIEWED HIS DATA?" Zhatan poured herself a glass of *asab* nectar but offered none to Sciver. She didn't care to be bothered while taking her meals, but wouldn't disallow it, either.

Sciver sneered. "We have."

He stood rigidly before her as she sat at her table and poked at the food on her plate.

"And?"

"The test is valid, but so far inconclusive. However, we believe there are other ways to test the theories, including one that would allow us to operate at warp speed."

Zhatan nibbled on a reconstituted freeze-dried berry. "We see. Do you know how to perform such testing?"

He nodded. "With time—"

"We haven't the time. They have rebuilt a fleet and could pursue war at any moment." Zhatan pushed away the nearly full plate, drank the rest of the nectar, then poured herself another glass. This time she just took a sip. "We've already talked to the Assembly about this delay. We shall not ask for another."

"They've not moved to attack us," Sciver pointed out. "We have evidence of activity that could just as easily be interstellar trade as buildup for war."

"Trading with whom?" Zhatan demanded. "For what purpose? The first time they began to rebuild their industrial base, did they not develop a military infrastructure? Despite being banned from that activity?"

"They were not allowed to take any such actions. They broke the treaty, we do not disagree. But they likely thought we would never come back."

"Did you not support us when we brought this plan to Kand? Did you not testify against Alkinth?"

"We did," Skiver said. "And we still support you."

"All of you?" Zhatan asked.

He hesitated.

"You know how they are," Zhatan spat. "We all remember. How many of us died, lost to eternity? We saved as many as we could, but this isn't the life we wanted." She gulped at the nectar again. Most of her enjoyed it. Those that did not had learned to remain silent on that point.

"Life is life," Sciver said. "We are not bitter that we live on in this way. At least we live on."

"Horrific!"

"Limited!" Tibis wailed.

"Painful!"

"Lingering desolation!"

"Isolation!"

"Misery!"

"We," Zhatan said, slugging down the rest of her drink, "are mostly bitter." She slammed the glass down on the table.

"What if they don't even remember those days?" Skiver asked. "We do—because *we* live on. They may not."

"Then we will remind them." She pushed away her plate. "You say these experiments can be done while we're at warp?"

"We believe they can."

Zhatan nodded. "Bring us Spock. Now."

LOOKING DOWN at the plate, the Vulcan could identify at least one tuber of Vulcan origin. The rest, a variety of alien fruits and vegetables that had been well presented, did not look familiar.

"Thank you," Spock said. "Your staff was kind enough to provide the ambassador and me a protein supplement which was sufficient."

"This was *our* dinner," Zhatan said curtly. "We'd offer you a drink but suspect you do not imbibe spirits."

"No, I do not."

"Sit." She motioned to one of the chairs at the table.

Spock lowered himself gently into the seat and placed his hands on his lap. "If you seek a progress report, I've shared the data with your lead scientist."

"We are aware."

Spock interlocked his fingers and waited patiently for her to indicate the reason for his being summoned. Whatever battle went on within Zhatan, he was not privy to it, but her hesitation suggested it was an extensive debate.

"Sciver says your tests can be performed while we're under warp power," she said finally.

Spock shook his head slightly. "It is impossible to execute these tests with an active warp engine in range."

"But there are other experiments you could do, which would achieve the same end, *and* allow us to continue toward our enemy."

Zhatan was careful not to ask a question, so he was equally cautious in his reply. "To what end, if my research is incomplete?"

Another long pause, and likely another debate among Zhatan's numerous and schizophrenic chorus of consciousnesses. "We will be under way as soon as the warp engines are restarted."

Spock raised a brow.

"Please," Zhatan said, "do not feign surprise. You were clever enough to convince us of a half-truth, and we were gullible enough to believe you. We are not amused, nor are we insulted by your actions."

Spock nodded, but doubted there was anything he could say to change her mind—minds—at this juncture.

"You are directed to assist Sciver with tests which can be performed while traveling at warp speed." Zhatan motioned for him to rise, and as he stood, the chair dematerialized. "You will delay us no more. Thanks to your matter/antimatter intermix formula, we should be under way within the hour."

"Zhatan, you are making a grave error." Hands clasped behind his back, Spock knew he would be monitored more closely than before. He would need to plan for that contingency.

"Perhaps," she said. "But it is ours to make." The edges of her lips curled upward and she motioned to the door. "You are dismissed."

Spock was escorted under guard back to the laboratory complex. It was possible that this would mean increased scrutiny not only of future actions but past ones as well.

Sciver was waiting for him when he returned to the dedicated consoles he and Pippenge had been assigned. The ambassador sat awkwardly, nearly immobile, as the Kenisian scientist stared him down. If this was meant to show his superiority, he was mistaken. Intimidating Pippenge took little effort.

"You've been ordered to assist me," Sciver said when Spock sat.

"I have."

"This one doesn't appear to be of any use." He nodded toward Pippenge.

Perhaps to the Kenisians' ends. Spock wondered how such a conclusion might manifest in action. Would the Maabasian be imprisoned? Killed?

"'This one' is a recognized ambassador to the United Federation of Planets." Leveraging his Vulcan serenity, Spock kept his voice quiet and even. "He and his people are signatories of a binding agreement with the Federation which assures a protective alliance."

Either uncertain of what Spock was saying, or confused as to how to respond, Sciver just looked from the Vulcan to the ambassador and then back.

To remove any ambiguity, Spock added, "You seek to end one conflict. It is ill-advised to begin another without good reason."

Sciver still looked perplexed. He understood the threat, but not the reasons for making it. "For this?" He gestured to Pippenge. "Why?"

"Because I value his life. By oath and by choice, I am sworn to protect it." Spock allowed that statement to settle, and eventually the Kenisian turned away.

"Please shut down all ongoing experiments," Sciver said over his shoulder. "We shall need your help in crafting *our* tests once we're under way at maximum level."

When Sciver was out of sight, Pippenge opened his mouth to speak.

Spock put up a finger, waited until he could no longer hear the Kenisian's breath, then said, "Forgive me, Ambassador. Vulcanoid hearing is quite sensitive. What did you wish to say?"

Lips pursed, Pippenge smiled tightly but sincerely. "Thank you, Mister Spock. Thank you."

"WELL, WHAT DO YOU SEE?" Stretched anxiously over the red rail that separated the upper bridge from the command well, McCoy looked up toward Kirk and Uhura at the science station.

The captain had been bent over the sensor cowl for a while, and judging by the doctor's tone of voice, he was anxious to hear what prompted the interest.

"Spock's alive," he told McCoy with an I-told-ya-so smirk.

"So sensors can pick up comm signals now?" McCoy didn't like the captain toying with him.

"Better." Kirk motioned Uhura back to the scanner. "Transfer coordinates to the helm." He leaped past McCoy and into the command chair. "Mister Chekov, alter course to location transferred by Lieutenant Uhura. Mister Sulu, best possible speed."

The doctor grabbed the arm of Kirk's seat and turned the captain toward him. "Jim, uncle."

"All right, Doctor. You've suffered enough." Smiling, Kirk gestured to the science station. "Uhura found a plasma discharge—same as the Kenisian vessel."

"And?"

The captain nodded confidently. "Bread crumbs, Bones."

"Oh, sure. Bread crumbs." McCoy looked at his boots and shook his head, then glared up at Kirk. "What the devil are you talking about?"

Still smirking, Kirk explained, "The amount Uhura found is not normal. The only explanation is a stationary vessel releasing plasma slowly or dumping it. It's Spock sending us a message."

"That's a hell of a leap," McCoy said. "What if it's just a ship that sprung a leak?"

"It's not, Doctor," Uhura said, still at the science station. "If it were, there would be telltale signs. This is pure warp-engine plasma; someone spilled it."

"Spock," Kirk added pointedly.

One side of his mouth curling down, McCoy didn't seem to buy that. "I hope so," he said quietly.

"Kirk to engineering. Mister Scott, we'll need you to stoke the boilers."

SCIVER STOOD at the main computer console which was linked to the *na'hubis* prototype mines. The screen in front of him pulsated with data as he ran his experiments. From where Spock was allowed to stand, he could see the tests were producing mixed results.

"You're aware of the problem," he told the Kenisian.

Grunting, Sciver worked on.

Mines were often used to focus a destructive force. In this case, they'd hoped to use a mine to limit destruction. Unfortunately, the Kenisians were basing their hope on a document that Spock had created.

Approaching the screen, the Vulcan pointed at a specific data point. "Here."

"I see it," Sciver said.

When properly stressed, both Zhatan and Sciver changed the personal pronoun from "we" to "I." As Spock had suspected, there was a primary personality that could be asserted, but was usually held in check by the other consciousnesses within each individual's psyche.

As test results confirmed the level of destruction the *na'hubis* weapon would cause, Sciver became more anxious, and his own personality revealed itself. "I could mitigate the explosive power," he said, then added, "somewhat."

After a minute he clarified, "*If* we had time to build a new delivery device." His exasperated tone, while having this discussion with no one in particular, suggested that Spock was listening to an internal debate spoken aloud.

One of Sciver's assistants pulled a large piece of equipment into view and asked him if it was acceptable.

"No!" he barked. "That won't help us at all!"

The burst of anger was disconcerting. Sciver was dealing with a weapon of immeasurable power. He was using sophisticated tools and probes to manipulate and test it. A rash action now could destroy them all. And by "all," Spock believed that meant a portion of the galaxy as well as the ship.

I may have miscalculated, the Vulcan thought. He'd provoked the Kenisian believing it would keep the scientist off balance, but he hadn't intended for Sciver to be working with the *na'hubis* in an agitated state.

"Remain calm," Spock told him.

Sciver turned slowly toward him, his hands frozen, hovering over his computer's controls. "I— We are calm."

Spock nodded slightly. "Good. In composure one can find concentration."

Pulling in and then releasing a long breath, the Kenisian smiled just a bit. "Yes. Thank you, Commander Spock. Would you help us?"

Bowing his head, Spock accepted the invitation. He moved to the console, and Sciver stepped out of the way to allow the Vulcan to work the controls. "This may not prove possible, but we shall attempt it." While he might have forged the document,

Spock did base the possibility it proposed on a scientific hypothesis.

The way Spock understood *na'hubis*, the experiment was unlikely to produce fruitful results. However, it was the only test imaginable which had a chance of working *and* gave him time to talk to Sciver.

"We must let this simulation run unencumbered by other processes."

The Kenisian nodded. "Of course." He cleared the other programs from the system, and they watched the data flow across the display.

Spock chose this moment to engage Sciver on a nonscientific level. Notwithstanding Doctor McCoy's belief to the contrary, Vulcan emotional disciplines didn't preclude one from engaging individuals on a personal level.

"Your task is difficult," Spock said.

Continuing to study the screen, Sciver said, "We appreciate your assistance, as we said."

"I don't refer to the *na'hubis*."

Slowly he turned to meet Spock's gaze. "You speak of . . . ?"

"Your Kenisian condition. The *shautish-keem*."

"Condition? You deem it an affliction?" Sciver frowned.

Offended? Perhaps hurt?

Spock was unsure. "I meant no offense. I've had an opportunity to touch the minds of others, and I have even melded with a community of individuals who were telepathically linked."

"And this distressed you?" The Kenisian was now looking at Spock and ignoring the data that scrolled rapidly across his computer screen.

Spock considered how he should reply. "On occasion," he began slowly, "it has proven somewhat *troublesome*. While my experience has been different than yours, I assume there is some inherent effort necessary in your situation."

Sciver sighed. "Your assumption is correct."

"Have your people always engaged in *shautishkeem*?" Spock asked.

The Kenisian shifted his weight uneasily. Any delay in answering was likely the internal debate Spock hoped would be raging within.

After five minutes, Sciver took in a deep breath and responded. "Not always, no. When the first of us joined another, the bond was only among the same clan. We knew each other. We loved, as only kin do, perhaps as only they can."

There was an ancient process, still practiced by some on Vulcan, of transferring one's *katra*— their living mental essence—to a close family member. The *katra* was then released into a *katra* ark, after a ceremony where relations were able to say their farewells. It was closure for Vulcans, and while not practiced by many, the process was revered.

Perhaps that is how *shautish-keem* began for the Kenisians. "Eventually, things changed," Spock said.

Sciver whispered, "The war brought change."

"And to whom does one trust their essence when their clan has been decimated?"

"Eventually *shautish-keem* was initiated when an attack was anticipated. If one's death came unexpectedly, their *ka'atrehs* were safe."

"A logical step for a race trying to preserve themselves," Spock said.

"Many found," Sciver said, "if they stayed in telepathic contact, it helped our defense and attack tactics."

"Those that didn't employ *shautish-keem* perished."

Again, the Kenisian agreed.

That explained how the Kenisians became such powerful telepaths; survival of the fittest. Or in this case, the best prepared.

"With time, we found that life could be lived within the form of another. It could be pleasant. Even if we were from opposing clans, we banded together against a common foe."

"Those who conquered you," the Vulcan said.

"Yes."

To avoid the conflicts within, the Kenisians needed an external enemy. How real was the current threat?

"But you struggle, you said."

"We thought, if two minds were better . . ." Sciver's sentence trailed off, either because he thought he revealed too much, or he didn't know how to precisely articulate the difficulty.

Spock pressed forward. "How do you cope with so many disparate personalities within you?" Zhatan had attempted to evade the same question, but she was a commander on a mission. Sciver was a scientist, engaging with another scientist. He seemed more open to a frank discussion.

"Like any group of individuals, we discuss. Debate. Deliberate. Not everything, of course," the Kenisian laughed. "We do not squabble with regard to which meal we'll have." His chuckle trailed off and toward the end became nervous. It seemed there was an argument even on the trivial.

Spock wondered how far he could push Sciver. He glanced at the computer display and saw the simulation they'd initiated was done compiling data.

The Kenisian scientist noticed it as well and turned back to the console.

Their candid discussion was at an end.

FOURTEEN

Ambassador Pippenge had not been patiently waiting for the *Enterprise*'s first officer to return. Instead, he had been getting them better rations.

"Look!" The ambassador eagerly showed the Vulcan a tray with two covered cups of liquid, two napkins, and three squares of the hardtack-like protein concoction they'd previously received. "I talked the assistant—Idran was her name—into giving us an extra ration. I thought we might share it." The glee in his eyes shone brightly at his own achievement.

Taking one of the small napkins, Spock picked up a protein biscuit and nodded his appreciation. "Thank you. Please indulge yourself, Ambassador. I find one sufficient."

As they ate, the Vulcan related his discussion with Sciver, as well as the results of the test. Spock had found the Kenisian's psyche to be more damaged than he had first believed. As for the *na'hubis*, he was unsurprised they'd made little headway, but he was more concerned about what they had found. It could spur the Kenisians on, rather than dissuade them.

"They have threatened my people," Pippenge said as he nibbled on the thick biscuit. "Yet I have pity for Sciver."

"Him, specifically?" Spock took the lid off his drink and sipped at the tepid, flavorless water. Like the biscuit, it nourished but did little else.

"No, all of them." The ambassador dunked his biscuit in the water to soften it, then took another small bite. "I struggle with my own feelings and sometimes those of my loved ones. Reconciling those is demanding enough. I cannot imagine incorporating the feelings of a dozen others, let alone hundreds."

"Nor I." The telepathy to which Spock was accustomed was unlike what the Kenisians had developed out of necessity and selection. Vulcans were trained as young children, each to their ability and at their own pace, to engage in the birthright of a mind-meld when they deemed proper. Because of his inquisitive nature and life as an explorer, Spock's own abilities had occasionally proven difficult. What the Kenisians bore seemed insurmountable in comparison.

His eyes darting around, seemingly focusing on nothing, Pippenge was suddenly distracted. "Message," he whispered.

Calmly, Spock placed his rations back on the tray and sat before the computer. Between the Kenisian tricorder he'd modified with the communicator components and Pippenge's computer implant which now could interface with the laboratory's equipment, Spock had managed to boost the range of his makeshift subspace transceiver. But because they had been unable to make contact with the *Enterprise* for some time, Spock had left an automated message broadcasting.

"Enterprise *to Mister Spock. Please respond.*"

Because his implant was the go-between, Pippenge was privy to the messages which could be read and replied to from Spock's console.

"*Enterprise*, this is Spock."

"CAPTAIN! IT'S MISTER SPOCK!" Uhura's wide smile was met with an equally relieved grin from Kirk.

He charged from his command chair to the communications station. "Let's hear it."

"Decoding now." She routed the coded message through the computer which would turn the heavily encrypted text into audio.

"Enterprise, *this is Spock.*"

From next to the command chair, McCoy cheerfully jibed, "Computerized voice, lacking all emotion, that's Spock all right."

"Reply," Kirk ordered with a relieved chuckle.

Uhura nodded fervently. "Go ahead, Mister Spock. We read you."

The captain twisted toward Jolma, who was back at the science station. "Track the signal, Ensign."

"Already on it, sir."

Jolma probably still needed more sleep—they all did—but he also needed to be back on the bridge. A few hours of shut-eye and a request to get back in the game is just what the captain would have done at his age. Though he couldn't remember the circumstance, it was probably what he *had* done.

Glad to have Jolma back, Kirk gave him an encouraging nod.

Because the transmission was interpolated from code, then transposed to audio, there was no static, no crackle, no loss of signal. "Enterprise. *Situation extreme. Simulations suggest a* na'hubis *chain reaction can be delayed but not contained. This may encourage the Kenisians to attempt detonation and then escape the blast radius.*"

The expanse of a normal explosion didn't pose a threat to a starship, and even the destructive abilities of supernovae didn't traverse the great chasms between star systems. But the nature of *na'hubis* was that it would disrupt space-time itself and at great speed.

If the Kenisians had found a way to slow the rate of expansion, thinking it possible to save themselves while destroying their enemies, they would not care about the cost to others.

"Send to Spock," Kirk ordered. "Relate all available information gathered." Knowing Spock would have prepared a detailed report, the captain believed the key to stopping the Kenisians would be contained within.

Uhura nodded, sent the message, and then waited. After a half minute she said, "Receiving now."

"Location confirmed, sir," Jolma reported as he punched a map up on the science station display. "They're on the move."

"Extrapolate from trajectory. Transfer coordinates," Kirk ordered. "Mister Chekov, plot an intercept course. Uhura, I need Spock's full report."

Returning to the command chair, the captain reassuringly clapped McCoy on the shoulder as he lowered himself into the seat. The doctor clearly sensed Kirk's enthusiasm and met it with a pleasant nod. Now they could be proactive. Since Spock and Pippenge had been taken, Kirk had felt like he was playing catch-up. Not anymore.

"THEY'RE ALIVE!" Pippenge sent a message to Spock's computer console through his implant that somehow had the ambassador's unbridled enthusiasm inherent in the text.

"That," Spock sent in reply, *"is a reasonable conclusion."*

Having already explained that the message originated from the *Enterprise*, Pippenge was now sure they'd be rescued. Not wishing to dampen his spirits, Spock did not detail how grave the situation was.

"What happens now?" Pippenge asked, covertly via the implant.

"Now we wait for Captain Kirk to read my report. He will have orders, and we will coordinate a solution."

The ambassador cheerfully pursed his lips.

Spock wished he could be as sanguine.

Sudddenly, the *Enterprise* replied, *"Your location confirmed. Report read and understood. Will intercept. If we fail to reach accord, act to disrupt personnel and process. Contact hourly as able."*

"Received and understood," Spock replied.

"What does it mean?" the Maabas ambassador asked aloud, but in a hushed tone. " 'Personnel and process'?"

"It means," the Vulcan replied to Pippenge's implant, *"if Captain Kirk cannot dissuade or threaten the Kenisians into rethinking their course, we must stop them from within."*

"WE WILL *NOT* be stopped." Zhatan shook her head very slightly, and her lips tightened into a smirk.

The image of Captain James Kirk filled the large screen opposite her. Clearly he was alive.

Unable to trace *Enterprise*'s exact location, Nidal

could only offer that the Federation ship was outside sensor range and therefore outside weapons reach. Neither revelation was comforting.

Despite their inability to fire on Kirk, many desired that option.

"*Kill him,*" Tibis demanded.

"*Yes, destroy him.*"

"*Deploy countermeasures.*"

"*He should be dead.*"

"*What happened?*"

"*What of the interceptors?*"

"*Let the commander handle this.*"

"*We have been in command before.*"

"*As have we!*"

"*Silence! I will handle this,*" Zhatan thought to herselves.

"*We know where you're headed,*" Kirk told her. "*The homeworld of the Sahntiek.*"

It was a name no Kenisian spoke, or thought, or wrote into their history. They had vulgar names for their conquerors, but refused to dignify them with what they'd called themselves.

"*How could he know?*"

"*He is more clever than we credited.*"

"*Has he been in league with them?*" Tibis wondered.

"*Has he warned them?*"

"Knowing our destination," Zhatan said, maintaining her calm as best she could, "and being able to keep us from it are two disparate abilities, Captain Kirk."

The *Enterprise* captain seemed to agree. He opened his arms a bit, as if including not just Zhatan but all Kenisians. "*You're a survivor, Commander. I know you want to live. And you want your people to live as well.*"

"Are you trying to bully us, Captain?"

Kirk shook his head. "*As you did the Maabas? Or us? No. It's* you *who threaten trillions of lives.*" He stood up and stepped closer in frame. "*Why?*" he asked in a near whisper.

"*Cut him off,*" Tibis ordered.

"*Enlighten him.*"

"*Say nothing.*"

"*Convey our passions.*"

"*Hold your tongue!*"

"*Tell him our intentions!*"

"*He is nothing.*"

"*Speak our peace.*"

Her hesitation lingered in the air, crossing the void of space. His unremitting gaze was intense, as if he was trying to look into her soul. "*Explain it to me,*" Kirk pressed. "*Make me understand.*"

"ZHATAN," the captain pleaded, "we can solve this together. We can save *everyone.*"

Her confusion seemed palpable, despite the distance between them. *"How can you help? You would stop us from—"*

"From destroying yourselves?" Kirk interrupted. "Just for the satisfaction of taking an ancient enemy with you?" He managed to keep his tone just this side of chastising; it was more imploring her to see reason.

"We can't expect you to understand," she said.

"You can," the captain told her more softly. "If you talk to us."

Once again there was a very long pause. Zhatan seemingly stared at him, but she was clearly lost in thought. From Spock's report, this was the tempest of disagreement within Zhatan, and she would eventually distill a reply.

"What would you tell us," she said finally, *"that would ameliorate thousands of years of pain? How would you restore millions upon millions of lives? What words could you offer that would give us justice?"*

Kirk shook his head. "What could *you* say that would justify to me, to yourself, to *anyone*, the deaths of innocents for acts you blame on the Sahntiek?"

"I don't . . . we don't . . . this isn't just about justice."

"I?" Kirk asked.

Suddenly the connection was lost, and the main screen returned to a starscape outlook.

The captain glanced back to Uhura and she shook her head. "Transmission cut at their end, sir."

Taking his seat, Kirk pushed out a sharp, exasperated breath. "That's just great."

"She's on the edge," McCoy said. "You heard her—the individual Zhatan is conflicted about this."

"I heard her," Kirk said. "But how do we know that Zhatan is less bent on destruction than any of the minds whispering to her?"

"I don't know," McCoy said, shaking his head. Arms folded, he pointed his chin toward the viewscreen. "Zhatan seems like she's being controlled. All those delays? Maybe the real Zhatan is starting to push back."

The captain agreed, but he couldn't count on it. "She may not have the strength to overcome them. For most of her life she's been a conduit for all these other . . . people."

"They're the problem." In McCoy's eyes Kirk could see the doctor's empathy. "Her own ancestors are pulling her toward hate, and into war. They hold all that bitterness, but she ends up feeling it."

Uhura stood and took a step toward them. "Many cultures end up passing down their hate to their children. How many worlds have seen decades of conflict because people can't let go of the past?"

"Letting go is easier when it's just history, but here the actual aggrieved individuals live on in their own progeny," McCoy said.

"No wonder they're poisoned toward peace." Kirk sighed and turned toward Uhura. "Get Spock back. We need a plan B."

She worked her console and nodded toward the captain. "Channel open, sir."

"Spock, I may have made matters worse. Doctor McCoy believes Zhatan is fighting for control of her own actions. Do you concur?"

"The doctor is correct. Zhatan is in a fragile state. Conventional discussion may not be possible."

"I'm correct," McCoy whispered.

"I'll have to ask you to employ something less conventional, Spock."

"Understood."

"DO YOU HAVE an estimate?" Zhatan asked.

Nidal checked her board and nodded. "They're entering the system now, and the *Enterprise* is within their sensor range."

"How many?"

"Twenty-seven. It's all that platform had left. We can send others, but not in time. And we'd have to divert them from other tasks."

Zhatan frowned. "It will have to do. We need not destroy them."

"Destroy them!" Tibis countered.

"Leave them to rot!"

"Withhold. Stay any attack."

"Kirk is right. Listen to him."

"Kill him. He stands in our way."

"Reconsider!"

"We only need to buy more time," the Kenisian commander told herselves. *"Sciver is almost ready. We can just disable the* Enterprise."

Nidal turned slowly around and faced Zhatan. "Will they have a chance to escape the *na'hubis* blast radius?"

"No!"

"Yes!"

"No!"

"Please!"

"Refrain!"

"Destroy!"

"We hope not," Zhatan told her, and she wiped a clammy hand on her tunic. "I hope so."

"INCOMING. SEVERAL CONTACTS!" Jolma called.

"'Several' isn't a number, Mister." The captain shot only a brief glance at the ensign. Muscles taut with anticipation, he edged forward in the command chair, his eyes on the viewscreen's tactical display.

"Twenty-seven, sir. Twenty-seven."

"Red alert, all hands to battle stations. Red alert," Uhura ordered.

"Evasive action." They'd handled the missiles

before—and many more of them—but there was less time now.

One of the missiles sped quickly toward them, thrusting toward the port nacelle. It bounced off the shields, spun about, and headed back toward them again as *Enterprise* twisted away.

"Shields holding," Forbes said, but nevertheless the explosion reverberated across the ship, shuddering the bridge.

Kirk spun toward Uhura. "Anything?"

One hand at her controls, the other on her earpiece, Uhura shook her head. "No response from the Kenisian ship on any channel, sir."

Another missile crashed against the shields just above the bridge. Then another. And another.

No matter how close they might be, Kirk had to fight back. His ship couldn't take the pounding. "Phasers, point blank. Fire!"

Explosions burst into more explosions around them. Bulkheads creaked; console circuits sizzled, sending sparks cascading across the bridge controls. Kirk was thrust from the command chair and felt some jagged piece of debris slice through his tunic sleeve and into his arm.

Acrid smoke bit at his throat as he scrambled upright, pulling Chekov up into his navigator's chair as he did. The captain moved to Sulu, who gasped for breath, having struck the console with his chest. "Bones," Kirk called, and McCoy, also struggling to regain his wind, shuffled toward the helmsman.

Pain arced along the captain's arm and crackled across his back as he twisted around, making sure that everyone else was accounted for. Somehow Jolma had made it across the bridge to help Uhura back into her seat.

Just as Forbes helped a yeoman to his feet, he collapsed. Blood dribbled down the side of his face.

"Bones!" The captain leaped up to steady him, trying to ignore the sting that came with movement.

McCoy took over, taking Forbes's left hand and pushing it tightly against the cut in his scalp. The gash was large and a mere bandage wouldn't suffice.

"It's wet," he said.

"What's your name?" the doctor asked. He knew, but wanted to see if the engineer remembered it.

"Forbes, Joshua," he said, then added, "sir," in a groggy afterthought.

McCoy nodded. "You're bleeding, Forbes. Keep pressure on it."

"Aye, sir."

On his way to the science station, Kirk moved past the turbolift just as the doors opened. Lieutenant Palamas stepped out, looking stunned to be on the bridge.

"Palamas? Good." McCoy motioned her over

to the engineering station. "You're a trained field medic. Help me get Forbes into the lift. It's an aneurysm."

"Yes, Doctor." She moved quickly to help him walk the barely conscious engineer into the lift. "You're going to be fine, Josh," Palamas told him.

Once in the elevator, McCoy draped the engineer over his left shoulder. Palamas moved to go with them, but the doctor handed Palamas his medkit. "No, stay here. Triage."

By the time the lift doors closed, Kirk was at the science station. "Status."

Hovering over his console, Jolma was shaking his head repeatedly, incredulous. "Unknown."

The captain glared at the ensign. He felt his mouth gape open and then quickly closed it. "Explain."

"The bridge has only battery power, lights, and life-support," Jolma said, coughing over his own words. "All other systems are offline."

"*All* other systems, Mister Jolma?" Kirk prodded.

"Aye, sir." He looked at the captain. "I—I don't know what—"

"All right, stand by, Ensign." Kirk moved toward communications. "What's smoldering?" he asked, then realized the list of what wasn't might be shorter. He grabbed a yeoman from the damage control team as she passed. "Find out what's burning, put it out." He then turned to Uhura. "Get me engineering."

She nodded and snapped toggles on her board, and when one connection didn't work, she tried another. Then a third. "I've got Mister Scott, sir. Internal communications are spotty. Subspace is out."

Wiping sweat and some soot from his forehead, the captain nodded his understanding and leaned toward the comm. "Scotty, go."

"It's not good, Captain. I can have sensors in a few minutes, but structural integrity fields are close to overloaded again. There's a bypass . . . emergency bulkheadsssss . . . I can't get to . . . doing."

"Are you all right, Mister Scott?"

"I'm—" The engineer was cut off.

"I'm sorry, sir, the circuits are fried," Uhura said.

Wonderful, Kirk thought sardonically. Chewing on the inside of his lower lip, he took a moment to survey the bridge. The crew diligently ran their system checks, the upheaval of just a minute ago now past and their duties foremost in their minds. There were no more explosions—no more impacts against the shields—so the missiles were likely spent. But by destroying them so closely, Kirk had done the *Enterprise* inestimable harm.

Spilt milk, he thought, still unwilling to dwell on the guilt he knew he'd feel later. This was his constant struggle—pushing away the distracting emotions until his tasks were complete. Right now, the *Enter-*

prise and her crew needed him, and he couldn't lose focus. "Uhura, keep trying to raise engineering."

As he moved toward the turbolift, Palamas got his attention from the environmental controls. "Captain? Yeoman Merrill has a compound fracture of the tibia. I need to get him to sickbay."

Joining them, the captain eased the yeoman's arm over his shoulder. "Let's go." He turned back to Uhura. "Coordinate repairs, Lieutenant. You have the bridge."

"Aye, aye, sir," Uhura said as the lift doors closed.

"WHAT HAPPENED to the *Enterprise*?" Pippenge asked aloud, understandably distressed. Since Kirk had simulcast his discussion with Zhatan, they knew that the captain had been cut off mid-message.

"Unknown," Spock said quietly.

"Perhaps we can explain." Sciver's appearance shocked the ambassador and even Spock was somewhat startled. He'd been so focused on communicating with the *Enterprise* that he'd not heard his approach.

"That would be appreciated," the Vulcan said.

"Long-range scans tell us your ship is disabled. We'll have no more interference from Kirk."

"I see." Spock glanced at Pippenge, who looked quite unnerved.

"Our tests are complete," Sciver said. "We would

have you review our data and assist in modifying the prototype, assuming you can be trusted to give us an accurate appraisal." The Kenisian scientist opened his arms and spread his hands apart. "You *do* still wish to limit the destructive spread of the *na'hubis* explosion, do you not?"

Spock rose. "I do."

Sciver gestured for the Vulcan to follow, and both he and Pippenge did so.

"Are you required for this?" the Kenisian asked the ambassador.

"Is there a reason he cannot join us?" Spock asked. "I am entrusted with his well-being." He didn't think it wise for them to be separated at this juncture and would do all in his power to see they stayed in close proximity.

Sciver accepted that and led the way.

Hand on his chest, Pippenge tacitly thanked the Vulcan, and Spock bowed his head in reply.

"We could have destroyed your vessel, you know," Sciver said. "We did not, to show you we don't want the destruction of those who have not aggrieved us."

How incapacitated was the Enterprise? One could assume that communications had been disabled but the ship was intact. Supposition was of no value. Spock had his orders, he knew what to do. Support from the *Enterprise* would be appreciated, but he could not count on it.

"Indeed," Spock told Sciver. "I'm prepared to help you."

UHURA HAD DONE THIS before. She'd rebuilt her communications console's circuits any number of times, and there were days she felt she lived in the access panel under her station. However, she'd rather see to the damage herself. Waiting for a tech and then relaying the problems was a waste of time, time the *Enterprise* did not have.

The life of a starship communications officer; after a time the work one did on their station shifted from craft to art. Uhura knew her circuits better than those who designed the components. The lieutenant had stretched their specifications and capabilities to their limits. She'd designed new materials and had them fabricated aboard ship. And now, what lay before her was too many burned circuits and fried connections.

Pushing herself away from the access hatch, she found Sulu offering her a hand up.

She took his help and rose to her seat. "Thank you." She brushed dust off the red engineering jumpsuit she'd taken from storage before she dove under the console.

"The captain left you the conn," the helmsman nodded toward the center seat, "so isn't fixing this someone else's problem?"

"In command," she said with a wink, "my job is to see things get done by the person best qualified to the task."

He smiled. "Oh, I see."

Uhura stood and stepped down to the command well where Chekov was working with a member of the damage control team.

"How're we doing?" she asked.

"We are needing intensive care." Chekov smiled wryly as he continued to work on a circuit node he'd pulled from the underside of the console. "Maybe three or five minutes."

"How's the helm?" Uhura asked Sulu as she returned to her station and balanced herself on the back of her chair as she straightened the leg of her jumpsuit.

"I'm good. Just waiting on Chekov."

"Give him a hand," she told him. "I need to get back at mine. I'm not going to fix communications from this chair, *or* that one." She nodded to the captain's chair, then slid back down to the deck and reached again for her toolkit. "This would be easier if someone in engineering could reroute certain circuits, but I doubt they can spare anyone just now."

"Are you sure about that? Maybe they could spare *someone*," Sulu said.

"I'll only be sure," Uhura said, crawling back under the console, "when I get the intercoms working again."

AS THE TURBOLIFT moved toward sickbay, Kirk thought it was extraordinarily slow. He checked the indicator.

"Something wrong, sir?" Palamas asked, trying to keep the pressure off Merrill's broken leg.

"Debris in the tube, power loss, or possible malfunction," he told her. "Slowing us down."

"I think malfunction. I ordered the lift to bring me to my battle station on deck ten, and it brought me to the bridge instead."

Trying to take the majority of Merrill's weight on himself, Kirk leaned in and repositioned the yeoman's torso against his side. "Emergency protocol. If the bridge is damaged, the computer reroutes an available cab in case the bridge needs to be evacuated."

"I didn't know that," Palamas admitted.

"Even clears a path to auxiliary control," he added.

Yeoman Merrill groaned softly.

"I gave him something for the pain," the lieutenant explained, "but I wasn't sure of the dosage."

"We'll be there soon, Merrill," the captain assured him.

When the lift doors finally opened, Kirk took Merrill's full weight on his shoulder and guided the yeoman into the corridor. "I'll take him from here," he told Palamas. "Hold the cab on this deck, or we'll lose it."

The captain met Palamas's eyes a moment, and what he saw surprised him. She was steady, ready to do whatever her captain needed.

"Aye, aye, sir," she said.

When Kirk got to sickbay, there was a line of crew curving out the door and down the corridor. Several medical techs were scanning people, treating them where they stood or taking them in for further examination.

The captain passed Merrill to the first crewman he saw, Ensign Nehring, a research scientist who, like Palamas, doubled as a field medic when at battle stations. "He has a compound fracture of the tibia. Take care of him."

"Aye, sir."

"How many?" Kirk asked, motioning up the corridor.

"Seventeen inside, sir." Nehring passed Merrill to the nurse nearest the sickbay doorway. "We're still doing triage."

The captain mentally winced. How many were injured overall? Had he lost anyone? There was no time for a full report. Kirk knew however many made it to sickbay, more hadn't.

Kirk gestured to Nehring's emergency medkit. It was more robust than the one McCoy had given

Palamas, and they might need it. "Can you spare this?"

"Yes, sir. No problem." Nehring grabbed the kit and handed it to the captain, but as Kirk reached for it, the medic gasped, "Captain, your arm."

Kirk looked down. His tunic sleeve was torn where the debris had slashed into his forearm. The gold captain's braid was cut in half, and crusted with dried blood. "I'm fine, Ensign." He'd forgotten about the gash and there just wasn't time to worry about such a minor wound.

"Let me just seal—"

Taking the medkit, the captain turned back toward the turbolift.

"That'll be all, Nehring. Carry on."

When Kirk returned to the lift, Palamas was waiting dutifully. Her eyes held a sadness, and the captain followed her gaze to the other side of the corridor. Repair crews were cleaning debris from the walkway as crewmen hurried by. Nothing unusual. But against one bulkhead was a blood stain. Perhaps one of the seventeen now in sickbay. Hopefully not one sent to the morgue.

He couldn't be thinking of that now. And neither should she. "Look what I found," Kirk said more brightly than he felt as he handed her the medkit.

As he stepped into the turbolift, she reciprocated his smile with one of her own. "Thank you, sir."

"Let's hope we don't need it." The captain took the lift control in hand. "Engineering."

They traveled faster this time, probably because debris had been cleared from the turbolift tubes. In under a minute the doors opened to reveal the engineering deck.

They entered main engineering to find a mad hive of activity. Crewmen in red moved crisscross from console to console, from one ladder to another, all carrying a tool or a replacement part or piles of circuits. Scotty stood in the middle of this pandemonium, focusing it and directing its flow.

Maneuvering around the traffic, Kirk and Palamas strode to the chief engineer.

"Just a moment, sir," Scott said to Kirk, then called to the upper tier. "Sanchez, you can't bypass that from there. You know better, lad."

The engineer sounded exhausted, and the captain noticed he was holding his wrist at an unnatural angle. Palamas saw it at the same time and pulled the scanner out of her medkit.

"He needs to sit down," she told Kirk, running the Feinberger from Scotty's left hand, up his shoulder, then back down. "You need to sit down, Mister Scott."

"I don't have time to sit," he said, then turned to a crewman behind him. "Remember you can't replace that circuit with power less than fifteen percent. Boost each auxiliary bypass to level six. That'll reroute enough away from the node you need to repair. If you don't, you'll blow the whole subsystem."

Palamas cast an exasperated look at the captain, then took Scott by the elbow of his good arm and guided him to the chair near the status board by the entry.

As he was practically dragged away, the engineer continued to bark out orders. "Mister Gross, if I see you hold that probe like that again, I'll have you replacing impulse points for the next year."

"Sit," Palamas ordered, and Scotty looked to Kirk for support.

"Doctor's orders," Kirk said.

"But, sir, I need to—"

"No, sir. Sit," Palamas ordered.

"You're as bad as Doctor McCoy," Scott said.

Kirk smiled at Palamas, but she was bent over the chief engineer studying the readings. He was glad he'd grabbed the better medkit. The chaos seemed less organized without Scott.

Kirk grabbed the arm of a passing engineer—who nearly clouted his captain on the jaw before he saw who'd seized him.

"Sir! Captain!"

Kirk took the man by his shoulders and pointed him at Scott. "Crewman Hong, you are now the chief engineer's legs."

"Sir?"

"I'm ordering Engineer Scott to sit here and not

move. You, Mister Hong, are to run where he tells you, relaying his orders as he instructs. He is not to get up from this spot until Lieutenant Palamas or I say so. Understood?"

"Yes, sir. Completely," Hong said, sharing an awkward look with Scotty.

The chief engineer sighed, but realized it was useless to protest. He nodded toward the auxiliary booth above them. "Tell Gudapati I want every change he makes to those intercooler circuits documented. If we don't keep our records current, it's like not keeping 'em at all."

"Aye, sir," the engineer said, and hurried off.

Palamas took Scott's middle finger and pushed it upward. He winced hard and yanked his hand away. "Definitely a broken wrist," she said.

Nodding, Kirk could see that his wrist was red and already swelling.

"Didn't the blasted scanner tell you that?" the engineer protested.

"I can help the pain," Palamas told Kirk, "but this kit doesn't have a splint."

"We can make one," Scott said. "Get Hong back here. We can—"

"No," Palamas cut him off. "We need a real wrist splint, and I shouldn't be the one setting it. The scaphoid bone may be shattered. That's permanent nerve damage if we do this wrong and possible diminished use of your thumb."

Now the engineer looked as if he was in mental as well as physical shock.

Now what? Kirk didn't like being off the bridge any longer than necessary, but the work that needed to be done would be done faster with Mister Scott in charge.

Moving to the nearest intercom, the captain hit the button with the bottom of his fist. "Kirk to sickbay."

Silence.

"Kirk to sickbay."

Nothing.

"Stay here. Do what you can," Kirk told Palamas as he moved toward the exit.

"Where're you going, sir?"

"To get McCoy."

FIFTEEN

"Don't you 'Bones' me, Captain! That won't end well—for either of us." Leonard McCoy didn't hold back when in his own sickbay.

"Doctor . . ." Kirk began again.

"Look at this place!" McCoy pointed at the overflowing examination room. "Another coolant leak on deck seven. We're overloaded and M'Benga and Chapel have already taken medics and supplies to triage on site."

Kirk knew what McCoy was saying was right, and inwardly he was embarrassed that he'd even asked. But *Enterprise* needed her chief engineer. "We're talking about Scotty . . ."

"I'm deliberately *not* talking about Scotty," McCoy barked. "I'm needed right here, right now. People could die if I leave."

McCoy was right.

"So unless you're injured, Jim," the doctor continued, "and with all due respect to your captain's braid—get out of my sickbay!"

Lifting his arm, the captain showed McCoy the wound he had ignored.

"You would have to be hurt, wouldn't you?" The doctor turned and grumbled to himself, "Figures he'd find a way to have the last word." He motioned to a nurse in a blue jumpsuit. "Sakura! Get over here. See to the captain's wound and give him a wrist splint kit."

"Can I have Sakura?" Kirk suggested.

"I need him. Palamas can handle it." The doctor stormed off to the inner ward.

Kirk smiled at Sakura as he approached. He took the captain's right arm gently in one hand while he scanned it.

"You'll have to forgive the doctor, sir," Sakura said in that tone medical people used when doing an examination, as if nothing was going to hurt, and if it did, it should be ignored. "He's . . . well, he's in a touch of a snit today."

"You heard all that?" Kirk motioned toward McCoy.

"Deck twelve heard it, sir." Sakura unsuccessfully tried to hide a smirk.

Under his breath, Kirk said, "I hate when he's right."

Sakura pulled out another instrument and applied it to the wound. There was a slight prickling sensation and Kirk watched as the gash began to heal. The nurse sprayed on a bandage that would promote healing.

"If it's any consolation, Captain, he hates it when you're right, too."

Oddly, that *was* comforting. Kirk had a list of concerns: his ship, Spock, Pippenge, the Kenisians, and the *na'hubis*. There was something reassuring about McCoy's consistency. If the doctor could take the time to bark at him, maybe the situation wasn't as grim as it seemed.

"Sakura! Stop lollygagging and get back here," McCoy called from across the sickbay.

Comforting.

RUNNING THE SCANNER over Mister Scott's wrist again, Palamas didn't like what she saw. The swelling wasn't only due to injury, but internal bleeding. That was likely the cause of his dehydration. "You've not been drinking enough," she told him.

She'd already asked Hong to bring some water. What was keeping him?

"Aye," Scott said, "a glass of water would be a sight for sore eyes." He began to rise, as if to get himself one.

"You can't go running about." She pressed lightly on his shoulder with one hand, but it was enough to keep the engineer in place. "You stay put. Captain's orders."

"Ugh," Scott groaned. "It's just a wrist."

Scott was clearly still in pain, so she loaded ten cc of a painkiller into the hypospray and gave him the dose.

"An injured wrist means you can disobey Captain Kirk? I'll have to remember that."

"I didn't say that," he sighed.

"Hong will be back with the water in a moment," Palamas assured him.

"I hope not. He should be telling Kozachok about that variance in the G-6 output."

"If it's above ten percent, they'll see it and reduce the power flow to compensate." Palamas smiled.

Brow furrowed, Scott looked up at her skeptically. "And how would ya know that?"

"Mister Scott, my field of expertise is archaeology and anthropology, but my *profession* is Starfleet. I went to the Academy." She scanned him again and tried not to frown a bit at his readings. "It didn't hurt that my uncle was an engineer's mate on a cargo vessel."

"You know engines?"

"I do," Palamas said warmly. "Is that so hard to believe?"

"No. You were cross-trained as a field medic, so I thought . . ."

"Only since coming to the *Enterprise*. I was at Starbase Ten for six months before being assigned here. You know what they do a lot of?"

"Starship repair." A weak smile turned Scott's lips.

"Exactly, Mister Scott." She gripped his good hand to check for clamminess. His palm was wet.

As he gave her hand a tight squeeze in return, his smile strengthened a bit, and he said, "Call me Scotty, lass."

For every degree of power his smile lacked, she brightened her own. "I will, if you continue to call me lass. It's very charming."

"I call every lass that," Scott scoffed.

She patted his hand. "So you do."

Hong appeared with the bottle of water, which she took and fed to Scotty, not letting him hold it himself.

The engineer croaked orders to his subordinate, who ran off as quickly as he could.

They were silent for a while, as Palamas continued to let Scott sip water slowly. He closed his eyes and relished it until jolted awake by the ship creaking around them. The structural integrity fields had been put through the wringer.

As had the chief engineer, who grunted in disdain. "Do you feel that?" He tried to rise again, but once more she easily pushed him back.

"Working now would be a mistake, Scotty," she said. "We have to wait for the doctor."

Weak but still annoyed, he sank back into the chair. "All right, Lieutenant. All right."

"Does everyone call you Scotty?"

"Aye."

"Now, don't tell me your mother called you 'Scotty.'"

"Don't be daft," he grumbled. "My mother called me—" He stopped himself, clearly not wanting to divulge the name. "Well, never mind what she called me."

Palamas smiled playfully, saying, "Well, now I have to know."

"Do you?" He laughed, and it was good to hear.

"I do." Palamas leaned down close. "Whisper it to me."

Scott stayed silent. He just sat, half smiling, half grimacing.

"You're not going to tell me?" she asked, mock-pouting just a touch, if only to amuse him.

He shook his head.

"Monty?" she offered. "I bet it was Monty."

"Uchh," he grunted.

"I'll take that as a no." Giving him another sip of water, she put her right index finger on her chin, exaggerating a thoughtful pose. Palamas didn't care what his mother called him, although she was curious. She was only more interested in keeping Scott talking, not just to keep his mind off any pain, but to keep him from working. "It wasn't just Montgomery. Sonny boy?"

Again, he shook his head and, judging by his bemused look, she was at least keeping him entertained.

"Is there some reason I'm not allowed to know?" she prodded.

Scott sighed. "Life on a ship," he said. "I tell you, everyone—well, maybe not Mister Spock—will be calling me what my mother did by the end of watch."

"I wouldn't mind this watch being over."

"That, lass, depends on how it ends."

LEONARD McCOY had worked in a war zone. He'd found cures for alien diseases on primitive planets. He'd damned near invented a few treatments he thought would never succeed. But just now he'd have traded it all for another set of hands.

"Sakura, finish that up and get over here!"

It was McCoy's fifteenth operation of the day, and there were more waiting. M'Benga and Colone were treating radiation poisoning and other injuries that were keeping them just as busy: burns, breaks, lacerations, and contusions.

None of the work was complex—he wasn't discovering an alien antigen—but by sheer volume, he and his staff were spread thin.

His current patient, Chief Touré, had a deep enough wound that he'd have to slowly close it. Except he didn't have time for that right now; all he could do was bandage it and keep the woman stable.

"Doctor?" Sakura was at his side, ready to act.

"Get me a pressure bandage refill, type forty-five."

"You have the last canister, Doctor."

"How can we be out?" McCoy barked.

Sakura began to answer but the doctor cut him off.

"Never mind. Go to my office. The cabinet to the left of the door. Middle shelf. There'll be a box of physical bandages. They'll have to do."

Immediately, Sakura dashed off.

A physical bandage wasn't as good as the chemical kind, which would bind itself to the organic matter beneath it and exert the exact amount of pressure needed, but it would do the job.

There were times McCoy eschewed technology, but not when it came to medical advances. The tools and machinery at his disposal were more than his life's focus, they were necessary for the well-being of those in his care.

When Sakura returned with the bandages, McCoy snapped the box open with one hand and let the lid drop to the deck. Sakura picked it up.

Unraveling the material, the doctor applied it, then pressed tightly until it grabbed hold. After ten seconds, the bandage would maintain whatever pressure had been applied. It was effective, if less comfortable for the patient than the usual kind, which would have given the patient more normal movement.

"At least it's not gauze," McCoy grumbled.

The nurse grunted his agreement, though

McCoy wondered if the younger man had even seen gauze outside of a museum.

McCoy was irritated because he had to use a non-spray-applied bandage. And yet, the material he did have was still complex and technical: soaked in chemicals that would bond with the skin and assist platelets in clotting. An advanced bandage that he was complaining about as if it was as primitive as mud salve.

As soon as Chief Touré was squared away, McCoy turned to his next patient, Crewman Roath. The medical tricorder said he had massive blood loss.

Quickly, Sakura and McCoy tried to suture his wounds, but the crewman wasn't reacting well to the treatment. At a certain point, a body could only help so much in its own healing process.

"Did you give him that Rigelian blood therapy?" McCoy asked.

"Yes, sir, as per your orders."

"Damn."

Despite being in shock, Crewman Roath began to stir.

"Am I gonna be okay, Doc?" he asked weakly.

"Of course you are, Roath." McCoy patted him lightly on the shoulder—one of the few areas that wasn't injured. "Don't you worry."

Even in a barely conscious state, the boy was still anxious, and McCoy shared a concerned glance with Sakura.

"Are you doubting me, crewman?" the doctor asked with mock indignation. "Is that what I see?"

"No, sir," Roath said feebly. "I . . ."

"As long as you take your doctor's advice, you're going to be fine. You hear?"

The young crewman nodded very slowly and slightly. "Yes, sir."

"So, you just relax and let me do my work."

"Okay," he sighed.

"You know," McCoy continued as he worked on the crewman's wounds, "worry ages us. It makes us tired, and we need you to be strong for recovery, not spending your energy frettin' on my part of the job."

Roath's lips turned up ever so slightly into the smallest of smiles. If he had energy, he might have chuckled.

"We'll get you all fixed up," the doctor assured him. "And then out of here. I can't have my sickbay filled with people taking up space who don't really need my care, you know."

Again, Roath tried to laugh but couldn't quite manage it. With a soft moan, Roath lost consciousness, and then the biobed indicated his passing.

This—*this* is what McCoy was always complaining to Kirk about. The loss of life, of young potential. A life of possibilities—gone.

McCoy couldn't allow tears to well.

"Who's next?" McCoy asked Sakura as he placed

his hand on Roath for a quick moment, wishing him a silent goodbye. "Come on. Who's next?"

"YOU REALIZE THIS will retard the destructive extent by only two percent more than the previous simulation." Spock inserted a program module into the side of the prototype mine.

Sciver pulled the module back out, double-checked it with his tricorder, then placed it back into its receptacle again. "With the rest of the *na'hubis* safe in storage, so long as we escape the initial blast radius, the cascade should dissipate after a time."

Raising a long finger of protest, Ambassador Pippenge asked, "How many star systems fall within the 'after a time' estimate you so casually assert?"

Spock raised an appreciative brow. The Maabas ambassador began as the spokesman for a xeno-phobic and protectionist people who were at the infancy of their embrace of the Federation. Now, he was advocating for the people of the galaxy, not just his own planet.

"We cannot be certain—"

"Seventeen," Spock interrupted. He nodded toward Sciver. "According to your own simulations."

"Most of those systems are uninhabited," the Kenisian pointed out.

"Six have a total of eight inhabited planets."

Handing Sciver the next component directly, Spock continued, "Of those, three have thriving ecosystems, two of which have intelligent life on an industrial, pre-warp scale. One other may develop such a civilization within the next thousand years."

The Kenisian scoffed. "You can't know that."

"How many lives?" Pippenge pressed.

"You saw the data." Spock wanted the Kenisian to answer—to say the number.

Pausing, he suddenly examined the mine component as if it were a foreign object. With Spock and Pippenge staring at him, Sciver eventually croaked out a reply. "Approximately four hundred million."

The Vulcan sensed the internal battle going on within Sciver. Unsure how many distinct personalities could be at play within him, Spock was certain that they were not in agreement.

The more that incongruity could be exacerbated, the better.

"Approximately?" The Vulcan cast a downward glance at the Kenisian. Zhatan was very exacting when she threatened the Maabas. She had the number of sentient inhabitants counted within one percent. A scientist should be able to articulate the specific number.

The Kenisian handed Spock back the program module. "Please double-check this."

Spock knew there was nothing wrong with

the encoding. "Of course." He took the unit and scanned it.

Now may be the appropriate time to attempt a meld.

With telepaths as strong as the Kenisians, the risks were great. But it could also mean the meld would be easier to perform and faster to achieve.

Cautiously, Spock surveyed the room. There were several scientists and technicians involved in various tasks. All were likely important to the mine preparation, and the only way to force their exit would be an accident of some type.

Scanning the area with his Kenisian tricorder, Spock found the plasma leak he'd created earlier. He quickly showed the data to Sciver, who used his own tricorder to verify it. Hopefully, Spock had been careful enough in his sabotage that Sciver would think it an accident.

"You must evacuate this section until the leak is sealed," the Vulcan advised.

Sciver protested, "We don't think it calls for all that—"

"For the safety of your team, I recommend otherwise. Free plasma in this quantity can wreak havoc with biological and technical systems alike. The room should be vented and the leak sealed. It shouldn't take long."

"But . . ." Irresolute as usual, the Kenisian hesitated. While Spock knew it was but one more example of the internal debate among hundreds of minds, he used the delay to prod Sciver.

"If you prefer, I will offer to stay and complete mine modifications, but I ask that Ambassador Pippenge and any nonessential personnel are removed from harm's way."

That Sciver didn't discount that notion out of hand spoke to the level of dysfunction in the multigenerational multividual. Doubtless there were many within Sciver who did not trust Spock, but a greater number either did, or had realized the Vulcan's deception and wished to aid him. Either way, the answer was, "Yes, very well."

Looking confused, Pippenge withdrew with the Kenisian technicians and left Spock and Sciver alone in the huge lab.

"Engineering. This is Sciver." There was no visible communications equipment, and so it was likely the Kenisian had technology similar to the Maabas's implant. "We have discovered a plasma leak. I will transfer the specific coordinates to you. Please see that the leak is controlled. Then alert us in the main laboratory so we can fully evacuate for decontamination."

Nodding to an unheard voice, Sciver looked at Spock. "We have time to install three more components. Please move quickly."

"I shall." Dropping his tricorder, Spock grasped the Kenisian man by his wrist and placed the fingers of his other hand to Sciver's face and temple. "My mind to your minds."

"GIVE ME YOUR ARM." In one hand Kirk held the splint he had gotten from sickbay. In the other he held the companion bone-knitter.

Scott hesitated.

"What's wrong?" The captain looked to Palamas, then back to his engineer. "Is it the pain?"

"Oh, no, sir. The hypo did its job." Scott glanced from the splint to Palamas.

"I see." Kirk handed everything to Palamas. "Lieutenant."

Smiling slightly, Palamas took both tools as the captain hovered close by.

"The splint just clicks on," Palamas said as she gingerly placed it around Scott's arm. "I'll rotate the wrist slowly until it beeps, which means it's properly set and ready for the bone-knitter." She slowly adjusted his wrist, ever so delicately. "Don't worry. I've used one before."

Kirk heard the beep of the splint and then the whine of the bone-knitter.

Several engineers rushed by, some glancing over toward the three officers, but moving on. There was no time to linger. They knew that Mister Scott was counting on them. The captain remembered being that green, an ensign so focused on his duty that whatever else was happening didn't matter, thinking that it must be so much easier at the top. The senior officers always had the answers, were always so cool, so calm and collected. If it wouldn't undermine the chain of command, he'd love to take one of his junior officers aside, say Jolma, and tell them how he felt right now.

The whine of the bone-knitter stopped. The captain turned back toward them. A wave of relief descended over Scott's face as Palamas locked the splint and returned the tools to the medkit.

"That'll take some time to heal, but the knitter gave it a head start. Does it feel better?" she asked.

Scott wiggled his fingers. "Aye. Thank you, lass." He stood up saying, "Now I need to work on that emergency bulkhead." The engineer motioned up the corridor. "Hull breach just beyond, so I'll need to get force fields in place before opening 'er up. Beyond that is the area I'll need to access."

"Scotty, we're not only blind, but deaf," Kirk said.

"We'll see to it, sir." The engineer motioned to Palamas.

"We?" she asked.

The chief engineer held up his splinted wrist. "Well, you're not going to abandon your patient now, are you, Lieutenant? I'll need someone to help."

"Captain?" Palamas looked expectantly to Kirk for help.

"She's had engineering experience, sir."

"I see." Kirk felt as if he was missing something. "If my chief engineer needs you, who am I to disagree?"

"Thank you, sir." Scott grabbed a large toolkit with his good hand, and they exited to the corridor.

"How long?" the captain asked. He'd feel better about their plan if he could contact Spock again, to be sure things were properly timed. And none of it would happen unless the *Enterprise* was warp capable.

"Once we get that force field up, it won't be long, sir."

"Thank you, Mister Scott. Keep me informed. I'll be on the bridge."

Kirk headed toward the turbolift as Scott and Palamas moved toward the emergency bulkhead that had dropped to seal a hull breach.

"Where do we start?" she asked eagerly.

"Jefferies tube just before the emergency bulkhead." The engineer led her to it and used the toolkit as a pointer. "You'll have to go up. I'll hand you what you need."

Without hesitation, Palamas climbed in.

"You sure you don't mind getting your hands dirty?" Scott asked as he opened his kit and took out a circuit meter.

She stopped and looked down at him over her shoulder. "Scotty, I'm an archaeologist."

He smiled. "Aye. I forgot."

"Well, don't worry about me." Palamas stopped at the end of the tube where the top opened onto relays, circuits, and conduits that twisted this way and that, all labeled with numerical or color codes.

"Steady yourself," Scott said.

Palamas placed one boot firmly on a narrow step and her other on the one below it. "Should I describe what I see?"

"*I* could describe what you see," the engineer pointed out. "To your left is a small, yellow node labeled 45D9. Do you see it?"

She found it, then peered down, saying, "I have it."

He took the circuit meter and placed it under the arm with the splint and grabbed a new circuit module from the kit, then pulled himself up the Jefferies tube. Halfway up, Scott handed her the meter. "Take this."

Palamas reached down. "This will tell me if the circuit is live."

"Aye. Place it near 45D9 and if it's green it's live. But it won't be."

The A&A officer followed Scott's instructions and when the meter neared the circuit, it flashed amber. "Yellow."

"Yellow means it's working but degraded. But that's the same as not working when push comes to shove."

Nodding, Palamas reached down to hand him the meter.

"Keep it," he said. "There's a little ledge to your left where you can stow it for now. You'll need it again."

Palamas eventually found it. Just a small outcropping from the tube that was probably an alternate hand-hold. It fit the meter perfectly.

"Take this one now." Scott reached up and held out a tool. She'd seen this one before. It would pop the circuit out without her needing to touch it as it was likely to be hot.

After she removed the bad circuit, there was an audible warble in the hum of the tube around them.

"What happened?"

"Don't you worry, lass. She just wants her circuit replaced." He handed up the fresh one. "But it'll get hot. Pull away the moment it's in."

Palamas stretched down and their hands met. Scotty passed her the new circuit and she smiled down at him. His forehead was damp with perspiration, and she noticed she was quite warm as well.

Swapping out the circuit module was as easy as he said, and the hum around them actually seemed happier than before.

Shifting one foot down, ready to leave the Jefferies tube, Palamas noticed Scott hadn't moved. "We're not done yet. That was just the circuit. Now we have to reroute the power that was routed away."

Pulling herself back up, the lieutenant settled in. "I suppose I should have realized if it was this easy someone else would have taken care of it."

Scott directed her to three conduits which needed to be passed to the previously failed circuits. It was as if he was reading from a technical manual, he knew just what she was looking at. He warned her off touching something before she even reached for it.

"Working on a starship is different than repairing a starbase," Palamas said as she manipulated the connections at his direction.

"It is," Scotty said. "You've got to see her as a living creature to really know her. And when she's in starbase, and all her systems are down, it's like she's having an operation under anesthetic."

"You never refer to the *Enterprise* as a thing, do you?" she asked. "Only 'her' or 'she.'"

"Lots of people do that."

"But you feel it," Palamas said, and found it quite endearing. "She's alive to you."

"Aye."

"You're a passionate man," Palamas said.

"The best engineers are." He smiled back. "Tell me about your uncle." He passed her another component. "Then fit this over the N131 cable and route it to the A544 receptacle. It fits but snugly."

"My Uncle Elias. I only got to see him when he was in port, which wasn't often. But when he was, we'd go everywhere together. He'd tell me about an engineering problem he had, or the interesting ship they had encountered. And he always brought me gifts."

"Working a cargo vessel, he must have had his pick."

"He was an engineer," Palamas reminded him. "He *made* the gifts for me." She struggled with the connection, but after putting some shoulder into it, Palamas managed to attach the cable. "That's how I came to Starfleet with some engineering aptitude."

She looked down at Scott and found him smiling. He said, "You love him."

Palamas nodded. "Loved, yes. He's passed."

"I'm sorry," the engineer said.

"Thank you. I never forget how dangerous this life can be. He knew it too, and he always said that he couldn't even think of doing anything else."

"How old were you?" Scotty asked. "When you lost him?"

"It was only four months ago." Her voice wavered and trailed into a whisper.

For a while, they said nothing. Finally, Scott told her, "I think he must have been quite proud of you."

Palamas nodded, and for the next few minutes, they worked silently. When they finished, the *Enterprise* officers were both tired, covered with sweat and coolant gel.

Scott backed out of the tube and Palamas slowly

climbed down. Near the bottom, she lost her footing and with his good hand he steadied her.

"Thank you. Not my usual duty," she said, nodding up toward the top.

"Ach," he scoffed. "You'd get used to it in no time."

"What's next?" Already cooling off, the lieutenant was ready for their next task.

The chief engineer motioned toward where the emergency bulkhead had been. It was now gone and the corridor beyond was revealed to them. "Doin' what the captain needs. Let's give the *Enterprise* back her voice and ears."

"I don't see a breach," Palamas said as they stepped into the corridor.

"Probably several micro fissures. Force fields will hold it until I have one of the lads come through with something more permanent."

Ducking into a vertical access hatchway, Scotty handed her the toolkit and took a ladder rung with his good hand, letting his splinted one hang to the side.

"Up or down?" Palamas asked.

"Down. Here's where the real work begins, Lieutenant. If you're up for it." Smiling again, the engineer seemed energized.

"I am if you'll stop calling me lieutenant. It's Carolyn."

"Carolyn," Scotty said, easily lowering himself

one-handed down the ladder as if he'd done it a million times, "follow me."

"SIR, SENSORS ARE back online," the chief engineer reported. *"The main communication relays will be online in two minutes. It won't take long to get under way."*

"Excellent work, Mister Scott. Kirk out." They weren't far from their destination, but getting there before the Kenisians was only part of the plan. The captain wondered how they would be received. The Sahntiek had been conquerors, and Spock's report said the Kenisians knew they'd rebuilt their fleet.

Before losing communications, *Enterprise* had been hailing the system, but without reply. The only thing Kirk knew they would find when they reached the Sahntiek was the fleet of starships Zhatan feared. Long-range scans had confirmed their existence.

After thousands of years—and much of it under Kenisian oppression—there was no telling what the attitude of the Sahntiek would be to outsiders. Would they refuse contact, as the Maabas had? Would they attempt to strike the Kenisians first, and in doing so destroy Zhatan's ship—along with Spock and Pippenge—which might also spark the *na'hubis* devastation that Kirk had hoped to avoid?

If Spock did his part, Kirk had time to warn the

Sahntiek before Zhatan's ship arrived. He might be able to resolve this without bloodshed. If they would listen to reason.

"MY THOUGHTS to your thoughts." The fingers of Spock's left hand pressed into Sciver's cheeks and temple. His right pushed Sciver's wrist tightly up toward his own chest.

"Indecent!"

"Intruder!"

"Violence!"

"Vul-kuhn?"

"Blood."

"Open your mind," Spock whispered.

"No! Leave us!"

"We move together. Our minds sharing . . ."

"Alien!"

"Violator!"

"Savior."

Sciver grunted, and Spock felt a fraction of resistance. Less than he expected.

"Our thoughts merge."

"Kill him!"

"Kill the Vul-kuhn!"

"Get him out!"

Sciver's free hand wrapped itself around Spock's throat.

"Repress him!"

"*Embrace him!*"

"*Save us!*"

Ever conflicted, the Kenisian didn't apply the strength needed to choke the life from Spock. The Vulcan encouraged and bolstered the side that supported his meld.

"Who are we?" Spock asked. A rush of emotions flooded toward him. Some had names, others just a wave of feelings that threatened to overwhelm him.

"*Ashnu!*"

"*Hutindra!*"

"*Oaebint!*"

"*Costre! Enict! Podor!*"

"*Histet! Bidras-eta! Colost!*"

Dozens of names, titles and identities, pushed forward. Desires and passions inundated them. This is what Sciver felt all day, every day. This was his existence.

"*Know us!*"

"*Be us!*"

"*Help us!*"

"Calm," Spock said.

Sciver repeated in a whisper, "Calm."

"We are Sciver," Spock said through gritted teeth. "I am Spock."

"We are Spock," the Kenisian added, "*I* am Sciver."

Within the blizzard of personalities, there was a physical being named Sciver. An "I" and not a "we." To release it from submission, its individuality would need to be awakened.

"Others have taken our identity." Spock re-arranged his fingers at Sciver's temple and pressed in again. "We must reassert."

"*No!*"

"*Control!*"

There was an inherent contradiction in the concept of a melded Spock and Sciver fighting for individuality. Despite that, Spock was succeeding, and the panicking mass of consciousnesses within struggled to retain their domain.

"*We must live!*"

"*Help us!*"

"*Be with us!*"

"*Isolation!*"

"*Leave us!*"

One hundred and forty-seven unique indi-viduals swirled around them. Thousands of years of memories, confused and churning, folding in on each other until they couldn't distinguish one from another.

"*Chaos!*"

"*Control!*"

"*Help us!*"

"*Noooo!*"

There were ancient disciplines that could filter the voices and govern the minds within him. Sciver knew they existed because Spock knew of them.

The Vulcan had shown him how it could be done. But now, Spock had to break the meld.

"Disparity," Sciver cried.

"Order! We need order!"

"Our minds, separating," the Vulcan whispered harshly. "Parting."

"No!"

"Come back!"

"Return!"

Releasing Sciver's wrist, Spock quickly pulled his fingers from the Kenisian's head as well.

Sciver began to shake uncontrollably, blathering. "Nuuhhhh—nuuuuhhh."

The torrent of personalities had been shown control could be imposed, then Spock left. With time all the minds could find coordination again, but Sciver was in shock from the experience and unable to do it on his own.

Guiding the man to a chair, Spock lowered him into the seat. "Sleep," he whispered, "is preferred." He pinched the proper nerve in Sciver's neck until he lost consciousness.

For Sciver, the internal torment would continue. But in the meantime he wouldn't be a danger to himself or others.

Recoding the components they had placed in the prototype mine took only moments. Should all other efforts fail, the *na'hubis* was now useless.

When he finished, there was no way for Spock

to contact the Kenisian engineers, so he left the lab.

Pippenge and the host of technicians were waiting in the adjacent corridor.

"You've been in there for some time," the ambassador said cautiously. "Are you well?"

Spock hesitated to answer. What he'd done was distasteful, no matter the necessity. He'd taken an individual who struggled to incorporate too many personalities into a functioning being and left him in disarray. By showing Sciver that control was possible, then taking it from him, Spock knew what he'd done was a violation. Necessary to save millions, but the remorse he felt—which Sciver had also felt—was difficult to control.

"I am adequate," Spock finally told Pippenge.

"Sciver?"

Glancing toward the door to the laboratory, Spock said, "Indisposed." He turned to the nearest lab tech and placed the fingers of his right hand on the upper left quadrant of her face. *My mind to your minds.*

Peripherally he saw the two other techs who were waiting look at one another and then move forward.

"I wouldn't do that," Pippenge said. "It may harm them both." There was truth to that, but the ambassador probably thought it a clever lie.

"*What are you doing?*" the technician's minds

wondered. This one was more curious than Sciver, who knew quite well what Spock had done.

This one was fascinated by the Vulcan and embraced the meld.

"You are different."

"You are similar."

"We would know you."

And then the tide turned and the chorus began to fight back.

"No! Stop!"

Sifting through the dozens of minds, Spock isolated the individual who was the form. "You are Murlit," he said. "Be Murlit."

After a brief struggle and an instinctive resistance to change, Murlit accepted the calm the Vulcan offered. And when he had, Spock left it, just as he'd done with Sciver.

Released from his mental grasp, she began to cry softly as he leaned her against the bulkhead. He reached for the next Kenisian, who flinched away in protest, but Spock caught the man by his arm and pulled him close.

My thoughts to your thoughts.

"We are Burgee," the man thought.

"No," Spock told him, and he distilled out the seven others who had survived within Burgee's body.

One had been a chemist, who gave the Kenisian his love of science. Another had been a musician who'd passed on his love for mathematics and song.

They'd been with Burgee as long as the individual could remember. They'd helped mold who he was. And Spock was now giving them the tools to co-exist in a sustainable way.

Burgee was content. He was grateful to Spock.

Until the Vulcan removed the barriers, and chaos began again—except worse than before.

Collapsing, the Kenisian man became catatonic.

Obviously seeing a pattern emerge, the last technician turned to run. Pippenge grabbed him, his long, gangly arms wrapping around the Kenisian. The ambassador's thumbs tightly interlinked, locking the man in place.

Applying his hands to the technician's head, Spock melded with the last of the three as Pippenge held him.

Our minds are one.

"*A new consciousness.*"

"*I am Spock.*"

"*We are the undying. We are within Talar.*"

"*Where is Talar?*"

"*We are Talar.*"

"*Release him.*"

"*Impossible. Who are you? Get out!*"

"*Let Talar control Talar.*"

"*No, he needs us! Leave us!*"

"*He does not need you. You need him.*"

"*Yes, we need him. Leave him to us.*"

"*No. He is an individual. He must live his life.*"

"He is us. We are him. Stop blocking us."

"No," Spock told them. *"No."*

Talar, the individual, was alone. Spock felt his others, but Talar did not.

"We are Spock?"

"We are Talar," Spock corrected, but then pulled himself back so that the Kenisian could feel what it was to be singular. So he might remember who he was.

"I am Talar," the man mumbled aloud, and smiled faintly.

"No," Spock whispered, and let the others come flooding back.

Talar groaned and slackened.

"What exactly did you do?" The ambassador released the lab tech to Spock's grip, and the Vulcan gently lowered the now-sobbing man to the deck.

"I removed the inhibitions of their many minds. I showed them themselves, then returned them to their chaos." His voice was soft and scraped like gravel. There was emotion churning within that was difficult to process and suppress. "And, in doing so, incapacitated them."

SIXTEEN

The *Enterprise* limped. Or at least that's the way it felt to her captain. She'd been traveling at maximum warp for too long. With many systems on bypass, the best Scott could offer was warp factor six but only for one more hour.

Would that be fast enough? It should be, but how much progress had the Kenisians made while *Enterprise* was being repaired?

Since communications had been restored, Uhura had tried to raise Spock, but to no avail. Nor had the Sahntiek replied to repeated hails.

"Are they receiving us?" The captain was hovering near the communications station, as he had off and on for the last twenty minutes.

"The signal is making it there, sir. We're not being jammed." She worked her console, trying a different frequency range. "I'm monitoring for any outgoing transmission from that system. Nothing, but they may be under some kind of comm silence."

That didn't bode well.

"Any telemetry from the probe, Mister Jolma?"

"Not yet, sir." The ensign turned to the left and flipped a series of switches. "Probe is still at warp."

The probe was limited. It was basically a ball of sensors with a powerful transmitter and a compact warp engine. But the captain hoped the probe could tell them something, anything.

As he waited, Kirk anxiously moved from the command chair, to the science station, to Uhura, then over to the engineering station to see how the *Enterprise* was doing. Scott was manning the station on the bridge as his people continued to work to shore up the systems.

"She'll hold together, sir," Scott said as the captain surveyed the displays.

Kirk nodded his approval and stepped down into the command well.

"Getting telemetry," Jolma reported.

"On-screen," Kirk ordered.

The starscape was replaced by a data display showing the star system they were approaching augmented with a graph pinpointing planets and satellites and artificial space structures. The fourth planet was inhabited. There was evidence of starship movement, and in orbit there was a fleet. The probe was still tallying the number of ships.

The Federation had no quarrel with the Sahntiek. Kirk did not want to make first contact this way, but he had no choice. What he preferred was stopping Zhatan before she even got to the Sahntiek system. He'd need to talk to Spock to know if that was possible.

"Reduce magnification," the captain ordered.

The image shifted to a wider view. The *Enterprise* was fifty-five minutes from the system. If Zhatan's ship maintained their current speed, they were two hours away. "We'll be cutting it close."

"They could detonate their weapon where they are now," Chekov said. "Wipe themselves, us, and the Sahntiek out in one explosion."

Kirk pushed out a breath and shook his head. "I don't think so." He motioned behind him. "They don't want their enemy to just disappear—alive one moment, gone the next. They want to explain the reason. Personally."

Intently studying the telemetry that flowed across the main screen, the captain leaned forward. *An hour doesn't leave a margin for error.*

Pushing himself out of the center seat and toward the engineering station, Kirk leaned into the rail.

"Mister Scott, we need to increase speed."

As he turned toward the captain, Scott's expression was carved with warning. "We can push the engines, sir, but the ship herself isn't up to much more. We've still got structural integrity problems." He shook his head. "I canna guarantee she'll hold."

Kirk had learned that being in command wasn't

just figuring out when to make which decision. It was knowing how to inspire the people under him—encouraging them to do what they could, so he could do what he must. Would Scott ever push the ship as hard as Kirk needed?

No. That's why a captain had to ask the impossible of his chief engineer.

"I have confidence in your skills, Mister Scott."

Scott nodded his relenting acceptance of his orders. "Aye, sir. I'll try not to disappoint."

Kirk smiled. "You? Never." He pivoted back to the command chair. "Mister Sulu, warp factor seven."

"Warp seven, aye."

THERE WAS an alarming simplicity with which Spock was now able to enter a Kenisian mind and pull on the proper threads to undo them. The ease was of a technical nature, but the emotional ramifications were far reaching. How could he justify his actions? They'd kidnapped him and the ambassador, threatened the lives of billions, perhaps trillions. And yet, it did not feel right.

Feel.

He and Pippenge had encountered several of the crew since leaving the laboratory deck, and all of them had fallen with relative alacrity.

The Vulcan had now touched hundreds and

hundreds of minds held within dozens of bodies. He'd pushed his way into the ship's auxiliary control room, where the ambassador stood guard as Spock configured a timed sabotage that would allow them to make their way to the bridge before it was noticed.

"What are you doing here?" A Kenisian guard forced his way past Pippenge and brought a weapon up toward Spock. "You are not cleared for access to this location."

"My apology," the Vulcan said as he nonchalantly sauntered toward the door.

As he passed the guard, Spock turned quickly and jutted out his hand, melding with the man.

Our minds are one.

"We are Chith'gol. Who are you?" The Kenisian didn't know of Spock, only that he shouldn't be where he was. *"What are you doing?"*

"I am Spock," the Vulcan explained telepathically. *"Your commander has abducted us, in an effort to extort cooperation."*

"Why?" Chith'gol asked.

"She wishes to harness an ancient devastation, but it is not possible. Her error will destroy innocent lives," Spock told him.

"This is true?"

"You are in my thoughts. You know the verity of it."

"We did not know," the Kenisian said. *"This outrages us."*

"How many are within you?"

"You meld with Chith'gol and Twibe, both of the clan Vomla."

Spock was surprised. *"There are but two of you?"*

Chith'gol smiled. *"You are in our thoughts. You know the verity of it."* He pushed Spock's hand away, and the Vulcan allowed it. The meld was broken.

"Chith'gol and Twibe, you are one."

"We are integrated," the Kenisian said with a nod. "You must be the Vulcan. There have been rumors. We were not to bother you if we saw you in the corridor."

"Why?" Spock asked.

"We were told," Chith'gol said, "you did not wish to be disturbed. That you were a special envoy."

"A lie," the Vulcan told him, gesturing toward Pippenge. "This is the Maabas ambassador. We have been held against our will and forced to act against our interests."

"It is distasteful to us," the Kenisian said, looking down at the deck and shaking his head. "Zhatan ordered this?"

"Orchestrated and ordered," Pippenge said.

Chith'gol bowed to the Maabas ambassador. "You have our apology, sir."

How many more like these? Spock wondered. Here were two individuals, in one body, that had managed to incorporate into a single being. Were the majority of Kenisians like Chith'gol? Seeing how conflicted those like Zhatan and Sciver were, how could their society function if the majority weren't like this man?

"We are attempting to stop this vessel before it reaches its destination," Spock explained, and Pippenge seemed taken aback by the admission. "Will you assist us?"

Staring at Spock a long moment, Chith'gol finally smiled. "I shouldn't," he said, "but I will."

"Why?" the ambassador asked, perplexed.

"The connection we have shared," Chith'gol said, motioning to Spock, "is difficult to explain. I know and understand his motives, and he is familiar with mine. I cannot, in so brief a connection, know all about his Starfleet or his friend named Kirk, but I can understand his character, and his moral code." Chith'gol told Spock, "For that I am sorry."

The Vulcan bowed his head. "We must act with haste." He explained to the Kenisian his plans and the modifications he made to the auxiliary control systems.

"My peer will be here soon." Chith'gol looked to the door, concentrated a moment, then turned back. "I've locked him out but he will countermand it," he explained. "When he enters, he will see what you've done and undo it."

"We shall wait."

Spock could have left the Kenisian man to handle his shipmate, as he trusted him to not betray them. But there was no guarantee that Chith'gol would be the victor in a conflict.

Despite the uncomfortable delay, Pippenge, ever curious, asked the Kenisian, "Why do you have but two consciousnesses within you? Why not more?"

As if this was a frequent inquiry from strangers, Chith'gol was ready with an answer. "I am from a small clan, and we do not believe in accepting non-kin *ka'atrehs*."

"Why do the others?"

The Kenisian answered honestly. "Others see a high number of consciousnesses as a matter of prestige. Commander Zhatan is master of this vessel as much for that as for her skill." Chith'gol shook his head and looked past Pippenge. "After the civil war, individual *ka'atrehs* that lived on within others acquired a vote in the assembly. That is when we took the darkest turn."

"How?" Spock asked.

Chith'gol's gaze was marked with deep regret. "The past became more important than the future. Fear and hate of our enemies outweighed love."

"That is an emotional conclusion, not a rational report of a historical event," the Vulcan said.

Smiling, Chith'gol didn't disagree. "I suppose so. But what of the *na'hubis* and its destructive purpose? Is that not evidence of fear and hate above all else?" His expression was suddenly worried, and Chith'gol moved toward the door. "Djow approaches."

Spock moved to the doorway and waited to one side. When the Kenisian entered, Spock stepped forward and grabbed Djow's shoulder with one hand and his forehead with the other.

"My mind to your minds, Djow."

Their thoughts swirled quickly together.

"Intruder!"

"The Vul-kuhn!"

"Calm us!"

"Leave us!"

"Join us!"

It was much the same as the previous Kenisian melds. Within moments Djow was mumbling softly to himself.

Gently, Spock lowered him to the deck as Chith'gol watched.

"Was that the fate meant for me?"

"Yes," the Vulcan admitted. "He will recover. But it will take time." He took the man's weapon and gave it to Pippenge. "Do you know how to use this?"

Examining it, the ambassador seemed to recognize it. "I think so. I'd rather not have to use such a thing. I am a man of peace."

A man of peace.

Chith'gol showed Pippenge the settings. "This stuns," he said, "and this kills."

The ambassador set it to stun.

"We must get to the bridge." Spock turned to Chith'gol. "Live long and prosper."

They returned to the corridor, leaving Chith'gol with his unconscious crewmate.

As they ran hastily along, Spock noted that the other Kenisians they'd previously encountered were gone.

The ambassador motioned to the areas of the deck where the Kenisians had been left. "Where did they go?"

"I assume they've been taken to their sickbay."

"Yet no one tasks us? Why has there not been an alert?"

Spock shook his head. "There may have been, but silently, communicated to implants much like your own. We were, in fact, interrupted just minutes ago."

"Chith'gol would have mentioned it."

"Perhaps." It was also possible, Spock thought, that the Kenisians were aware the crew was being disabled, but didn't understand why. "They may think there is a disease spreading. All they are finding are crew members in various states of unconsciousness or emotional disarray."

Hearing someone heading down the corridor, Spock moved the ambassador into a dark alcove to hide. Spock preferred to limit the number of crew with which he had to engage.

Unwittingly, the Vulcan exhaled after the crewman had passed quietly on.

"Are you unwell, Mister Spock?" Pippenge

asked. "You seem quite adept at whatever you're doing with the Kenisians, but I sense it is taking a toll on you."

"*Doing with*" *was not accurate*, Spock thought. *Doing* to. "I am not under any physical strain."

As they continued up the corridor, the ambassador pressed, "Mental, then?"

"Mental" wasn't the right word to describe Spock's state, but he didn't wish to share that with Pippenge. *Philosophical* strain was perhaps the best way to quantify his anxiety. That he *felt* anxiety suggested that his emotional control was insufficient.

"There is a task at hand," Spock said eventually, temporizing. "Personal discomfort is of no matter."

After a few more detours into alcoves, and once into what was likely someone's empty cabin, they found themselves at a lift. According to the schematics Spock had seen, it would lead to the bridge.

"Why do we hesitate?"

Spock gestured to the door. "There is no external panel. Like the doorways we've seen, this is telepathically controlled, likely for security purposes."

"Wise," Pippenge said drily. "Can you open it?"

"I shall try." The Vulcan closed his eyes and began to concentrate. He brought his left hand's fingers to his own temple and thought about the door. He wasn't asking some unseen force to open it, but visualizing it open. He imagined what the space looked like, tried to imagine every aspect: the curve of the floor, the very white walls, and the very dark gray carpeting.

When the lift doors parted for them and Spock's eyes opened, it was just as he'd imagined. Every line, every detail. For the picture he had in his mind to be that exact, there must have been a mechanism that accessed his thoughts and fed him the image. Again, he appreciated the technology.

Spock took the ambassador's elbow and led him in. "We must move with urgency."

"Why?"

As the lift doors closed, Spock explained. "The control is telepathic, but the mechanics are not. Someone may be alerted to an unauthorized lift heading for the bridge."

The cab moved swiftly, zigzagging more briskly than the *Enterprise*'s lifts.

The doors opened to reveal two Kenisian guards waiting for them. Zhatan stood to their left, just in front of her command chair.

Frowning harshly, she motioned them forward.

"We've been expecting you."

SEVENTEEN

The Sahntiek were quiet as the *Enterprise* approached the edge of their system. Once they dropped out of warp, the alien ships came in force. Three oddly shaped vessels, looking somewhat like gorilla heads with small warp nacelles attached. Their weapons charged, all three somehow looked angrily at the Federation starship. If they'd not already been at red alert, Kirk would have called for it.

"Jolma, report."

"Multiphasic disruptor arrays, Captain," the ensign reported. "Five torpedo tubes on the lead vessel, two on the others. I have readings that suggest a tractor-like weapon that rips ships apart, also on the lead. Heavy shielding, armor . . . but it seems very discordant."

Spock would have given the most important information first, and in the most concise way. Jolma was less organized in his report.

"Explain," Kirk ordered.

"Power signatures are all over the place. Usually a ship has one or two. I'm reading five." The ensign hesitated.

"You're onto something, Jolma," the captain encouraged. "Keep going."

"Sir, I think these ships are powerful, but an amalgam of a lot of different technologies."

That makes sense, Kirk thought. "The Kenisians weren't allowing the Sahntiek their own technology. Maybe this was their answer."

"We're being scanned," the ensign reported.

A conquering race would be comforted by what they found. *Enterprise* had been battered. While she was on the mend, sensors would probably reveal her degraded state.

Uhura half turned toward the command chair, left hand holding her earpiece. "Captain, we're being hailed."

Finally, they're breaking their silence, Kirk thought. "Put them on."

On the viewscreen, the image of the vessels was replaced by a single, craggy visage. This wasn't an alien Starfleet had encountered before. Sharp features cut a thick brow but a weak jaw, all edged in a fuzz of short hair. If the Klingons ever designed a stuffed toy, it might look like this.

"For what reason do you transgress our space?"

"I'm Captain James T. Kirk, commanding the Federation *Starship Enterprise*. We mean no transgression, but seek the leaders of the Sahntiek on a matter of urgent concern."

The alien on the screen turned to someone out

of frame and guffawed. Heartily. *"The Sahntiek?"* He laughed so hard it became a cough that collapsed in a harsh chuckle as he slowly regained his composure.

Kirk glanced at Scott, who shrugged. Neither knew what was so funny.

"Debarr, he wants to talk to the Sahntiek," the alien commander said to his offscreen comrade, and both laughed.

Annoyed, and knowing that time was short, the captain said, "I take it you're not the Sahntiek."

Choking over his own mirth-filled throat, the alien calmed himself down. *"Ah-hahaha, no, we are most certainly not. I am Admiral Rueft Martish of the Grepund Confederacy. The Sahntiek left this system of their own accord."*

Kirk had never heard of the Grepund Confederacy. "When was that?"

Martish turned again to Debarr. *"When did we arrive in this system?"* He laughed some more, and then, without hearing an answer, addressed Kirk again. *"Ah, I remember now. They pleaded with us not to force them from their homes, but they had no fleet. Some wonderful cargo vessels which we graciously allowed them to use to remove themselves from our new system."*

"After our third attack," someone added from the Grepund bridge. Probably Debarr.

Kirk nodded. "I see." This was a dead end. They

were wasting their time, and by now Spock should have made the Kenisians ready for the *Enterprise* to intercept them. It was time to leave.

"What is your matter of urgent importance, Federation Starship Enterprise *Captain James T. Kirk? Do you wish to challenge us and avenge your friends, the Sahntiek?"* There seemed to be another roll of laughter ready to erupt, but Martish held himself back.

"No," Kirk said drily. "Thank you. We'll leave."

Another guffaw, and Martish shook his head. *"I don't think so. Not yet, anyway."* He gestured and *Enterprise's* deflectors flashed.

"Tractor beam," Scott said. "Right through our shields."

Strong beam. How the captain reacted was very important. That the Grepund were easily amused didn't mean they should be taken lightly.

Standing, Kirk tapped on the back of Sulu's chair. "All stop," he whispered. There was no sense taxing the engines or the structural integrity fields. Loudly, but without anger or fear, the captain faced the viewscreen. "We are not friends of the Sahntiek, nor are we enemies of yours. And that is to your benefit."

"Is it?" Martish said, a cruel smile twisting his lips. *"We like to decide for ourselves what benefits us."*

"Release my ship," Kirk said.

"But I like your ship," the Grepund admiral said.

"You have an interesting engine design. We want to study it."

"Something can be arranged." Kirk smiled this time, and not in a friendly way. "We have many examples we could show you."

Martish sneered at that threat. *"Debarr?"*

"Captain," Uhura said, "long-range communications are being jammed."

Kirk nodded. The Grepund didn't want to risk having to contend with a larger force. They didn't know how many Federation ships were in the area.

"Thank you, Lieutenant." The captain nodded. "They just don't want us calling for reinforcements. They also don't understand what happens if we're not heard from. I don't blame them."

"You don't? That's a relief," Martish said. The admiral wasn't buying what Kirk was trying to sell.

Fair enough. Kirk turned his back to the screen and made a slashing motion for Uhura to cut the communication.

"Mister Scott." The captain went to the rail by the engineering station. "How strong is that tractor beam?"

"Less than ours. But you heard Jolma. They're not interested in towing, they're interested in tearin'. And with our damage, it might not be that hard to do."

Kirk wondered, *Why rip apart the* Enterprise? He didn't doubt that the Grepund used the strategy to instill fear for strategic purposes.

"Admiral Martish is hailing, sir."

With a smile, Kirk told Uhura, "I'm busy."

"Aye, sir."

"THEY CONTINUE to refuse," Debarr said.

"I can see that," Martish grumbled. "You're certain of your scans? No armor at all?"

"Did I question your support when I was admiral?" Debarr spat. "Trust me to my tasks." Martish should never have been allowed his turn in command. Who'd ever heard of such a ridiculous arrangement? A leader should be determined by skill, not by riches or votes.

"You had me scrubbing plasma conduits," the admiral barked as he took a swig from his flask. "Who could foul that up?"

"Somehow you managed it," Debarr mumbled. Becoming Admiral Drunkard's lieutenant wasn't the most humiliating part. Because the buffoon had stumbled upon the defenseless Sahntiek, he'd gotten the majority of the planetary rights. It would be difficult for Debarr to regain command under this arrangement. He couldn't complain. A similar find had allowed him to take control of their group. Of course, he was better at it.

"Scan them again," Martish ordered. "Make sure it's worth our effort."

Debarr shrugged and poked halfheartedly at the

console. "What I need is their control components. I tire of this hybrid mess. We replace so many parts with dissimilar technology that I am not even sure if anything of the original is left."

"We don't want them for replacement parts," Martish snorted. "We want parts someone else will pay for." He grinned. "Or their Federation will pay to get back."

"Sure." The lieutenant was noncommittal. He needed parts more than the small share of a profit they might or might not be able to obtain.

As he ran the scan, Debarr wondered if Martish saw himself commanding their small fleet from the bridge of Kirk's ship. Probably. That would be a sight. He would never fit in that command chair.

"There would be very few ships able to match us, if we had that vessel," the admiral snickered. "Especially that slimy big-eared lout who cheated us out of half our last bounty."

"You made the deal with him," the lieutenant reminded Martish. "He just held you to it."

"Don't defend him, Debarr," the admiral ordered. "Give me what I asked."

Reviewing the data that filled his screen, he did as Martish asked. "Same scan as before, Rueft. Mass of fourteen *edars*. Overall length, seven *parps*. Highly energized shielding array, deflector type, but no armor, as I said. Conventional phased particle weapon banks, six forward torpedo tubes and one aft torpedo launcher. Matter/antimatter dilithium warp engine configuration." He turned back and asked, "Do you still want it?"

The admiral took another drink and wiped his mouth with a dingy sleeve. "Oh, very much so."

"I DOUBT he wants to tear this ship apart," Kirk said, moving around the rail and up toward Scott. "He wants it intact."

"Who are they?" Jolma asked.

"They look like scavengers or pirates," Sulu offered. "Find a system you like? Take it if you can. See a ship you want? Take that too."

The captain agreed. "The Sahntiek couldn't stop them—they'd been kept hamstrung by the Kenisians for centuries. Easy prey." Kirk wagged a finger at his helmsman. "Pirates." He pivoted toward the science station. "Jolma?"

"Sir?"

"Scan for life-signs. How many people are aboard those ships?"

The ensign stood and leaned over the sensor cowl. "Scanning. Twenty-three on the first ship, sir. Twenty-seven on the second, and twenty-five on the third."

"Seventy-five?" Scott scoffed. "Across three ships? They'd have to be heavily automated."

"You know what pirates don't like?" Kirk rubbed his fingers with his thumb. "Sharing their booty."

Returning to the command chair, the captain nodded to his engineer. "Tractor beam, Mister Scott. They've got hold of us? Let's hold on to them."

Enterprise reached out and grabbed the lead Grepund ship. A warble shuddered through the warp engines.

"Aye," Scott said. "Power fluctuations. We're both going to have trouble maintaining a lock."

"That's the idea." Kirk wouldn't take a hail from Martish now even if it came with flowers.

Whatever the reaction on the admiral's bridge, there was probably a lot less laughter.

"The other ships are peeling away, sir," Jolma reported. "Weapons still hot."

Inching forward, the captain knew what he did next was going to cause damage to his own ship. It couldn't be avoided. If the Kenisian ship arrived, and the Grepund somehow managed to end up scavenging the *na'hubis*, that would be a new level of disaster. "Sulu, starboard, one-quarter impulse."

"One-quarter, aye." The helmsman tapped lightly at the controls, and *Enterprise* pulled their captor with them.

The ship creaked around them. Stresses were building, but it would be the same for Martish's vessel.

"Let's dance," Kirk said, with the smallest of smirks. "Sulu, increase speed to one-half. Alter course on the Z-radius at plus-five degrees. Scotty, pull us closer to one another."

As *Enterprise* twisted, the Grepund ship was dragged along. The rolling target would be difficult for her sister ships to fire upon, especially as they drew closer to one another. At least not without hitting one of their own.

"Stress points are building, Captain," Scott called out. His wrist still splinted, the engineer ran his board one-handed, but expertly. "We're going to twist something off ourselves or them."

Kirk hoped they had the same concern on the pirate ship. "Right now, I'm betting we're taxing their automation. It can't hold on forever."

"Aye, sir," Scott said. "But we've got a tiger by the tail. If either side lets go, we're likely to ram each other."

Good point. The captain rubbed his chin and wondered if they could reverse course fast enough to avoid a crash. "What about adding some torque to the tractor beam?"

"Hmm." The engineer considered it a moment. "Aye, it might work at that." He glanced up at the overhead as another shudder groaned across the bridge. "If they break their beam, ours will twist them out of the way."

"Do it," Kirk ordered. It didn't hurt that the added rotation would put more stress on the Grepund ship. Unfortunately, it was putting more on *Enterprise* as well.

"Why don't the other ships do something?" Jolma asked.

The captain glanced up at him. "Piracy, Ensign. If we defeat Martish, they'll clean up the pieces and their share goes from one-third to one-half."

It appeared that the Grepund ship remained stationary, but the viewscreen showed the starscape twisted around it. Occasionally one of the other pirate vessels would spin into and out of view.

"Captain, they're hailing again. Urgently requesting contact," Uhura said, a bemused tone coloring her voice.

"On screen, Lieutenant."

Martish appeared. His bridge looked hazier than before. Somewhere, Kirk thought, several consoles had probably overloaded and spread smoke. It looked like their fans had pulled most of it out, but a lot remained.

"What do you want, Kirk?"

The captain placed a hand on his chest. "What do *I* want? I wanted to leave."

"Release your tractor," Martish demanded, his voice coarse from the smoke.

"You first."

"We must shut down our beams simultaneously or we'll collide," the admiral explained.

"Yes. I'm aware of the physics," Kirk said coolly.

"Then will you?"

The captain leaned back in his chair as nonchalantly as possible, given the audible strain on his ship. "Are you going to stand down and leave us to go on our way?"

"*What is so urgent?*" Martish demanded. "*What did you think you'd find here?*"

As churlish as the so-called admiral was, he wasn't an idiot. Whether he'd heard of Starfleet or not, he knew an official ship from a large government when he saw one. The *Enterprise* wasn't just salvage Martish wanted. Now he was curious.

That the captain didn't need.

"I thought I'd find the Sahntiek. I didn't. I'd rather not have to deal with you, but if I must . . ." The captain leaned forward, clenching his jaw. "That's your mistake to make."

For whatever reason, Martish broke off communications. Maybe Kirk's attempt at intimidation had worked.

When the bridge shook around them, the captain knew it hadn't.

"They're trying to knock out our tractor emitter," Jolma said.

"Shields are holding," Scott reported. "Reinforcing."

"He's not as clever as I thought," Kirk told the engineer. "Prepare to shut down tractor beam." He turned to the helm. "Set course two-one-one mark eight and stand by."

"Course set," Chekov said.

"On my mark." The captain ordered, "Drop tractor and full impulse, *now*."

Bulkheads trembling, *Enterprise* groaned and her engines whined. The Grepund ship sped past them closely, crackling its shields against hers.

"Martish's ship is having attitude problems." Sulu peered into his tactical viewer. "They're spinning out of control."

"Alter course again," Kirk ordered. "Keep out of their tractor range."

As the *Enterprise* maneuvered, the captain knew he had to keep them from being grabbed again. She couldn't take the strain. He also couldn't warp away to the Kenisian ship and bring the Grepund into that situation.

Kirk had to deal with Martish quickly and with finality. He spun toward the science station. "We need to disable those ships."

"Aye, sir." Jolma took that as his cue to review the sensor data on the Grepund vessels. "The lead ship—the admiral's—is the most heavily armored. The other two have more limited protection."

Kirk swiveled back toward the helm. "Those are our targets. Let's thin the herd."

"Aye, aye, sir," Sulu and Chekov said in unison.

As *Enterprise* bore down on the first of the two weaker Grepund ships, the captain's shoulders tightened with anticipation. "Increase power to the forward shields."

"Aye, sir." Scott jabbed at his console and motioned to the crewman at the secondary engineering station to continue the transfer.

Kirk tightly gripped the arms of the command chair. "Fire."

Enterprise sent blue bars of energy crashing against the pirate's massive hull.

In return, the enemy ship's disruptors crashed into the *Enterprise*'s port nacelle. The impact reverberated across the ship.

From the corner of his eye, Kirk saw Jolma straighten from his scanner. The captain turned and moved toward the rail between the command well and the science station. "Ensign?"

"His friend is coming around for a pass. Bearing three-zero-four mark twenty."

Chekov snapped a few of his controls. "Confirmed, sir. I have them."

"Torpedoes, full spread."

Hot globes of energy spat forward, slamming into both Grepund vessels, covering them in chemical flame.

Both ships were staggered for a moment, but gathered themselves and sped toward *Enterprise*. "Evasive," Kirk ordered.

Sulu and Chekov raced through a series of maneuvers, twisting the ship on one axis, then another.

In unison, the two enemy ships fired a volley of torpedoes. Three glancing blows shot past them. One made contact, sizzling against the shields.

"'Evasive' means to evade, gentlemen," the captain said, returning to the center seat.

"They're trying to box us in, sir," Sulu said, exasperated. Despite their size, the Grepund ships were more maneuverable than they seemed.

Another rumble through the deck plates— they'd been struck again by the enemy's disruptors.

If the pirate ships were heavily automated, it meant their engines weren't well tended. That would be where they were most vulnerable. "Target the nearest one's engines," Kirk ordered. "Full phasers."

"Target locked," Sulu said.

"Fire!"

Enterprise sliced toward port, ripping phasers into the enemy's port side. First it broke through their shields, then into the nacelle.

A massive explosion rumbled outward, surging into the shields.

Kirk gripped the arm of his command chair. "Brace!"

A bubble of energy rammed into them. Sparks cascaded from an overhead panel. Uhura reached under her console for an extinguisher to put out the fire.

"Shields down sixty percent," Scotty called.

The captain held himself in the command chair

as the bridge continued to rumble around them. He hadn't expected the Grepund ship to explode. The resulting shockwave was impossible to avoid.

"Helm's sluggish," Sulu said.

Jolma's voice was surprisingly calm. "One Grepund ship destroyed. Martish's ship is coming about. The other one is pulling back, looks like it's limping home."

By destroying one, they'd damaged the other—and themselves.

"Damage report." Kirk turned to Scotty, who was now standing behind the assistant engineer who worked the main engineering station. Just now, one hand wasn't enough.

The status screen above the engineering station was discouraging. "Shields are weakened. Down to thirty-seven percent. Torpedo launch systems are out. Only one phaser bank is responding. We can't take much more and walk away, sir."

"Understood, Mister Scott." The captain huffed out a breath. "Scotty, I want ten torpedoes moved to the hangar deck."

"Aye, sir."

"Have them set with delayed proximity fuses."

The chief engineer nodded and smiled. "Aye."

"Come about, Mister Sulu," Kirk said as he returned to the command chair. "Show them our aft."

———

"THEY'RE TURNING to run." Martish laughed as he smeared the soot off his sweaty forehead.

Debarr spat a bloody tooth onto the deck. "Did you notice that my face was crushed into my console?"

The admiral looked at him blankly. "No. Why did you do that?"

"Because you *fell* on me," Debarr yelled.

"That was Gorm's fault for getting his ship destroyed. I told you to turn us into the shockwave."

"If I slice open your fat gut, do you think turning into my blade would save your spleen?"

Martish waved him off and wedged his body tightly back into the command chair. "Never mind that. *Enterprise* is weakened. Hail them again, and we will discuss terms of their surrender."

Cupping one hand over his mouth so that blood didn't drip onto his controls, Debarr hailed the Federation ship.

As they waited, the admiral took another drink. He relished the image on their main screen. A powerful ship, running from them. "Look at that," he said pointing to the image. "They fear us."

"Not enough," Debarr said. "They still don't reply."

"Get back in range. We need to disable them."

Moving to comply, the lieutenant glanced at the distance indicator for weapons lock acquisition. "Rueft?"

"What?"

Debarr leaned back, turning, but raised a finger toward the screen. "They're not moving away. They're moving *toward* us."

Martish demanded, "Why would they do that?"

"I—I don't know," the lieutenant said as he scrambled to aim the disruptors. "Wait." He checked the console and then rechecked it. "They've stopped. Still just outside weapons range."

Martish blinked at the screen, and Debarr gulped down a mouthful of blood.

"Could they be dead in space?"

The lieutenant shook his head. "No, sensors say their propulsion systems are online."

"Perhaps their bridge has a breach and their captain is dead," the admiral mused. "That would explain their silence."

"It wouldn't explain their odd maneuver."

Waggling a finger at the Federation ship, Martish had made his decision. "Close to weapons range. We will spur them to move or determine their motive."

"I do not think this a wise course," Debarr said.

After another sip from his flask, Martish said, "I didn't ask what you thought. I am in command."

"Fine." The lieutenant, who was once an admiral, smacked the controls and they sped forward. "Be in command!" He got up and turned toward the door. "You can fly the damn thing too."

"Come back here, you ingrate. This is mutiny!" Martish struggled to get to his feet.

When he looked forward, several black orbs filled the screen. By the time he realized they were topedoes, it was too late to reach the controls.

ONE EXPLOSION after another blanketed Martish's vessel, hiding it from *Enterprise*'s view. Kirk's chest tightened with anticipation and when the explosions cleared, the Grepund ship was listing to one side.

"Jolma?" The captain looked up expectantly.

"She's disabled."

"And the other one?"

"In retreat," the ensign said, "returning to the Sahntiek system."

The captain turned to his chief engineer. "Scotty, what kind of speed can you give me?"

"No more than warp three, sir. She just can't take more."

Let's hope it's fast enough.

EIGHTEEN

"You're welcome." Zhatan lowered herself slowly into her command chair as she motioned for the guards to bring the prisoners forward.

"W-welcome?" Pippenge's nerves, which had been steady, reemerged

"We didn't kill you," the Kenisian commander said, but seemed displeased with her own decision. "Yet. So, you're welcome." Finished with the Maabas ambassador—perhaps for the last time—she looked to the Vulcan. "Tell me what you've done." She wasn't asking. Safe on her own bridge, guards holding weapons on them, Zhatan was in command.

Spock would have to do something about that.

"You will have to be specific, Commander. I have done many things."

Behind her coal-black eyes, he could see her fume. "Silence!" Zhatan snapped. "Tell us what you've done to Sciver and the mine!"

Deliberately trying to provoke her, Spock maintained his unemotional demeanor. "You've given two conflicting orders. Which shall I give priority?"

Her eyes glazed over. Yet another Kenisian internal debate, he assumed. Eventually, Zhatan recovered herself. "Tell us now how to fix the mine, or we *will* end you."

Spock raised a singular eyebrow. "Indeed? Since detonation of the mine would include that outcome, your threat is hollow."

The Kenisian commander stood and motioned for the guards to aim their weapons at Pippenge, which they quickly did. "And if we order the ambassador's death? What then?"

"Logically, if the mine kills us all, that includes Ambassador Pippenge." Spock bowed his head slightly at the Maabasian. "You'll forgive me, sir."

"I— Yes, of course."

Fists balled at her sides, Zhatan swallowed hard. She stood there, shaking, saying nothing until finally she unleashed a torrent of angry words on Spock. "You are a liar and have stolen our precious time! If you truly understood us, you would know why we must take these actions."

The Vulcan found himself at a loss for how to proceed. The captain could talk his way out of the most difficult of situations using a mix of logic and passion, the formula for which had eluded Spock.

His orders were to disable the crew and leave the ship intact, because anything else could set off the *na'hubis*. His efforts, so far, had been fruitful.

While he might not admit this to either the captain or Doctor McCoy, Spock asked himself, What would James Kirk do?

"You are correct. I do not understand," he told her. "I'd like to, but cannot fathom the depth of destruction you seek to cause." As Spock stepped toward her the guards tensed, but she waved them off. "Explain it to me, Zhatan. Elucidate."

She shrank down into her seat as he took another step toward her, but she didn't order the guards to stop him. Likely, Zhatan was thinking that the answer to fixing the prototype mine was in his mind, and she would have the solution if she melded with him.

Or, perhaps the arrogance of some personalities within her thought they could subdue him. Whatever the reason, Zhatan was drawn to Spock's tacit offer to meld, though she didn't move toward him.

Holding out his hand, Spock pulled the Kenisian commander up, close enough that his elbow had to bend for his fingers to meet her cheek and temple.

"My mind to your—" Spock grunted in pain. Unlike the other melds, this was an uneven connection with coarse edges that bit at his psyche. He dove into the whirlpool of her minds, and she pushed into his thoughts as quickly.

"We . . ." he rasped.

"Are . . ." she whispered.

"Of Kenis," they said together.

They drew one another close, and Zhatan's fingers wrapped themselves around Spock's head as he brought up his left hand to press into the other side of her face.

"We . . ." he moaned.

"Have . . ." she continued.

"Been decimated," they voiced.

Hate—pure, white-hot hatred—crushed into Spock, boiling his blood and knitting agony down his spine.

"We . . ."

"Are . . ."

"Tibis!"

Tibis. A singular among the many, but not Zhatan. She fed them moments, memories that sliced through their minds, slivers of recollections that burned as they burrowed into him: children watching their parents die, families burned alive, hospitals vaporized, ships destroyed, starvation, radiation . . .

"We—"

"Are—"

"Vengeance!" Tibis screamed through their lungs.

"Your vengeance," Spock accused. "Not Zhatan's."

"We are Zhatan."

"We are?" the Kenisian woman asked.

"You are not," the Vulcan compelled.

"She would not live if we had not survived," Tibis said.

"She lives," Spock choked out. "Let her live."

Zhatan and Spock pressed harder into each

other. His hands felt as if they had melted into her temples. Hers felt like they'd become a part of his forehead and jaw.

Tibis was a force. She may have been a person at one time, or just an amalgamation of several like-minded consciousnesses which banded together to control Zhatan. Either way, Tibis held sway over her to a great degree and was ready to wield it.

"Release us," Spock said.

"Help me," Zhatan murmured.

There were sounds around them, calls from the one named Nidal and chirps and bleeps from equipment, but they were pushed aside. There were odd-but-familiar feelings, an electricity that buzzed nearby them, tickling their collective skin. They disregarded that too. Only their anger was important. Only their rage.

THE KENISIAN SHIELDS were down just when Spock said they'd be. That didn't mean the *Enterprise* could fire on the vessel—they dared not—but it granted them access. In six pillars of light, Kirk, McCoy, and four security guards beamed directly to Zhatan's bridge.

Pippenge gasped, looking shocked and relieved as the Starfleet security guards stunned their Kenisian counterparts.

The woman at the helm stood, but had no

weapon. When Kirk pointed his phaser at her and nodded for her to move away from her console, she did. Oddly, she too looked a mixture of surprised and relieved.

With his free hand, Kirk pulled out his communicator and flipped it open. "Kirk to *Enterprise.*"

"*Enterprise. Scott here, sir.*"

"Bridge is secured, Mister Scott. Begin transporting boarding parties. Secure the *na'hubis* mines."

"*Aye, sir.*"

The captain snapped his communicator closed, and returned it to his belt as he moved toward the command chair.

Entwined in a mind-meld, Spock and Zhatan looked catatonic. McCoy immediately had his medical tricorder out and was running it over them.

When he scanned them for a third time, Kirk prodded, "Bones?"

"I don't know, Jim." The doctor snapped his tricorder shut. "Spock could be in trouble. Zhatan's an incredibly strong telepath."

"Stronger than Spock?" the captain asked. "Can we pull them apart?"

McCoy shook his head. "That's not a good idea."

VOICES HE RECOGNIZED, McCoy's, Kirk's. She feared them. Some respected them. They all knew them and were curious. Tibis hated them.

"Are they fighting one another?" Pippenge's voice.

The ambassador, a vile man, a brave man, an insipid man, an honorable man, a curious man, a frightened man.

"I can't tell." Kirk's voice.

The captain. Stubborn. No, determined. Clever. Too clever. Wise. No, naïve. Experienced. Frustrating. A survivor.

"Zhatan, listen to me. Let Spock go."

We are Spock.

We are Zhatan.

We are Tibis.

We are many.

We are survivors.

We must endure.

"We are Kenisians. We will have vengeance."

"Spock isn't a Kenisian," Kirk said.

Captain? The captain is here.

"He may be lost in there, Jim."

The doctor. McCoy is here.

"But he's still there, somewhere."

We are Spock. We are Zhatan. We live.

"Understand us, we want revenge," Spock and Zhatan said in unison.

"There is no revenge!" Captain Kirk said.

Frustrated. Angry. Passionate. But so are we. We are Tibis. We are Zhatan. We are Spock.

"There will be revenge," Spock and Zhatan said in unison.

"Zhatan, listen to me. The Sahntiek are gone. Obliterated by another race. The fleet you found isn't theirs. It belongs to their conquerors."

"*Lies.*"

"*No, the captain is honest.*"

"*No, he is deceitful. He is not Kenisian.*"

"*Spock is not Kenisian.*"

"*The Vulcan can be controlled.*"

"The Sahntiek?" Pippenge again. "Are you certain, Captain? They were *our* conquerors."

STILL MELDED TO SPOCK, Zhatan turned to the Maabas ambassador. Something in his voice pulled her. "Y-you understand us?"

"I believe I do." Pippenge stepped toward them. "We had a common enemy."

"You hate them? You want them dead." Zhatan was sobbing now. She and Spock were melded; still grasping each other, the Vulcan looked on the verge of tears.

"They *are* dead." The ambassador looked to Kirk, who nodded his agreement. "As are those of my people whom they killed."

"The past is the past, Zhatan," Kirk said.

"Our dead are at peace," Pippenge whispered.

"Peace," Spock groaned. "Send Tibis away, Zhatan. Send her away."

"You have within you the memories, the anger, of hundreds of people wronged by a people long since turned to dust." Kirk lowered his phaser and came within a meter of the Kenisian commander and his first officer. "The Maabas are at peace because they knew when to let go of their past. They've buried their dead. Yours are still holding on to you."

"Holding us back," Spock and Zhatan said in unison.

"Yes. Their hatred doesn't have to be yours." Kirk slowly placed one hand on Spock's elbow and pulled him away from the Kenisian as far as he could without breaking their connection. "Those acts weren't done to you—but to people who should have said goodbye when their physical forms were gone."

"We must survive," Spock whispered and Zhatan spat.

"Survive," Kirk said. "But don't demand the deaths of others to fuel your hate."

"Find peace," Pippenge said. He moved to Zhatan and pulled one of her hands off Spock and cupped it in his own. "Have the courage to move on. Don't burden your progeny with your pain."

"Spock," Kirk said, "help her."

"Help *them*," Pippenge said.

Zhatan turned to Spock, letting her hands fall to her sides. "Help me. Please. Help me."

The Vulcan pulled her close again and reached deep into her minds.

———

THERE WERE HUNDREDS of consciousness within her, but a large mass of them called themselves Tibis.

"You will not silence us, Vul-kuhn," they told Spock. *"We are Zhatan more than Zhatan is."*

"You are most certainly not," Zhatan protested. For the first time she was angry at herself. Angry at Tibis. *"You have perverted us. You have manipulated us with your hate to the point where we can no longer love!"*

"Who made you what you are?" Tibis questioned her. *"Your love of* asab *nectar comes from where? Your ability to command. Your desire to join the fleet and be a soldier. From what well do those needs spring? From us."*

Spock saw this was true. As with Burgee, some of the *katras* within had molded the individual whose brain was being shared. Burgee was encouraged toward the academic. Zhatan had been pushed toward war and hate.

But how different was this from a child listening and learning from their parents or the others they revered? For good or ill, the young heard many voices. How much they listened and heeded should have been a personal choice.

"This will not help you, Zhatan. We are not only Tibis, and without us our entire race would have died at the Sahntiek's hands."

"She is an individual," Spock said. *"And you are not."*

"We were," Tibis spat bitterly. *"Now she is* our *individual."*

That was the key. Tibis was clearly not one mind.

As Spock had suspected, they were a political ideology. Not a set of emotions or memories, they were a philosophy given voice within the minds of others.

This was the root of all Zhatan's hesitation, all her internal debates and constant confusion. Tibis was not content to be within Zhatan. They wanted to *be* Zhatan.

"*I am not yours,*" Zhatan said, fighting for herself. "*And you will be silent. You will finally be silent, Tibis, or I will* make *you so.*"

"*You haven't the ability,*" Tibis told her. "*And your Vul-kuhn friend cannot help.*"

"*That is untrue,*" Spock informed the commander. "*I can help you, and you can help yourself.*"

"*Teach me, Spock,*" Zhatan asked. "*Free me.*"

THEY STOOD SILENTLY for several minutes, barely moving. McCoy shook his head when the captain suggested separating them.

Suddenly, they parted.

Head bowed, a shaken Spock stepped away and nearly collapsed into McCoy's waiting arms.

Zhatan, lips quivering, turned to the woman who stood before the helm. "How goes the ship, my love?"

"Unabated," the woman answered, her voice wavering hopefully. "Ever unabated."

EPILOGUE

Captain's log, supplemental.

The na'hubis *has been disposed of in a safe man-*
ner. Commander Zhatan, exercising her authority as
Kenisian Ambassador, has returned to the Maabas
homeworld to negotiate a good faith agreement.

"How are you, Commander?" Kirk had arrived in
the transporter room to bid farewell to Pippenge
and Zhatan. They were going to join President
Moberte at the negotiation table. Spock stood at the
transporter console, with McCoy just to his side.

Slowly pulling in a long breath, the Kenisian
commander looked shakily at Spock. "I—it sounds
odd to use this word—am recovering."

"No more multividual?" Kirk asked.

"On the contrary." Zhatan tapped her temple with
two fingers and offered Kirk a brief smile. "Most are
still with me. Although many have disincorporated and
their thoughts are gone. One group in particular could
not bear for me to be in control and have vanished."

"How does that work?" McCoy asked, and when

Zhatan hesitated to answer, the doctor glanced to Spock.

The Vulcan looked to her for approval, and when she nodded, he explained, "When the Kenisians first used this method, it was practiced only between members of the same family. At some point, the entire Tibis clan disguised themselves as an individual, and they were passed down with others. Eventually they split and spread, successfully influencing many others. The strain on Zhatan's mental disciplines was extreme. It is extraordinary that she did not go mad." She smiled at Spock as he continued. "The commander and I were able to erect a mental barrier to that clan. Having lost control over Zhatan, they chose oblivion over subjugation."

"You're in charge?" Kirk asked Zhatan.

"I am." She looked at Spock, smiling brightly. "There are Vulcan mental disciplines that were lost to us, or perhaps kept from us. I have learned them and will teach them to my people. I suspect I am not the only one who was subjugated. Others of that clan, or similar such movements, are among us, but we shall see to their end."

The captain wasn't sure other Kenisians would be as eager as Zhatan to accept individuality. "Will your people want to learn?"

"I don't know," she admitted. "We will have to discuss it. There is already a debate among us—

internally and externally—as to when it is time to die." Her eyes held a sadness and looked past Kirk at some far-off thought. "We've let a long goodbye become an unnatural afterlife."

"Immortality," Spock said, "can grant eternal life to bitterness and hate. No civilization can long survive under those conditions."

"Agreed." Zhatan joined Pippenge on the transporter platform. "Our Vulcan friend is wise," she told the ambassador.

"Our?" Kirk asked.

Zhatan smiled and motioned between herself and Pippenge. "Our," she said, then tapped her head, "not *our*."

"We intend to share our world with the Kenisians," Pippenge said, arranging his robes as he centered himself on the transporter pad. "We know they have another world, but we would like to welcome them back to this one. We believe we can both benefit. The Maabas can learn firsthand from those who've given us so much knowledge through their ruins, and perhaps we can teach them something as well."

Relieved and exhilarated by the unexpected outcome, Kirk said, "An excellent resolution, Ambassador." He bowed his head to Zhatan. "*Ambasadors.*" Moving toward Spock at the console, the captain took on a more formal tone. "The Federation will be sending advisors to help and would like to negotiate a treaty with the Kenisians as well."

"We are honored, Captain." Zhatan raised her hand in a Vulcan salute. "Speaking for myself, as well as those I've sworn to represent, I wish us all peace and a life not quite as long as we've become accustomed to."

When they'd first met Zhatan, she smiled from arrogance. Now, her grin was mirthful, full of humor.

Kirk bowed his head formally, saying, "Good luck. Energize."

Two forms dematerialized, and as the familiar hum faded, the captain turned to his friends.

"Peace and harmony," McCoy said. "A few days ago I wouldn't have thought it possible."

Shutting down the transporter console, Spock stated, "Peace is always possible, but unlikely when anger overwhelms all."

"Are *you* at peace, Spock?" Kirk wasn't sure what prompted the question, other than he knew his first officer hadn't seemed himself.

When the Vulcan didn't answer, McCoy pointed out, "You *have* seemed out of sorts."

As they left the transporter room for the corridor, Spock was circumspect. "I melded with a total of thirty-seven Kenisian individuals, a composite of four thousand, three hundred and fifty-two distinct personalities."

"That's in your report," Kirk said. "I was asking how you *feel*."

"How I feel," the Vulcan murmured.

"Yes."

Spock didn't reply.

Silently they waited for the turbolift to arrive, and only once inside did he speak. "Disabling the Kenisians as well as their vessel necessitated great exertion." Spock paused to gather himself. "All wounds, with time, either fester or heal. Mine shall heal."

Kirk grabbed the controls and twisted. "Deck five," he ordered, then looked to McCoy before meeting his first officer's eyes again. "You're wounded?"

"Not physically," the doctor said softly.

"Spock?" Kirk prodded.

When the Vulcan didn't reply, McCoy cast Kirk a sideways look, but remained atypically silent.

The lift doors parted and the Vulcan exited. "Gentlemen, if you'll excuse me, I am off duty." He nodded to McCoy. "Recuperation by meditation, rather than potion, Doctor."

McCoy nodded cautiously.

As the lift doors closed, the doctor shared a concerned glance with Kirk.

"He'll be fine," the captain said. Because Spock always had been.

"Are you sure about that?"

Kirk wouldn't meet the doctor's eyes. He stared at the lift indicator. "Spock did what he had to do. He knows that."

The doctor shook his head. "I don't know if that's true. He assaulted people, one by one—thirty-seven in all—face to face."

"Mind-melds," Kirk argued. "He didn't physically injure—"

"A clout to the jaw is worse than any other kind of force?"

"Zhatan was happy with the result," Kirk said, but the words were hollow, and he knew that Spock had crossed a line. "The Kenisians are better off."

At that, McCoy grunted his disapproval. "Maybe they are. But is Spock?"

ONCE IN HIS CABIN, the Vulcan lowered himself slowly into a chair and closed his eyes. The purpose of meditation wasn't to clear one's mind but to focus it.

The agony of Zhatan's many personalities, which had been quelled or coerced into silence, had taken its toll. Control over the Tibis clan had proven demanding.

Vulcan emotion was harsh, sharp, and dangerously brutal. This was why, as a people, they had embraced Surak's philosophy of logic; they needed to control their emotions or purge them.

Attempting to compel and resist the sentiments of thousands of minds in a matter of hours was nearly incomprehensible. Perhaps if he were not half human, Spock would have been more proficient at compartmentalizing his feelings.

Feelings. Something he had but did not want.

Spock knew there were a number of melds where a plurality of the personalities involved did not embrace his involvement. They did not want to meld with him, and they did not welcome his presence.

It was necessary, he told himself. Had there been another way to save millions? Was there an alternative he had missed? Perhaps he'd not searched hard enough to find one.

Morality, he believed, was a set of values used to guide one's choices. Emotions should not be part of the equation. *But what do you do when your values shape an emotional revulsion to an act which you believe is necessary for a greater good?*

Emotional revulsion.

A feeling.

Opening his eyes, Spock flipped a switch on his computer. "Computer."

"Ready."

"Connect to Vulcan Science Academy library archive."

"Working. Ready."

He took a data card and slid it into the slot under the screen. "Locate and record all data related to *kolinahr.*"

"Working."

The task would take time. Not merely the data collection, but the decision itself was not to be taken lightly. One did not embark on such a journey without much study and deliberation.

But the first step needed to be taken. Leaning back, Spock closed his eyes again and steepled his fingers.

With time, and effort, all wounds can heal.

ACKNOWLEDGMENTS

Any novel you read is a collaboration between writer, editors, and copy editors (who all did a fantastic job of guiding and supporting me on this book) but also family and friends who understand the time it takes to write—and rewrite—and allow one the time to do so.

So my deep appreciation must be extended to Margaret Clark, Ed Schlesinger, Scott Pearson, and Paula Block, for their amazing work, as well as Greg Brodeur (who still listens to my plot ideas and gives me his advice) and Rigel Ailur (for fast beta reading and awesome comments).

I also have to thank my family: my wonderfully supportive wife, Simantha; our son, Joshua; my brother Josh and his wife, Tamara (and their kids, Delilah and Alden)—all of whom understood my limited ability for family time while working to meet a deadline. Okay, Alden and Delilah are too young to care, but when they are old enough to read, they'll see this and give me extra hugs. At least, that's the plan.

CHEERS,
DAVE GALANTER

ABOUT THE AUTHOR

Dave Galanter has authored (or co-authored with sometime collaborator Greg Brodeur) various *Star Trek* projects, including *Voyager: Battle Lines*, *The Next Generation* duology *Maximum Warp*, and *The Original Series* novel *Troublesome Minds*, as well as numerous works of *Star Trek* short fiction.